# FALLEN CREST HOME

### THE 6TH IN THE FALLEN CREST SERIES

NYT & USA Bestselling Author
# TIJAN

Edited by Jessica Royer Ocken
Proofread by: Chris O'Neil Parece, Paige Smith,
Kara Hildebrand, and Amy English
Formatted by: Elaine York, Allusion Graphics, LLC/
Publishing & Book Formatting, www.allusiongraphics.com

# DEDICATION

To everyone who fell in love with Fallen Crest High and have
continued to love this series! The support has been amazing
and I don't know what I'll do when that last book is done.

To my readers, just thank you from the bottom of my heart!

# CHAPTER ONE

I got back from running early in the morning. Everything was still dark, the slightest hint of light was starting to creep over the lawns and the pavement where I jogged.

The last two weeks I'd gotten into the habit of waking around four in the morning, rolling out of bed, and pounding the cement five minutes later. I didn't know what it was—running in the dark, running when no one could see me, or even just knowing I was out ahead of everyone else—but I'd become a dark figure blending in with the other darkness.

I loved it, and when I'd return to my stepmother's house, I was usually still feeling that running high. I'd start the first pot of coffee, and as the machine began to spit and churn, I'd slip out to the front porch to finish stretching. The first morning, I was just about done and planning to head back inside to pour myself a cup when the door opened. I think Malinda had been woken by the coffee smell, like a vampire rising at the first whiff of blood.

My stepmother appeared, her rich chestnut hair looking like she'd hastily raked her fingers through it, and a glaze of sleep still over her eyes. She had two cups and handed me one, sinking down onto a porch chair before tightening her robe.

This morning was the same as that first time.

I was just lowering my leg from behind me when she appeared, giving me a warm smile. "Hey there, my little chickadee." She pulled the ends of her plush robe tighter together before sitting.

"Morning."

I sat on the chair next to her, propping my feet up so I could rest my coffee cup on my knees. It warmed my hands, and I inhaled the smell.

"You ran extra long today?"

I stiffened. I hadn't realized Malinda knew when I got up or that today had been an extra hour earlier. But I should've known. She was the stepmother extraordinaire.

"Don't say anything, would you?" I asked her.

She gave me a knowing look over her mug. "To your father or to those two young men who protect you like they're guard dogs?"

"Both?" A girl could hope.

She laughed, sipping her coffee. She patted my knee. "Does Mason know?"

"That I got up early?"

"That you're running so much every morning. I know you're going in the afternoons, too." A second knowing look. "And why you did a two-hour run this morning."

Ah. There it was. "I didn't know anyone else knew." I shifted on the seat, ignoring the pounding that was starting behind my temples. Every time I thought of *her*, it would start.

It'd been with me the whole run.

"I overheard a phone conversation between Mason and his father, and it didn't go well."

I glanced over to her. Did that mean Mason knew, too?

She sipped her drink, getting more comfortable on the bench. "Did you know James is forcing him and Logan to be his groomsmen?"

I did. "I'm worried the same will happen to me."

"No, no, no." Malinda shook her hand in the air. "She'll be lucky if you even attend the wedding. Analise won't push her luck. She might have..." She paused. "...*issues*, but she's one smart cookie. Trust me. You don't need to worry about that."

Her words should've been a relief, but they weren't. Only two people fully understood the lengths Analise would go if she wanted something: myself and Malinda's husband, David—otherwise known as the man who raised me. There was a reason we were both scared of the woman. Malinda, though I loved her dearly and was so grateful she'd come into my life, hadn't been around during Analise's darkest hours. Yes, my mother had gone away for almost two years to get help. Yes, she seemed to be doing better and had been back in Fallen Crest for an entire year and a half, and yes, she'd left me alone, for the most part. But she'd left the treatment facility and was living not just in Fallen Crest, but across the road, and I was here now, too.

I avoided her this long, but time was up. I couldn't anymore.

Mason and I were spending the summer in Fallen Crest because he had an internship with his father's company to fulfill a requirement for his business degree. He even had approval to return to school later than normal—not until the week before classes instead of earlier for football training like usual. A personal trainer was supposed to come out to make up for any practice he was missing, but it wasn't needed. If I was insane with my running, Mason was equally crazy with his training. He was in the gym for three or four hours a night, and I felt the proof every time he was on top of me, under me, and inside of me.

My body heat rose now as I thought of our lovemaking the night before. It had a different feel to it. There was a desperation and hunger I hadn't felt in a long time. Like we couldn't get enough of each other, like we knew there were things set in motion that could tear us apart.

I didn't believe that was true, but it still made me tense.

Mason's dad and Analise had been on a trip to London for the past three months, but they would be home sometime today.

Malinda sighed, yawning. Her smile was tired, but filled with warmth. "You really don't have to worry about her. I've talked to Analise over the last year and a half. She's accepted that everything has to be on your terms. You choose when and *if* you want her back in your life. She won't pressure you. She won't even say hello to you in public if you see her. You can approach her *if* you want to do that. It's all you."

Despite what Malinda thought, to say Analise was mentally stable would've been an overstatement. To say she wasn't a danger to me was another overstatement. There was a laundry list of things she'd done, and hitting me and threatening to destroy Mason's life were among the last she'd gotten to before she went away to the hospital.

The one silver lining was James Kade, Mason and Logan's father. When Analise left David, she and I moved into the Kade mansion, and two families were born: I joined Mason and Logan, and Analise partnered with James. Both Analise and James were cheating assholes, but at least James proved how much he actually loved her. Theirs was a match made in heaven as far as I was concerned.

Mason and Logan had their own issues with their father, but the relationship was a bit more congenial than mine with Analise.

The exhaustion from my run was starting to set in when a pair of headlights lit up the street. My hands tightened around the mug, but years of training took over. I always froze up when Analise was near, but that transferred to a ready feeling. *Okay, Mother Dearest*, I thought. My lips parted and a half snarl formed. I could feel my lungs expand with my deep breathing. I was ready. I was willing, and whatever she was going to send my way, would get sent right back at her.

Two black SUVs slowed before the Kades' gate. It opened slowly, and both SUVs pulled into the driveway. The gate closed behind, and our view was obstructed, but I knew what that meant.

My mother was officially back.

# CHAPTER TWO

My shower door opened and Mason's hand touched my hip, sliding across my back as he stepped in behind me. I felt the cool draft for a mere second before his heat warmed me and he closed the door. His arms came around me, and I leaned back against him. I moved my head so the water wouldn't blind me, and there he was.

Strong jaw. Beautiful green eyes. Black hair cut short, and a physique toned to perfection from all his training. Gorgeous.

His eyes darkened as his hands slid around my waist and up over my ribcage. I gasped, but didn't look away. I couldn't. Moments like these, Mason felt like my life force. If I broke contact, there went my strength. It wasn't a regular feeling now, not like it had been before when Analise tried to break us. But in this moment, I felt it. I inhaled it, arching my back to give him a better hold on me and myself an opportunity to savor this connection.

So many had tried to come between us. So many had failed.

It would be Mason and me forever.

I turned around, pressing against him. Every inch of me fit into him, like a glove. All his hard ridges and muscles were home to me.

I wound my arms around his neck. "Morning."

His eyes darkened even more. "Morning." One hand fell to my hip. "You ran this morning again."

A delicious shiver zipped through me. "I'll still go with you later, if you want."

His other hand crept up to the back of my neck. He held me there, anchoring my head as he studied me. I saw a slight trace of concern.

"You're running too much."

So he *had* known. I tried to pull away, but he wouldn't let me.

"Don't." He added a soft plea, "Please."

I stayed in his arms with the water beating down on us.

"Malinda said something this morning, too."

He nodded. "Your mom's back, isn't she?"

"You knew?"

"I figured. I was supposed to start my internship with one of my dad's partners, but he texted this morning saying he'd be there." A corner of Mason's mouth lifted. "He asked if I wanted a ride to work."

I matched his half-grin. "Did you reply?"

"Right," he mocked. "Because I'm the perfect, good son who drives to work with his father."

"Well, James can always dream."

Mason chuckled, pressing his lips to my forehead. He swept his hand down, tucking my hair behind my ear. For a moment, he held me, resting his cheek to my forehead. I could feel his tension. He was worried, and I couldn't fault him. Analise had been out of my life for two years, and things had been good. They were damned good, but now we were back home. Back on her turf. A wedding was happening in two months, and everything good could be unraveled.

It wouldn't be, though. I was bound and determined not to let anyone hurt us.

"Everything will be all right," I said softly. "You know that, right?"

He smirked. I felt his lips curve against my skin. "You haven't even seen her, and you're already running like you used to."

That was true. I let out a breath. "Okay. I promise I'll stop running…" I looked up at him. "As much."

"I don't care how long you run. I just want you to be healthy."

"I will."

He gazed down, still studying me intently. Then he softened and his lips came down to rest on mine. "Don't let her in your head."

"I won't. I promise."

He cursed. "I'm already sick of her."

"Let's forget all about them, her and him." I lifted myself up on my toes, sealing my mouth to his, and he answered by clasping his hands under me. He raised one of my legs so I could feel him right there, and just like that, everything was gone. It was just he and I. The way it should be.

I closed my eyes, feeling him enter me.

This. Him. Me. This was all I needed. I wound my arms around his neck and started to move with him.

In. Out.

Mason thrust inside of me. This man—he wasn't a boy anymore. I felt like I'd grown up with him. Side by side. From the first time he touched me until now, it was always the same.

Dark and primal pleasure filled me, and all I could do was gasp as he kept going.

In.

Out.

Back in again.

The harder he went, the deeper he slid inside, and I felt my climax coming. A low, guttural scream built in the back of my throat. I arched my back, sweat mingling with the shower's water, but I couldn't hold out any longer. I was going to come.

Mason watched me. I saw the need on his face, just like I felt it inside of me.

This was the same fervor we'd felt last night. I sensed it in his rough kisses, his grip on my neck, my hips, the way he was fucking me.

I wanted to let him dominate me, but my knees began to weaken, and I couldn't hold off any more. I grabbed the showerhead and pulled myself up. Mason's eyes flashed as he caught me and lifted me the rest of the way. Then he was inside of me again. I rode him this time, with my legs wrapped around his waist and using the showerhead for leverage. When that wasn't enough, I wrapped an arm around his shoulders and rested my hand against the tile.

His kisses were demanding, owning me.

I moved my hips up and down, a delicious tingle making my body tremble. He was right where he was supposed to be: as one with me.

Soon we were both convulsing.

A wave hit me hard, making my body jerk, but Mason held me all the while. Pressing a soft kiss to my lips, then my forehead, he tucked his head against my shoulder and waited until we stopped shaking.

"You okay?" he murmured, nuzzling against my ear.

I let out a weak laugh. "Is that rhetorical?"

He grinned, kissing me before lifting his head. His eyes found mine. "Was I too rough?"

I motioned to be let down, but Mason walked me out and sat me on the bathroom counter. He started to step back, but I caught him, keeping him between my legs. Looping my arms around his neck, I leaned back against the mirror. I didn't give a damn about anything in this moment.

"Only in the best way ever, and please be like that again."

He laughed softly, bending down to trail kisses over my shoulder. He whispered there, his lips moving over my skin, "I've missed waking up next to you."

A pang of regret stabbed me. "I'm sorry."

He shook his head, looking into my eyes again. "No. I get it. I do. I was just stating a fact." He frowned, his thumb rubbing over my forehead like he was smoothing out a worry line. "What are you doing today?"

"You mean while you go off and work with your dad?"

He groaned, dipping his head back to rest on my shoulder. "Yes, I mean that."

I made sure to shrug with my other shoulder. "I suppose you shouldn't be the only responsible one in this relationship."

"You're going to get a job?"

I nodded, speaking to my biological father. "Garrett gave me a trust fund, but I need to do something. I'm sure I could work at Manny's, but I don't know. I think I might want to do something else this summer."

His hand slid up my back. "I'm sure whatever you do, Logan will try to hang out at all the time."

I nodded. "He's in Paris with your mom, right? Did Taylor go with him, or is he seeing her after?"

"Both. My mom took the two of them on the trip, but when they get back they're spending a week with Taylor's dad. I think they're going camping or something. And that brings up another item—Helen called me this morning. She asked me to move into her house for the summer."

Lovely. Wonderful. Stupendous.

My boyfriend was moving out for three months. It didn't matter that he was literally going across the road. Helen Malbourne was not a fan of mine.

I leaned back and let out a disappointed sound. "If it's not my mom, it's your mom. Do you realize the only parents who haven't tried to get between us are our fathers? Does that mean something?"

He gave me a soft grin. "What are you talking about?"

"You moving into your mom's house. How's this going to work? You're going to end up sleeping with me every night anyway. What's the point?" I looked at the floor.

"Yeah, I will, because you're moving in with me."

I lifted my head again. "What? Your mom hates me. I didn't think I was allowed to live there."

He leaned close to me again. I leaned away until my back was against the mirror and he hovered over me, his lips a mere inch away from mine.

"And to quote my pain-in-the-ass brother…" He cupped the back of my neck, his fingers sliding into my hair. "'Fuck my mother.'" He dropped his mouth to mine in a hard kiss, one that had my heart pounding. "What do you think? Want to live with me, just you and me?"

"No Logan?"

"Not for the first month."

"No Nate?"

13

"He's at a movie shoot with his parents."

"No one else?"

His eyes flared with lust again. "Just you and me."

I could only look at him. We'd never lived alone. The most we had was a weekend away. But this time—I was almost salivating over the idea. It felt right, like we should've been doing this all along.

"Yeah." I nodded. "Yeah, I'd like that."

"Yeah?"

"Oh yeah." And then his mouth was on mine again, and he carried me to the bed. Once again, we couldn't get enough of each other. No matter how many times I touched this man, I'd only ever be yearning for the next touch.

As he moved inside of me, my legs and arms wrapped around him, my mind raced until I turned it off and surrendered. I gave in completely to Mason.

# CHAPTER THREE

"Hey, girl."

I was waiting in a rickety lawn chair near the bonfire pit outside of Manny's. There were three others to choose from, but they all looked to be in the same miserable state—holes in the middle, frayed at the ends. I was surprised they were still able to hold people upright. As I tipped back in mine, kicking my feet up to rest on bricks surrounding the unlit bonfire, I felt it dip under my weight.

I jerked upright. "Shit, Heather."

A low, smooth chuckle sounded as one of my best friends—correction, one of my *only* female friends—sat down next to me, pulling out her cigarettes and lighter. Heather leaned back like I'd just tried to, crossing one foot over the other on the stone pit as she exhaled the first drag. "I think you got the one I leave out in case Logan shows up. I'm hoping it'll tip him one of these days, just so I can have a good laugh."

I shook my head. This was the old dynamic, and a part of me relaxed inside.

"I thought all that was done?" I murmured, tentatively sitting back again. "You're happy with Channing. He's with Taylor."

She'd been fitting her cigarette to her lips, but paused and pulled her hand away. "What are you talking about?"

"This sexual flirting thing. I thought it was over."

She grunted, lighting her cigarette now. "When Logan stops giving me shit, I'll return the favor. He still dishes it out, and it's not in the flirting way you say it is." She sounded annoyed. "Somewhere along the line we became like brother and sister, but I already have a loser brother who *won't leave me alone*!" She leaned backward, closer to the side door of Manny's where she ran the diner part of the bar and grill. A second later her brother yelled back.

"Stay in your lane, Heather! I manage the bar. You run the grill. Back off me. You'd be up shit creek if I stopped coming to do my job."

She laughed softly, sitting normally again. "My stupid brother. I don't need another one, besides Brad, I mean." Then she frowned, focusing on me. "How is Little Kade doing? Did the missus come with him for summer break?"

"He and Taylor took off to Paris for the first couple weeks."

That got her attention. "Paris? I didn't know Taylor was rich."

"From what I hear, it was on Helen's dime."

"Damn." Heather's head craned back an inch. "Is Mommy Dearest there with them?"

I nodded. "As far as I know."

She grunted, taking a drag. "So Nightmare from Mommy Street sprung the new girlfriend all the way to France for a trip...and you've gotten what from her?" Her eyebrow lifted. "A big fat nada, right?"

If she was hoping to get a reaction, she was barking up the wrong tree. Yes, Helen Malbourne had always hated me with Mason, and yes, she seemed to adore Taylor, the love of Logan's life, but that didn't bother me.

I shrugged. "You really think I would go on a trip with her?"

"Touché." Her eyes narrowed as she flicked her cigarette into the empty fire pit. "Since we're on the topic of nightmare mothers, have you talked to yours?"

"I see Malinda every day."

"You know who I mean."

And there was the look. She was waiting for me to break down, or throw my chair across the pit, or take off running for six hours every day. It was the same look everyone had been wearing since my mother came back.

I was tempted to give her the middle finger, but all I did was sigh. "She's here."

"That's all you're going to say?"

I rolled my shoulders back. "What do you want me to say? She's back. There's nothing I can do about it. It is what it is."

"She lied to you all your life about your dad."

Yep. She'd done that. David wasn't my actual dad.

"And when your real one came around, she blackmailed him into leaving."

The lady was dedicated.

"Then when you started dating Mason, she threatened to turn him into the cops for having sex with you."

Oh yeah. Statutory rape could be a bitch, but Mason wasn't two years older than me. He was only one. I found out that nice little bit of information later. I hadn't needed to worry that his entire future could've been ripped to shreds by the woman whose loins I came from.

I was good with this. Really. It didn't bother me to hear a list of all the shitty things Analise had done before finally disappearing into a mental hospital for two years.

Then Heather dropped the last bomb. "She killed your unborn siblings, and you were the one who found her."

In a pile of blood.

I called 911.

I was eleven.

I suppressed a shudder at that one. "What do you want me to say? She's back. She's going to marry James, who is also Mason's father. There's nothing I can do." I cooled my tone. "I refuse to let her matter to me."

"Good for you." Heather saluted me with a pretend drink, her hand curled around an invisible glass. "Now get wicked drunk so you can tell me how you really feel."

I snorted and covered my face with my hand. "I can't believe I did that."

"Thank God you did." Heather grinned, a dry note in her normally husky voice.

I eyed her, waiting. This was when she'd normally return to her shift, but this was our first visit since Mason and I got home to Fallen

Crest from college a week ago. Yes, that made me a small coward. Heather Jax had been one of my most loyal friends since high school, and she had the ability to cut through the bullshit.

Mason and Logan held the same qualities, but I lived with them, so they weren't constantly calling me out. They were just watching, waiting.

A second shiver wound its way down my spine. I ignored it. It was a habit fast becoming a daily routine.

"Why don't you tell me about you and Channing?" I asked. "You two married yet?"

I meant it as a joke, but her eyes shifted. Her lips pressed into a strained line. "He wants to. He's nuts. That's what he is."

"Are you joking?" My mouth hung open. "Channing asked you to marry him?!"

She rolled her eyes. "No, but… Well, yes. He asked me a while ago because we had a pregnancy scare, but it was only a scare. No baby. I thought he'd drop it."

"He didn't?"

"He didn't." She was so glum. "He wants to settle down. I think it's mostly because he's raising Bren since their mom died."

"Wait. What?"

Channing Monroe? An older brother? Now like a dad to some little girl? This wasn't an image I could wrap my mind around. Mason and Logan had run Fallen Crest Public High School, and Channing, a model look-alike, had done the same with his high school, Roussou Public.

Roussou was the neighboring town and our usual rival, which had sometimes led to bloodshed back when Brett and Budd Broudou ran Roussou. Channing had worked with Mason and Logan and helped take control of Roussou. It helped that Brett Broudou eventually realized how much of a psychopath his brother was, and now Budd was currently residing in prison for attempted rape. Channing kept his town in check, but I wasn't so sure about him raising a child.

"Isn't he running a bar in Roussou now?" I thought that was what Logan had said one time.

Heather nodded, letting out a loud breath of air. "Yeah. Like I have time to play house. I'm running this place since my dad retired and going to community college. I don't have time to raise some teenager. Besides, the girl is tough as nails. She doesn't need or *want* a mommy replacement. Trust me. I've been there. I don't want to deal with another me."

"Whoa." I couldn't get over it. "Channing's like a dad…"

"More like a big brother extraordinaire, but he tries. She's got her own crew, though. She'll be fine." She held up a hand. "And don't get ahead of yourself. Channing is not just being the model big brother extraordinaire. He's got some stupid shit going on the sidelines, too."

"*Heather!*"

She raised her hand, her middle finger extended, but her brother couldn't see from where he yelled her name.

"*Get in here!*"

She collected her cigarettes and stood. "I'm five feet from where he's standing. You think he really needs to scream at the top of his lungs?"

"I heard that," Brandon shot back. "You do the same to me, Heatherkins."

"Do not call me that!" she snapped, reaching for the door. She paused before heading inside. "Hey, I'm going to this thing for Channing later. He's fighting in a big event tonight. If you're super bored, come with me. It'd be nice to have another female friend there."

There was no thinking required. If I stayed home, I'd go nuts wondering when Analise would strike.

"I'm in."

# CHAPTER FOUR

"You're where?"

I was leaning against Heather's car in the middle of a field, surrounded by a couple hundred other cars, and all around me was bass-heavy music, yelling, and a scream every now and then. I had my finger plugging my other ear, but I still strained to hear Mason over the phone.

"Channing's fighting tonight," I told him. "I'm going with Heather and her brother."

"Wait. What?"

I paused at hearing the snap in his voice. "What's wrong?"

"You're at a fighting event?"

"Yes." My mouth turned down.

"In Roussou?"

"Yes." My frown deepened. I could feel the wrinkles starting in my forehead and the wheels were churning. I hadn't even thought about it, but once it hit me, I wanted to smack myself there.

"Oh no."

"Yeah," he bit out over the phone. "Are you kidding me, Sam? You're there alone? It's dangerous there. I still have enemies in Roussou and you're alone."

"I'm not." I glanced over at Heather and Brandon, but I knew he wouldn't care about them or even about Channing and all of his friends. When he said alone, he meant he or Logan weren't with me.

I cringed, gritting my teeth. "I'm sorry. I didn't think about it. I just didn't want to go crazy at home."

He sighed, or I thought he sighed. I was guessing what the sounds were on his end about eighty percent of the time. "Can you wait until I'm done here? I can leave early. I don't give a shit what my dad says."

Oh. Well, fuck. Again. "I'm already here." I rushed forward, "I'm sorry. I am. I didn't think and to be honest, I only thought there'd be like thirty people here." I looked around. "There's gotta be around a hundred or so."

"A hundred?"

"Yeah." Holding the phone more tightly to my ear, I turned around. I could see a large stage alongside a couple of tents. There was one really large tent to the far right. I wondered if that was where the main event would happen. There was a smaller stage set off in the corner, and people walked around with drinks, food, and even balloons. If I didn't know better, I'd think this was some sort of music festival. I knew better, though. So did Mason.

He was groaning now. "You're there without me, Logan, or Nate."

"I know," I said quietly. "But hey—Heather's kind of a bodyguard. I'm sure she'll protect me." I rested my shoulder against the car, half-turned so I could watch people walking by. "Channing is here, and so are all his friends. Besides, I really doubt anyone will recognize me or even remember who I am." I sounded ridiculous. Who the hell was I? A nobody. People knew Mason and Logan. They didn't know me.

He cursed again. "I know people in Roussou aren't all happy with us. We did a lot of damage there and got away with it. That's how they see it."

"Yeah. Well." My stomach twisted. "Do you want me to ask Heather to bring me back?"

There was no hesitation. "No. I'm coming there. James mentioned something about an after-work meeting he wanted me to attend, but I'm ditching it."

"Okay." A lump formed in my throat. "Wait. Should I be worried now about you? It'll just be you coming."

"I'll see if I can find some friends, but be ready when I come. We're not sticking around long."

"I know. I'll be ready." I dropped my voice, "Be safe, okay?"

"Same to you."

"Love you."

"Love you."

We always said our goodbyes that way. Disconnecting the call, I put my phone in my back pocket and headed to where Heather and Brandon were waiting a few cars down, on the outskirts of a large crowd.

Heather read my face and lifted an eyebrow. "He was pissed?"

I nodded. "I didn't think."

She grunted. "I didn't tell you. Blame me. I didn't think either." Her eyes narrowed on me. "Do you want to go back?"

I shook my head, sliding my hands into my pockets. "He's coming here."

I didn't tell her we were leaving right away.

A part of me was glad I came. I was hoping to change his mind. This was something I did on my own, and in a very weird way, I was enjoying being here only as Samantha Strattan and not as Mason's girlfriend or Logan's sort-of-sister. I hadn't done something on my own in a long while.

It felt nice.

Once we'd gotten here, an excited buzz had begun low in my gut. It had gotten steadily stronger since. I was here with friends, and what I'd said was true. Nothing would happen. I was sure of it. Channing and his friends didn't mess around.

Heather threw her arm around my shoulder. "Got to admit that I'm being selfish right now because it's nice to have you here."

I put a reciprocating arm around her shoulder and laughed at how ridiculous we must have looked. Then two shirtless guys wearing white shorts with green dots on them walked past us, each carrying a stuffed flamingo. They had blue paint on their faces.

Maybe we didn't look that ridiculous.

---

# MASON

Sam was going to give me a damned migraine by the end of the day.

I cursed and texted Channing. **Sam's there. Can you have someone watch over her? I'm sorry to ask, but I'm worried some fuckheads will do something to her to hurt me.**

He responded right away: **Already on it. Heather gave me the heads-up she was coming. Sorry, man. If she's still here after my fight, we'll get everyone out asap.**

**Hoping to be there long before then**, I replied.

**You watch out too then. Jared Caldron was Budd's #2, and with Brett gone, he's stepped up. We've gone head to head more than I want to admit. He's a fucking snake.**

I remembered Caldron. **Thanks. I'll be ready for him.**

"Mason."

I put my phone away as I saw James crossing the lounge with another man. This fucking guy…he looked vaguely familiar, but I couldn't quite place him. He was dressed like my dad: custom-tailored suit and brightly colored tie.

I shook my head. Why the ties? All the businessmen I'd met today had solid looking ties, but the colors bugged me. Pink. Hot pink. Soft pink. Purple. Green. Blue. It was like all of them thought they were making a fashion statement. Or were they just rich? No… As James approached with this guy next to him, it struck me—it was their arrogance. They were broadcasting their special place in life: at the top with a secretary sucking their dicks and a miserable, alcoholic wife at home, where she'd never leave.

That was how it used to be for my dad. Not anymore, but I saw it again now.

I hated that arrogant, elitist attitude. I'd just forgotten how much after being away at Cain for three years.

"Mason," my dad said again. He clapped the guy on the back. "This is Stephen Quinn. I don't know if you remember, but you know his son."

It all clicked then.

Adam Quinn. The dick who'd tried to take Sam from me when we first began dating.

I scowled. "I know his name. You don't have to say it."

"Mason."

That was my dad's way of reprimanding me. *Be good, Mason, or you'll be kicked off this internship.* I tried to mask the scowl; I really did. Maybe it was knowing that Sam was where I should be, or worrying something was wrong with her and I couldn't find out right now, or maybe it was just the reminder that I truly hated this guy's sniveling son, but whatever it was—I knew the scowl wasn't leaving.

My dad would have to deal with it.

His eyes skirting from my dad to me, the guy cleared his throat. He held out his hand. "Uh, no offense taken. James. If I'm remembering correctly, my son had a thing for your son's girlfriend." He leaned toward me, offering his hand. "That was then. Adam has a wonderful girlfriend now."

Like that was supposed to appease me.

I shook his hand anyway, flicking my eyes to my dad. *See? I can play nice. Sometimes.*

James' mouth was a flat line of disapproval, but he said, "Yes, well, I'm glad I introduced the two of you. Stephen, I'm assigning my son to the hotel project." He looked at me like he was trying to convey a message.

I frowned.

"And your son is working with you as well, isn't he?" he continued, gauging my reaction.

*Fuck that.*

Stephen laughed. "Oh, yes. Adam's been with the company since high school, and I've been giving him more and more responsibility. He'll be in charge of handling promotions for the hotel."

"You're opening a hotel in Fallen Crest?"

My dad turned to me, purposely keeping his features neutral, but I saw the warning lurking under the surface. He was putting me on this, and he didn't want me to mess it up. I had a few choice words for him, but I held them back. They could wait till we were behind closed doors.

"Yes, out on the golf course, and it'll be connected to the country club," James explained. "There'll be a lot of cross-promotion going on. I was hoping to have that be your sole project this summer."

The subtext was: You're working with Adam Quinn. Deal with it.

I narrowed my eyes, but there was nothing I could say. He'd talked about a big project he wanted me to help with, but he never said anything about working with other people in the community.

My dad and Stephen turned to go, but not before my dad said, "My office in ten minutes, Mason? We can go over the details there."

I went to wait for him. I needed to tell him I'd have to cut work early, but once we were inside with the door shut, he sat at his desk and started with, "Are we going to have a problem here?"

"I hate that guy's kid."

"I gathered that." Acid dripped from his voice. He folded his hands on his desk. "What I asked is if we're going to have a problem."

I held his gaze; I sensed other shit going on. "Why are you putting me on this project? What are my responsibilities going to be?" There was a reason. There had to be. I wasn't known for getting along with people, especially when they went after those I loved. It didn't matter how long ago it happened. Adam showed his colors then. I doubted they'd changed.

James sighed and leaned back in his leather chair. "Adam Quinn is dating Becky Sallaway. I believe she was friends with Samantha as well."

I nodded. *Those two together? How did that work?*

"I'm telling you this because Stephen Quinn has maneuvered himself into a close and personal friendship with the commissioner and the mayor of our community—two people I want on my side. I need on my side."

"Then making me work with his son is stupid. I hate the piece of shit. I'll probably punch him at some point."

"You're going to have to refrain, but that's not why I'm putting you on the project. There've been rumors that Stephen is doing something illegal, and I think the other two are involved as well. He's got a tight group that's locked out the rest of us in the community. Except…"

"Except maybe his own son," I finished.

"You're the only one in my camp who has ties to his son. Yes, you were enemies, but that kid is going to take over his father's empire. You won't be playing football forever, Mason. I'm aware this is your backup, but it's here should you want it. And I need you to do this for me."

I was wary, but he had some points. I'd have to work with people like them eventually.

"What do you want me to do? Find out what the illegal shit is?"

"You could've used better language, but yes—find out what the illegal shit is. Do you think you can do that?"

"Were you hoping to use Sam for this, too? Because she's out. I'm not letting you use her like that."

He held his hands up. "I know. Sam's out. I agree. It's too tricky, especially with Analise. I've been away, Mason. And losing the inside track with some key people in our town was one of the consequences. I need to get back in there, and information is always power."

He had a point there for sure. *Fuuuuuuck.* I'd have to be cordial to Adam. I might even have to be nice.

"Seriously? Adam Quinn? It had to be him?"

"I didn't pick the players." My dad gave me a faint grin. "If I had, it wouldn't be you."

I rolled my eyes. "Well, be glad Logan's not around. That's one thing in your favor."

He paled. "I never thought about that. You're right. He would've blown it up within one day." His hands flattened on the desk. "So you'll do it?"

I nodded. "Any way to stick it to the Quinns, I'm in."

"Thank you, Mason. Really."

"When does this project start?"

"Now."

I shook my head. "Nope. It's gotta be tomorrow. I have to go do something."

"You're leaving? Are you—"

He caught my warning look and decided on a nod. He pointed to the door. "Fine. I'll see you tomorrow morning. There's a seven o'clock meeting at the country club anyway. Go straight there. You'll be working there most of the time anyway since it's the closest to the hotel."

I stood to leave.

"Mason," he called after me.

"Yeah?"

"It's nice to have you on board."

That was unexpected. I held up a hand. "Don't thank me yet. I've not done anything."

"That's not what I meant."

I knew what he meant. I just ignored it. I wasn't working here for a better father/son relationship. I was here to fulfill a requirement, and that was it. But first, I had to deal with a different problem: the woman I loved.

# CHAPTER FIVE
## SAMANTHA

The crowd doubled since my call with Mason. I assumed something came up at his internship because it'd been a while since we talked. I texted him once asking if he was still coming, and he replied that he had to make a small detour. That was two hours ago, and since then the sun was beginning to set, so a dusky feeling came over the air, mingling with the smells of beer, sweat, and greasy food. The music from a nearby stage pounded my ears, but I enjoyed it, leaning back on the bed of the truck where Heather and I sat.

Channing and his friends were talking and laughing. A couple sat in lawn chairs, holding drinks and watching the girls walk past. A few of those girls stopped to talk, then skimmed their eyes over to Heather and me. It was amusing to watch, because I could tell which girls were interested in Channing. When they saw Heather, they kept right on going.

We were set up at the corner of the parking lot with the fight tent a few yards away and a stage on the other side of that, so people were coming and going from the parking lot and checking out whoever was fighting inside the tent. As groups of guys passed, some stopped and greeted the guys with Channing. Most either nodded, pounded each other on the shoulder, or fist bumped. Some others stopped and raked Channing up and down, sneered, and kept walking.

A guy was doing that exact thing now. He had a group of seven or eight around him, but unlike the others who'd looked at Channing's friends—and had been ignored or joked about—this guy got a different reception. Everyone lowered their drinks, and Channing stepped out in front of his friends. They came to attention behind him, ready and waiting to see what would happen. A couple had girls trying to talk to them, but when they saw the guy, the women immediately quieted, stepping away.

Heather nudged my arm, leaning close. "That's Jared Caldron. You need to watch out for him."

I assessed. His hair was in a blond Mohawk, and he was a little shorter than Channing, so he'd be an inch or two below Mason's height, too. His face was round, but weathered with a deep tan. He had some scars around his mouth and at the corners of his eyes. I didn't want to think about where those had come from. He reminded me a bit of a troll I'd read about, but with a badass attitude. Sharp grey eyes smirked back at Channing. He held a 32-ouncer in his hand and wore a sleeveless and already dirtied T-shirt. It was baggy enough that as the wind moved past, it lifted the fabric and two pierced nipples peeked out. Ripped jeans completed the ensemble. Most of his friends wore something similar, and most of them were taller than this guy. A few were more muscled, but a couple were just heftier—with beer bellies. They had some girls with them, but I wasn't paying attention to them.

"Why do I need to watch out?" I asked Heather. "Who is he?"

She was already close, but as the guy's eyes moved to us, she leaned even closer. She lowered her voice as he watched us. "He was Budd's best friend in high school."

Channing spoke up, distracting Heather from whatever else she'd been about to add. "Move along, Caldron." Channing shifted so he blocked the guy's view of Heather and me. "Unless you want to start the fight early."

"Get off it, Monroe." The guy had a light voice, which surprised me, but he was definitely cocky and the leader of his group. "That's Kade's woman, isn't it?"

I gulped. This is what Mason had warned me about.

"She's with us, and it's none of your business."

Caldron snorted. "Yeah. Right. But good to know."

"Move along. Now."

The command came out softly. I shouldn't have been able to hear it since Channing was a few feet in front of us with his back turned, but somehow the entire group heard. Channing's friends seemed to become even more alert, as if it were a warning signal and the next word spoken might be their command to attack.

I found myself holding my breath. *Maybe I should've left instead of waiting for Mason to come here.*

"Yeah, yeah." He moved forward a couple of steps, and his eyes found us again. He spoke to Channing. "But this ain't high school any more. There's no Brett to keep us in line, remember? You remember that, too."

For a second time, Channing shielded us from the guy's view. His arms hung loose by his sides, but he gripped the beer in his hand harder, starting to crumple the can into a ball. Then he stopped, like he was waiting for something else to happen.

Time seemed to stand still, though it was only a few seconds until Caldron grunted once and then moved away, still glancing over his shoulder at us. His friends followed, as well as the girls who were with them, laughing and almost tripping on their heels.

Heather shook her head. "Beth Clovers. She's an idiot. Who wears hooker heels to walk around on grass, dirt, and mud?"

I didn't answer. I was still watching Caldron and his friends. I followed until they were swallowed up by another group. I glanced to Channing. He had looked back at me, and I half expected some comment about how I shouldn't have been there. Nothing came. His eyes flicked to Heather's before one of his buddies said something. An easy smile came to his face, and he turned, punching his friend on the arm. Then all was forgotten.

The tense moment was gone.

"You need to stick like glue to me tonight," Heather instructed.

I nodded. After seeing that, there was no way I'd risk even a trip to the bathroom alone. "Got it."

"When's your boy coming?"

That question came from one of Channing's friends. I didn't remember his name, but he was bald with two large flame tattoos that circled his head. I'd stared at the back of him before when we were moving through the crowd. The entire group seemed to be waiting for my response.

"I'm not sure, actually. He mentioned a meeting after work, but he was going to ditch out of it."

"Well, give us a head's-up, yeah? We'll go meet him."

"Word's out now," Channing added. "People know you're here, so they're going to be expecting him, too. Logan and Nate are both gone, right?"

I nodded. The phrase *bad timing* didn't cover this. Fucked-up timing was more accurate. "He said he would try to find some others to come with him, but..." This was Mason. More than likely, he'd come alone because he wanted to be at my side.

Channing seemed to be on the same wavelength. "Text him. Tell him you want to know when he's arriving."

I nodded and took out my phone, but then I heard Mason's voice next to me, coming up the side of the truck. "I'm here."

And he wasn't alone.

My mouth dropped. "Matteo?!"

Mason's football teammate grinned back, running a hand over his shaved head. He was dressed almost the same as Caldron, with a white, sleeveless shirt over jeans, but that was where the similarities ended—no nipple rings and instead of looking like he'd been mudding all day, Matteo was clean and trimmer than the last time I saw him.

He grunted, slapping a hand on Mason's back. "This one called me with perfect timing. I was about to board the plane for home, but he talked me into hanging out in the infamous Fallen Crest for a few weeks." His dark eyes lingered on Heather, and he held his hand out. "Don't know if we've met yet. I save this one's life on the field."

Mason laughed. "You would, if you weren't too slow. You're on the front line."

"Whatever." Matteo rolled his shoulders, seeming nonplussed. Two dimples winked back at Heather. "For real, my soul brotha connection must've been working both ways. Hello, friend of Sam's that must be a friend of mine, too." He stepped forward, his hand still extended.

I glanced at Channing, but he didn't look like he cared. He was laughing with the rest of his friends. The reception was a lot less tense than it had been with Caldron. They knew Matteo wasn't a threat, in any way, and a beat later, Heather confirmed it.

She looked at the hand, then turned to gaze at the crowd. "I think you might want to point that hand toward my boyfriend; his fighting is the main attraction tonight."

"Oh." Matteo withdrew his hand, looked around, and waved at Channing. "Hello, friend of Mason's who I hope will be a friend of mine, too." He jerked a thumb in Heather's direction. "No disrespect. I'm a soul brotha here to help cover my man's back, just off the field this time."

Channing grinned, moving around a lawn chair. "No problem." He nodded to Mason. "Just one?"

Mason lifted a shoulder, his eyes lingering on me. "It was last minute."

"And who's better than me? Huh?" Matteo added.

The others went back to what they'd been doing before: flirting, watching girls, or talking. Channing lowered his voice. I couldn't make out what he said to Mason and Matteo, but both looked at me with serious expressions. I felt a nervous fluttering in my stomach.

"He's telling them about Jared," Heather said.

Jared? Oh yes. Jared Caldron.

"He's bad news?" I didn't need to ask. I already knew. I felt it in my gut.

"Oh yeah. Budd tried to rape Kate, remember? Who do you think gave him the idea?"

The fluttering feeling grew, and ice flowed through my veins. "Nice to know."

"Don't worry, though." Heather lightened her tone. "You're safe. The guys are just being cautious. Caldron's had it out for Channing since back in school. Channing started the crew system to help push Budd and Brett out of the power they thought they had."

"Crew system?"

"Yeah, it's like a soft version of gangs. He had to. Once he formed his crew, others joined up and allied together. Budd lost a lot of power the end of his senior year. It wasn't all about protecting Mason and you, but some of it was. Budd couldn't take it out on Channing. If he did, he'd risk the wrath of all those crews. I think it was another reason he focused on hurting whoever Mason's girlfriend was."

The fluttering now grew into a full-sized rock, sitting right there at the bottom of my gut.

I let out a shaky laugh. "I'd forgotten what it was like that year in school."

It'd been scary at Fallen Crest Public, but I knew it was way worse at Roussou. Their town didn't have the factories and companies Fallen Crest did, which provided more money.

"Kate and those bitches." Heather had been right there with me. "She's still around, you know?"

"What?"

"Kate. She's working at the salon in Roussou. She got alienated from her friends after that year, so she officially moved to Roussou. Transferred to Roussou from Fallen Crest for school and everything. I think she's in the trailer court with her boyfriend now."

I rolled my eyes. "Lovely."

"I hate to say *white trash* because some might consider me white trash, but that girl really is. If she's not doing hair, she's at Channing's bar or drinking in her trailer." Heather thought for a second. "Or in front of the trailer. That court's not bad either. I've got a friend who lives there, and she hates when Kate does that. Makes the whole place look bad, you know?"

"Channing has a bar?"

"It's his dad's, but he took it over this year."

"Because it was time?" I wasn't really thinking about the conversation, just going along until I heard her answer.

"No, because his dad's in prison."

That got my attention. "What?"

"You didn't know?"

I shook my head. "You've never said."

"Oh." Her head lowered a bit. "Sometimes I don't say things because I don't want you to look down on me."

"What?" That came from left field. "Why would I do that?"

She looked at Mason and then to Matteo, and I saw what she meant. Channing and his friends were fine, dressed in jeans and T-shirts, and Mason and Matteo weren't dressed differently. They both wore Cain University shirts, Matteo's without sleeves, and both had on jeans. But it was the look of them. I couldn't put my finger on it, but it was obvious Mason had money. And Matteo stood out, as if he was a league above them or something.

I hated thinking like that, but this was how Heather saw them.

This was how Heather saw me.

"I'm not rich."

She half-snorted, half-barked out a laugh. "You literally have a choice between which mansion to live in for the summer: your dad's, his dad's, or even your biological dad's." She held her hands up. "Nothing against money. I don't look it, but we're doing well with Manny's." She shifted, her hands curving around the truck's edge as she leaned forward. "But we're not in range with you guys. So yeah, I think sometimes I don't say things because of that."

My tongue had never felt heavier than it did at that moment. "My mom used a wire to perform her own abortion. She threatened to turn Mason in for having sex with me so he'd be classified as a sex offender when we were in high school. There's nothing that makes me better than you. Trust me."

"I know. I do. And I know you don't think that at all, but..." She paused, sighing heavily. "Sometimes it's intimidating."

"What is?"

I was getting whiplash. I'd never expected any of this from her.

"Watching how far you're going to go with Mason and Logan, and knowing I'm going to be in the same place can be…humbling sometimes."

*Humbling?* I was honestly floored. "What are you talking about?"

"Nothing." She gestured to the guys beginning to gather together. Channing broke off to join them as Mason headed our way. "The first fight must be starting."

"Heather." I touched her arm.

She hopped off the truck's bed as Mason arrived. "Nothing. Forget what I said." She gave Mason a smile. "I'll give you two some space."

Matteo stood behind Mason, and she clasped him on the shoulder. "Come on, lover boy. I'll introduce you to some friendly girls you can get to know."

"I knew there was a reason I was attracted to you." He looked her up and down again, but the lecherous gleam was gone. "You're a home girl, aren't you? You get guys, in here." He gestured to his chest.

Heather tipped her head back, her dirty blond hair rippling, and she winked at him. "More like down there." Her eyes dropped to his groin. "I grew up with my dad and two brothers. I understand guys."

Matteo groaned, his hands coming to his chest. "I'm feeling the ache right here. Why do you have to be taken, and by someone who seems cool as shit?"

She laughed. "Come on. You like the name Tiffany?" Her voice faded as she pulled him around to the front of the group.

I knew she did that to give Mason and me more privacy, and the humbling feeling she'd mentioned now landed smack on my chest. I felt grounded to the steel of the truck beneath me. I reiterated some of what she'd said to Mason.

"She's a good friend to you. Loyal."

"I don't feel good enough for her. Not anymore."

"And that's why you're a good friend to her." He dropped a kiss to my forehead, his hand curving around and resting on the small of my back. "Come on. We can talk later. Just stick close to me."

I angled my head back to stare up at him. "We're staying? I thought you wanted to go right away."

He shrugged, glancing to where Channing was standing. "I kind of want to see him fight."

There was no 'kind of.' He wanted to. I could hear it in his voice, and I knew a part of Mason missed those days. It felt simpler back then. They could fight and not care about the consequences. Things were different now. Futures had to be considered. Decisions made now could harm someone's career.

I slipped my hand into his and squeezed. "I'm sorry."

"For what?"

"For coming here and not thinking about what I was going to be walking into."

He shrugged again. "It's okay. I got Matteo here and we'll deal with whatever happens."

I saw how he was watching Channing. He wanted to support his friend and I glanced to my friend from the reminder. I didn't feel like the good friend to her.

"Come on." He pulled me off the truck and his hand rested snug on my back.

He started for the fighting tent, but I stopped him. "Heather doesn't talk a lot about Channing or even about Roussou with me. If there's any part of you blaming her for bringing me here, don't. It's my fault. I should've known, and a part of me didn't because I don't talk to her about this part of her life. I haven't been a good friend to her."

Mason's eyes held mine, sparking a different feeling inside. The nerves were still there, but they mixed with another kind of tension. We'd returned home, and now that we were here, we needed to face the music. It didn't make sense to me, but what I'd said was true. I couldn't be friends with Heather if I only got half of her. That wasn't being the true friend I thought I was.

My mouth felt dry, and I didn't say any of those words to Mason, but he'd been watching me. And as if he'd read my mind, as I was sure he could, his eyes softened.

He tucked a loose strand of hair behind my ear. "I know, but I can't lie. I don't like owing someone else for covering my back. It's nothing against Channing. I like him. I respect him, but he's not family. Logan and Nate are, and neither one is here." His fingers laced with mine. He started forward, leading me. "And I have to be very careful what I do. Any leaked video could be the end of my career."

That was the feeling I had—the other kind of nervousness. My stomach dropped to my feet, with the rock and everything.

Looking around, I noticed again how many people were paying attention to us. I'd felt like this when Mason was in high school, and it had only gotten worse in college, but standing here now, among this rougher crowd, it was different. People wanted to know Mason so they could use him at Cain. It wasn't like that here. These people wanted to hurt him.

And I was one way for that to happen.

I'd been so stupid.

# CHAPTER SIX

The heat was almost suffocating when we got inside, and Heather waved us over to their corner. They'd taken up position near an opening in the tent, so a small breeze wafted in, giving us some respite. Channing wasn't there anymore, but his friends moved in around us. Or mostly they moved in around Mason and me. All of them, Mason included, glanced around, and I had to kick myself again.

I'd forgotten how much he was hated.

As if reading my mind, Mason gave my hand a reassuring squeeze. I slipped my fingers between his, and despite the heat, he pulled me in front of him. We stood like that, holding hands, my back resting against his chest. I caught Heather giving us a grin as a loud cheer rose up.

A guy wearing a white robe hopped into the makeshift boxing ring. As the crowd continued to cheer, he thrust two fists in the air, and they really let loose. He began bouncing around, doing a little jig with his feet until a guy yelled from the sidelines and tossed him a microphone. The robe guy stopped and caught it, and then suddenly the tent grew quiet. He pulled his hood up, standing smack in the middle of the ring, and gripped the mic. We could hear him breathing.

"Are you guys ready?" he whispered first.

There was silence. A guy yelled out, a beat later, "Yeah!"

"Are you guys ready?" he asked, a fraction louder, not quite a whisper.

"Yes!" The same guy yelled back, joined by others.

Fists started shaking in the air and more called out, "Let's go! Let's start."

"I said—" He shoved his hood back and raised his face. "Are you READY?!"

*"Fuck yes, motherfucker!"*

I jolted, bumping into Matteo, who stood next to us.

The guy behind us had roared that, and when he noticed my reaction, he flashed me a grin. "Sorry. I get heated."

I nodded. "Noted."

The announcer yelled something into the microphone, but I couldn't hear him. The crowd drowned him out, but I gathered he'd announced the first fight.

After a fast knockout, he introduced the second and third fights the same way. I had to step outside to see if the ringing in my ears would go away when the volume decreased, or if it was permanent.

I still wasn't sure ten minutes later when Heather motioned me back in. The last fight was starting, Channing's fight.

The crowd was insane. The bloodier the matches, the better. The announcer stepped back into the ring. He held his hands up, and the crowd quieted. Mason gripped my thigh, and I stepped back into him. Just feeling him steadied me.

Heather looked over her shoulder. I followed her gaze, and there was Channing. He wore no shirt, and his black sweats hung low from his hips. Channing was a good-looking guy, and I could see what the others were seeing. He was ripped. But as he stood there, swinging his arms back and forth and jumping lightly up and down, it wasn't him that I was seeing.

I saw Mason.

He was the one getting ready to fight.

He was the one everyone was watching.

He was the one everyone wanted to fight.

I could feel an underlying pressure from those around us. People kept glancing at Mason, and I knew Caldron was glaring from across the ring. People really did want to see Mason fight. Yet another wave of self-loathing came over me. I shouldn't have come here. What was wrong with me?

A new roar rose from the crowd, and I turned to see Channing heading for the ring. His opponent climbed in from the other side.

After another round of announcements, the fight began. I still couldn't shake the sensation of Mason being involved.

As Channing ducked, I saw Mason ducking. He hit the other guy with an undercut, and I could almost feel Mason's hand tensing. Channing danced back, evading punches and returning with his own. This went on until eventually, the other guy wore out. Then Channing went in for his win. He ended the fight in one round, delivering a knockout punch right before the bell rang.

The guy fell, and he didn't move.

Channing was the winner.

The crowd went nuts, and I saw lust in Heather's eyes. Her lips parted, and she gave her man a slow and seductive grin. He was watching her as well, his own eyes already darkened. If I hadn't been sure before, I was now. Heather was in love, and she was never going to leave his side.

I leaned back against Mason. His hand held my waist, anchoring me to him. All my friends were settling in, finding the ones they loved. Logan had Taylor. Heather was finally done with the back and forth with Channing, and I'd found my soulmate long ago. We'd all dealt with hurdles and obstacles, and now it was time to get ready for the future.

We left the tent and waited as Heather congratulated Channing on his win. I slipped my hand inside Mason's front pocket. He looked down at me, a soft smile on his face. He knew what I was feeling.

I was ready to go home. I was ready to feel him inside of me.

We waited, though. Channing's friends wanted to celebrate some more, and Channing greeted others who were still coming up to offer their own congratulations. Matteo had a girl in his arms. I had no clue where she'd come from, but her hands were wrapped around his waist, and he'd thrown his arm around her shoulders, holding her tight to his side. Heather was next to Channing. She wasn't sticking to him like glue, but after seeing a few wolfish looks shared between the two, I knew we could go. Heather wasn't going to be ready to leave any time soon.

I squeezed Mason's hand.

He glanced down. "You ready?"

I nodded and jerked my head toward Matteo. "What about him?"

"Uh..." Mason shrugged. "I'll have a word, but I'm pretty sure he wants to stay."

That was fine with me. I went over to Heather and let her know we were going.

"You guys okay to walk back alone?" Channing asked. "We can walk with you."

Mason came up behind me. I could feel his heat, and one of his hands found my hip again, burrowing in under my shirt. "We can call if we run into trouble."

"Just watch out for Caldron. Now that you're here, he can taste the blood in the water."

"I've been watching. He and his buddies took off for one of the band stages a few minutes ago."

Channing nodded, resting against Heather with his arms crossed over his chest. "They've been drinking all night. I had some of the guys keep an eye on them, too, but they're only starting. Just keep an eye out. If one of them notices you leaving, they're going to take a shot. You're here without Logan and Nate. It's the best chance they'll get, and they know it."

"We'll be watching." Mason nodded at him again, starting to pull me away. "Thanks for watching Sam before, and congrats on the win."

Channing grinned. "I'd like to see you in the ring. Something tells me you'd hold your own."

Mason mirrored his smile, but didn't say anything.

I waved at Heather, and she waved back, but she was already melting into Channing's side. He lifted his arm to encircle her shoulders as we stepped away from the group.

The area outside the tent was still filled with people walking around, but since the last fight was done, the main crowd had migrated toward the other tents that had bands playing in them.

We could hear the music while we'd stood with the group, but as we walked down the line of cars, it began to fade. It was quiet compared to the crowd we'd just left, and an almost eerie feeling came over me.

"You okay?"

I sighed, holding tight to Mason's hand. "Why aren't you madder at me?"

He stopped, turning around to look at me. "What do you mean?"

"This." I indicated where we'd just been. "This place is dangerous for you."

He lifted a shoulder. "It is what it is. We could've left before. I wanted to stay, too, and you wanted to spend time with your friend. There's nothing wrong with that. Besides, the enemies I have here are partly my fault," he added. "We didn't have to fight back so much with Broudou back then. We did some stupid stuff. Lighting cars on fire? Shit. Logan wanted to torch their barn even." He paused, frowning. "I think he did light it on fire."

I didn't say anything. A barn was nothing compared to the fraternity house.

"Don't beat yourself up. It's a pile of shit, and you might've helped bring that pile of shit to my doorstep, but it's not your pile of shit. It's mine. You can't look at it any other way."

"A pile of shit?" I teased, bumping my hip into his. "You're sounding like Logan."

A faint grin lifted his top lip. "Don't tell him that. I'll never hear the end of it. He'll start proclaiming that I secretly want to be him." He grimaced, but I caught the look that passed in his eyes.

He missed his brother.

I murmured, "I miss him, too."

He looked down, and we shared a look with music and moonlight as our background.

Then I heard, "You left without saying goodbye? *Tsk, tsk*, Kade."

Jared Caldron stood behind us, a bat in his hand.

# CHAPTER SEVEN

Three more guys filtered from the cars to stand behind Caldron, and I turned around to see another three standing behind us. We were boxed in, unless we ran through the cars, but as Mason's hand took hold of my arm, I couldn't gauge what he wanted to do. He moved me behind him and stood sideways, with cars behind us.

"Whatever beef we had is over, Caldron. It went to prison with Broudou."

Jared came forward, his hard eyes glinting a boiling anger. "Right. Because you had nothing to do with that, and your little girlfriend there didn't either."

"She didn't."

"Bullshit." The guy's nostrils flared, and he started toward us, bouncing the bat slowly in his hand. He stopped a few yards away, lowering his head. "Kate squealed. I know you set her up so Budd would think she was your girlfriend, and this one here—" he pointed the bat at me "—had that clerk call the cops as she blew up his truck. You're both the reason he went to prison."

I might've gotten used to how safe Cain was, and I might've been shocked at the reminder how unsafe Roussou was, but my nerves and fear quickly dissipated. I was adjusting on the fly, and I almost growled. My nails sank into my palm as my hand formed a fist in Mason's grip.

"Budd went to prison because he was going to rape her," Mason said calmly.

"Bullshit."

I surged forward. "I was there!"

Mason caught me, keeping me in place with a cement arm around my waist.

Caldron laughed. "You've got spunk—more than what I remember from high school."

"Don't talk to her." Mason sent him a glare, adding under his breath, "Sam, stop."

"Don't talk to her?"

I stilled, hearing Caldron's mocking tone.

"Who the fuck do you think you are? I can't talk to your woman?" He snarled. "Boy, I'll do anything I want to your woman."

Two more steps. He was within arm's reach now.

Mason tucked me behind him again. His hand gripped mine, and I realized he was guiding it somewhere. Down. Down. To my pocket. He pressed my hand around my phone. I was so stupid. Cursing softly under my breath, I turned and hunched my shoulders, trying to hide the phone as I sent a text to both Brandon and Heather. I hoped one of them wasn't too drunk already to notice their phone blowing up. I sent another text to Matteo. I didn't have Channing's number, or I would've sent him one, too. After that, I said a quick prayer and moved my hand away. I was hyperaware of the phone, and when it didn't buzz back, a feeling of helplessness hit me hard.

I blinked back tears.

Mason was outnumbered. He hadn't had to fight in so long. This wasn't good.

"Look." Caldron threw his arms out, swinging his bat wide as he gestured to his friends. "This talking thing we've got going was just a stall tactic. I needed time to make sure the rest of my friends got into position."

The rest of... I looked around again. The six friends now had another four added to their numbers. So it was eleven to Mason. No. Eleven to two. I was fighting, too.

"Now that's all done." He flashed us a smile. "Let's get to dancing." He hadn't finished his last word before he was swinging the bat, but Mason ducked. The bat cleared his head, and he twisted, catching Caldron's arm with both hands. He shifted, pulling Caldron to lie across his back. His toes were just grazing the ground. Caldron's eyes went wide. Panic flared for a second, but then a murderous rage came to the forefront, and he started to struggle.

Mason adjusted his hold, ramming his elbow into Caldron's face before wrenching his wrist to the side.

Three things happened then:

The bat fell to the ground.

I heard a snapping sound as Mason broke Caldron's wrist.

And the ten friends rushed in.

What followed was a blur. I was terrified, desperate, irrational, and scared. But I surged forward, my hands already in fists. I was going to help, and I didn't care what I had to do to keep him safe. My vision tunneled. I could only see Mason and feel the impending assault when he knelt down and scooped up the bat.

He tossed it to me.

I caught it, surprised.

He grunted before turning and hitting Caldron with one last good punch. "Aim for their knees." And then, as Caldron's body hit the ground, unconscious, Mason began exchanging punches with the others.

I blinked once, tasted the salt from my tears, and felt someone's hand on my shoulder. I stopped thinking then and fell to the ground in a kneeling stance, sweeping out with the bat. I swung it with all of my might and heard a crunching sound as it made contact. Someone yelled and fell next to me. That was my first victory. I enjoyed it for a split second before I was plucked up in the air.

There was no strategy after that.

I fought. I fought hard. I swung with everything I had. I kicked. I bit. I scratched. I made my body go limp on more than one occasion to get out of someone's hold. They didn't punch me, but I was slapped and knocked to the ground. I saw stars, but I jerked upright, aiming for the groin and receiving an ear-splitting sound as my reward. I didn't know if it was a squeal or a gasp, or even a scream. I could only hear the thumping of my heart. It drowned everything out, and I was back on my feet again. I had no time to stop and think.

I had to fight.

I had to hurt.

I had to protect.

Feeling someone behind me, I let loose with the bat, a scream erupting from my throat. Someone caught the bat and wrapped an arm around my waist. I tried kicking out. He dodged my feet and said hurriedly in my ear, "Damn, Strattan. It's me, Channing. Stop!"

Channing.

He was friendly.

*Stop.*

I sagged in his arms, looking for Mason. Where was he? He was circling a guy, still fighting.

I started forward, but Channing caught my arm. "Whoa. Chill."

I growled as I yanked my hand free and started forward again, but Channing grabbed my arm once more.

He got in front of me, holding his other hand up. "Whoa, whoa, whoa. Look. He's fine. We're here. He's got that. Look. Look, Sam."

My senses began to calm. The black around my eyesight faded. I could see more normally, and the buzzing in my ears subsided. I gulped for breath, tasting salt and dust in my mouth.

Channing was right. Mason's eyes were deadly, but alert, his mouth set in a flat line. His shoulders were tense, but he looked in control. His opponent was a heavier-set guy. He probably outweighed Mason by fifty pounds, but as he threw a punch, Mason evaded it easily and slammed back with one of his own. The guy faltered, falling to his knees. Mason reared back, his hand coming down hard, and a moment later, the guy collapsed to the ground.

Mason knocked him out.

"Shit."

I glanced at Channing, who'd spoken beside me. I heard the awe before he broke out in a grin, heading toward Mason.

"Fuck, Kade. If football doesn't do it for you, and if you're not going to become a millionaire businessman like your daddy, you've always got fighting as a backup." He laughed again, shaking his head.

"You and your girl took on ten of Caldron's crew." He swung around. "Heather, you should be taking lessons from Sam here."

I looked and sure enough, Heather was right next to me, her hands holding her elbows. She gave me a shaky smile. I saw the fear in her eyes then, and another moment of reality hit me like a slap across the face. The adrenaline had been a nice blanket surrounding me, but it was gone now, and I gasped, feeling aches and pains all over my body.

I doubled over. "Fuck."

"Sam!"

Mason was there, his hands gentle on me as he helped me stand back up. "You okay?" He inspected me all over, brushing back my hair, feeling over my arms, legs, and stomach. When he was certain nothing major was wrong, he pulled me to his chest.

"Are you okay?" He buried his head in my hair, at the crook of my neck.

His hug was gentle, but I crushed him to me. He wasn't the only one who needed reassurance.

Holy. Fuck.

Eleven to two.

I felt him peppering soft kisses to my neck. "Who knew you were such a badass with a bat, huh?"

A slight laugh slipped out, causing a new burst of pain through my chest. But it felt good. Damned good. I leaned back so I could see him. "You okay?"

His eyes roamed over me, his love and concern evident there. "I'm fine. Worried about you."

"I'm good."

Those two words didn't feel right, but I wasn't capable of speaking further at that moment.

———

"I don't think Caldron will seek you out for a rematch."

We had all regrouped at Heather's house, which was now overrun with Channing's crew. Some of the guys had migrated to the front porch, where their girlfriends were now hanging all over them. Channing leaned against one of the kitchen counters, his arms crossed over his chest as he spoke to Mason.

He turned to watch as Heather wet a washcloth before bringing it to me where I sat on Mason's lap at the table. Since the fight, we'd barely separated. I needed to keep reminding myself he was okay.

She handed it over, and I pressed it to a cut on my face. I winced, but Heather's painkiller was already working. The pain was considerably less than it'd been at the event.

Mason watched me as he replied to Channing. "I know, but he got his ass kicked. Budd was going to go after Sam no matter what. I can't put it past Caldron now."

Heather sat next to me, eyeing my bruised hand. "You sure you don't want to get that checked out?"

I nodded. "It looks worse than it is. It's not broken. I can tell."

"Okay." But she didn't seem convinced. "I can't believe you took down three of those guys."

Mason smiled. "Apparently, she's deadly with a bat."

I grinned, my chest feeling lighter with his teasing. "You said to aim for the knees. That worked with the first one. The rest I had to improvise."

"I'm pretty sure I saw you head-butt a guy's junk." Heather got up for another washcloth.

Channing laughed, tugging Heather into his arms as she passed him. He took the washcloth from her hand and tossed it into the sink. "She's fine. You've given her ten different washcloths. Your friend is okay."

She bit her lip, eyeing me from the shelter of his arms.

"I'm fine. Really."

Her eyebrows furrowed together. "I saw one of those guys kick you in the ribs. I think you should get that checked."

"Ribs?" Mason turned to me.

I didn't remember that, but I touched my side and found she was right. I hissed as I touched a swollen spot. I could move around okay, though.

"I'm sure I'm fine. I didn't even notice till now."

"Maybe we should go in," Mason countered.

I looked at him and was about to protest, but then I saw some of his bruising. If I looked as bad as he did, I understood why Heather was so worried.

I sighed. "Maybe we should both go get checked?"

He nodded.

As we stood to go, Channing gestured to one of his friends. "Congo can drive you guys there."

Congo?

A short, bald guy came over. He clipped his head at us, flashing blinding white teeth. He was so tanned, even the whites of his eyes seemed too bright.

"Wouldn't want either of you to lose consciousness on the drive over," he said.

Heather moved forward. "I can go with you guys."

"No." I touched her arm. "I'm fine. Really."

She was so tense, but she melted at my touch. Then she was hugging me, her head resting where Mason's had been earlier. I could feel her trembling.

"I was so scared," she whispered. "You didn't see yourself, Sam. You were…" Her body twitched again. She couldn't finish her statement. "I never should've invited you to come with me."

"Stop. I mean it." I pulled back, keeping my hands on her arms. "I chose to go, remember? If anything, this is my fault."

She began to shake her head, and I opened my mouth, ready to take more of the blame, when Mason pulled me away.

"Both of you shut up. Caldron's my enemy. Stop with the blame game. You're giving me a headache." He touched the small of my back. "Come on, Sam. The sooner you're checked out, the sooner we can go home."

He was right. Home. Bed. His arms. That was the list of where I wanted to be.

I said one more time to Heather, "I'm fine!" and hugged her a last time before turning away and following Mason outside.

Matteo was waiting next to Congo at the car. I didn't know the specifics of the fight, and I hadn't realized Matteo had fought with us, but his cut lip told me he had. Before I slipped into the backseat with Mason, I reached through the opened window and touched Matteo's shoulder. "Thank you."

He shook his head. "Don't thank me. I was deep in pussy and booze. I got in a few good hits at the end, but not enough. I never should've left your side." He spoke to Mason as Congo started the Escalade. "I'm sorry, man. I let you down."

Mason waved him off. "This was my fight, not yours."

Anything else Matteo was ready to say, Mason must've changed his mind because he closed his mouth. As we pulled away, Mason lifted his arm for me, and I leaned into him, my head resting on his chest and my eyes closed.

I could've stayed there forever, but soon enough I was pulled away to go into the hospital. A couple hours later, we checked out. The x-rays showed we were both fine, and I was back in his embrace.

Everything was just as it should be.

# CHAPTER EIGHT

## MASON

The girl at the front desk gasped when she saw my face the next morning. I couldn't blame her. I'd woken to a pounding head, black eye, busted lip, and aching ribs as well. Fucking Caldron.

I didn't want to shock this receptionist too much, so I kept my shades on. "James Kade said to be here at seven. I'm Mason Kade."

"I know." Hearing my dad's name and mine seemed to settle her a bit. She glanced around. "My manager said you'd be coming in, along with another guy. I'm supposed to show you to the conference room you'll be using."

"And the other guy is here," a voice announced.

I turned to see Adam Quinn standing next to me with his hand raised. He was about to slap me on the shoulder.

"Lay one hand on me and I'll break it, Quinn."

He looked the same as in high school. I knew girls thought he was pretty with his height and blond hair, but he still looked like a preppy douchebag who wore sweaters tied around his neck like some Ivy League pedophile to me.

He stepped back, looking at my face. "Your dad said you've been back a couple weeks. What shit have you already gotten into?"

I shifted to face him directly. He was trying to see my eyes through my shades. "You still got a hard-on for Sam?"

"What?"

"Enough with the bullshit. Let's just cut straight to business." I rested a hand on the desk. The receptionist looked like a deer caught in headlights. "I hear you're with that Sallaway girl, but I was there. I know how obsessed you were with *my* girl. So do you still have a torch? Are you and I going to have another problem like we did back in school?"

A strangled laugh slipped out, and he cleared his throat. "Jesus Christ, Mason. We're working together. I assumed you'd be over your issue."

"*My* issue?"

His head lowered a fraction of an inch. He sighed. "No, I don't still have feelings for Sam. Fuck's sakes, I'm with Becky. Remember her? She was friends with Samantha."

He seemed to be genuine when he said he didn't still have feelings for Sam. I was watching. Quinn was sleazy, but he was a piss-poor liar. I would've seen a reaction from him. I clapped him on the shoulder. "We can get through this." I turned back to the girl at the desk. "You can show us that conference room now."

"Nope. That'd be my job."

A tall, skinny woman dressed in a business skirt held out a hand, flashing us both a smile. Her black hair was pulled back into some type of bun, and she had a bird-like nose with a small chin and dark eyes.

"I'm Maxine. I'm in charge of cross-promotions with the country club, and that means I'm in charge of you two. I'll be the person you go to if you need anything, okay?" She gestured with her head for us to follow as she started down a hallway. "The hotel is almost complete, but your fathers want you to have a room set up here as your office. The conference room I'll show you is now yours to use. You'll both be given keys for the property." A second right, then she opened a door into a basic business room.

A table ran the length of the space with black leather chairs around it. She pointed to a smaller table in the corner that was loaded with coffee and water, as well as baskets and trays of food.

"Those will be changed every day. If you'd like lunch brought in, just call the front desk. They'll have it arranged, and as I said, if you need anything, let me know." Two business cards lay on the table. She touched them. "Here's my contact information."

She pointed out the white board behind her and showed us how to use the projector. Once Orientation 101 was completed, she folded her hands in front of her. Scrutinizing first Quinn, then myself, she lingered on my bruises. "We usually schedule a small press conference to announce a new partnership, but I'm assuming you'll want that postponed?"

"Quinn can do it," I told her. "He's pretty."

Adam coughed, frowning at me. "Uh, pretty sure they'll want Mason Kade there."

"He's right." There was a different look in Maxine's eyes now, something close to a gleam. "Your dad wants to use your name. A football star is a big draw for publicity. They'll want you to be there, but I don't imagine you want the state of your face getting out. Soon-to-be-NFLer Gets Beat Up. Those headlines would double our publicity."

Adam looked away, his shoulders lifted in silent laughter.

She noticed. "What?"

I smirked. "You think I'm the one who got beat up?"

"Oh." The corner of her mouth dipped down, just briefly. Then her shoulders rolled back. "I just…you look like you did. That's all."

"Being the one on the receiving end of his punches in high school a few times, I'll say this for Mason." Quinn gave me the smallest of nods. "There's only one way you'd know if he was the one who got beat."

"What's that?"

He grinned at me. "He'd be in the hospital."

This fuckhead. I narrowed my eyes. He was being complimentary. He was being easygoing. "I still hate you."

He laughed. "I have no doubt, but we're not enemies right now so…" He indicated the table. "Maybe we should act like project partners instead?"

## SAMANTHA

"Hey there, my sister."

I lowered my book as my stepbrother Mark opened the front door and came out to the porch, a smirk on his face. He looked freshly showered and smelled it, too, as he gestured for me to move my legs so he could sit next to me.

I scowled. "I was comfortable."

He shrugged, stretching his long legs in front of him. "You'll get over it. You know where my mom is?"

I shook my head. "She was gone when I came over this morning. I assume she's at the country club. One of her friends has a new obsession with wedding events."

He groaned, tipping his head back and pinching the top of his nose. "Great. My mom will start thinking she's a wedding planner now." He glanced at me. "Is she starting to harp on you and Mason?"

I hid a grin. "Because we both know she's not harping on you and Cass."

Mark was Malinda's son, and he'd been staying at his girlfriend's house since he came home for summer break. Cass was a point of contention. Malinda hated her, and Mark wouldn't break up with her. I'd been a little sad when I learned he'd be staying there instead of at home. Mark was the only one from Fallen Crest Academy, my old school, who got along with Mason and Logan. Plus, it would've been nice to spend time with the guy who actually was an official brother to me.

He grunted, stretching out even farther. "I think she's hoping to help your mom with her wedding, actually."

I straightened in my seat. "Are you serious?"

He nodded, yawning. "She likes to try to be on good terms with everyone." He gave me a reassuring grin. "I wouldn't worry about it. She's probably doing it to spy on Analise more than anything. My mom won't let yours hurt you again. She was bawling the night of the Christmas party last year."

I was taken aback. That was the first time I'd seen my mom again, and I hadn't been fully prepared. "That wasn't Malinda's fault."

"But she saw your mom hurt you, and it was under her roof. You know how she is."

I frowned. I didn't like hearing that at all. "I'll talk to her."

"No. Leave it. She'll worry anyway. Just let her do her thing. That settles her, at least a bit."

"Oh. Okay."

"Oh!" He suddenly shot up. "Hey, today's the day, isn't it?"

"What day?"

"The day Adam and Mason work together. Right? Or did I get that wrong?"

I'd walked into the bathroom this morning to find Mason looking over his wounds from the night before. I'd forgotten he had to meet up with Adam this morning. I should've felt some sympathy for my boyfriend, but as I took in the sight of his hardened and ripped body in only his boxers, that was the last thing on my mind. Even though we were both hurting, a minute later I'd been on the counter with my legs wrapped around his waist as he was sliding inside.

My neck grew hot. I coughed. "Oh yeah? That was today?"

He rolled his eyes. "Like you didn't remember. I half-thought you'd be there, spying on Mason while my mom's spying on some wedding."

There was already a scheduled wedding to spy on, but I didn't say that. "Right. Like I'm the type to do that?"

"Uh, yeah. You are. When it comes to Malinda, anyone is the type. I know how she can talk a rock into pretending to be a pet dog. My mom's got skills." He shook his head. "Skills I wish I had."

I was going with a gut hunch here. "Cass problems?"

He cringed. "Let's not discuss my girlfriend. What about you? Mom said you're staying with Mason at Helen's now?"

I nodded. It still felt weird being in her house. Mason had said I was welcome there. Logan would've said the same. But the person who owned the house probably had a different opinion. And I couldn't shake the uneasiness I felt being there, especially with Mason at work during the days now.

Hence the reason Mark found me on my stepmother's porch.

"Uh, let's skip that topic, too."

He grinned crookedly. "Okay. Enough with this. Let's go do something."

I was down. Whatever it was, I didn't care. No Logan. No Mason. No Heather even. (Too soon after last night's debacle. She would've broken down in apologies again.) I was in dire need of keeping my days occupied.

Maybe that was why I found myself making a suggestion as we got into his car.

"We should get a job together somewhere."

# CHAPTER NINE

## SAMANTHA

Four hours later I found myself with a garbage stick, a trash bag, and a red vest over my clothes. I glared at Mark, who wore the same getup.

"When you said the local carnival, picking up trash wasn't what I had in mind."

He frowned over at the beer garden, the place he'd said we should try to get a job. "Me either."

"Come on, you two. Unless you're reading the midway, get your asses in gear. There's trash to be picked up." The guy who hired us on the spot, after a good laugh, pointed for us to get going. "Everyone starts at the bottom. And if you find some hooch, bag it separately. We recycle that shit."

The guy wasn't wearing a shirt. He was probably in his later fifties, and he had tanned and oiled skin with tattoos up and down his arms. A raggedy baseball cap was turned backward on his head, but his eyes were sharp. He skimmed the booths even as he turned to leave us, and a moment later he barked out, "Doggie, put that back. I don't want to find your kick empty later on."

The worker waved at him. "Stop blowing your pipes. I'm fine."

They shared a couple more exchanges, but I couldn't make it out. The words were jumbled together.

"Hooch?" Mark looked around at the ground. "They recycle alcohol? What the fuck?"

Another worker started laughing as he passed. "Slum." He pointed at a piece of plastic on the ground and picked it up. "The really cheap shit. Keifer likes to be the definition of a cheapskate. It's this crap he wants." Brushing off some of the dirt, he handed over a plastic smiley face. Then he looked us over, taking in the trash picks and bags. "I would've marked you if you weren't holding those things."

"This?" Mark lifted the trash stick.

The guy nodded, narrowing his eyes slightly. "Just make sure he pays you at the end of each day."

"Wait. What?"

The worker was moving on. He raised a hand in an absentminded wave before veering around a booth and into another one. Apparently, he manned some type of climbing game. People tried to climb up a rope ladder to ring a bell, but it kept flipping around, and they fell off.

Mark watched the same two people trying a second time and cursed under his breath. "Sorry, Sam. It seemed like a good idea."

If I was being honest, finding myself picking up trash at a carnival seemed to sum up the last few weeks for me. What was I doing? Heather had a job. Mason had an internship. Even Logan had a new purpose in life: Taylor. And me? My purpose seemed to be more about avoiding Analise in case she tried to talk to me than doing anything productive.

I speared an empty paper cup. "Let's do the day and see how it goes." I grinned at him over my shoulder. "It's not like either of us has anything better to do."

"Uh." He lifted an eyebrow, picking up some "hooch" and putting in a different bag. "I beg to differ. We have people to avoid. That's why we're here. It's not like we have country clubs, private pools, or empty mansions to relax in. Nope. We don't have any of those to take up our time."

Private pools, empty mansions, and country clubs were exactly the places I wanted to avoid. I flipped him my middle finger. "I can't tell if you're being sarcastic or not, so I'm just giving you this. I'm channeling my inner Logan."

He laughed, scooping a bunch of napkins and cups into his trash bag. "Speaking of the sex machine, when's he coming back?"

"Mason thinks a few weeks."

I felt Mark's eyes on me as he mumbled, "Bet he'd come back earlier if he heard about those bruises you've not mentioned to me yet."

I stilled. I knew my cheek was red and swollen, along with some scratches on my neck. There were other marks under my shirt, but those weren't any of his business either.

I jerked up a shoulder, turning my back to him. "It's nothing. Something stupid." That'd been my fault in the first place.

"Adam texted me. He said Mason's covered in bruises and has a busted lip."

Fucking hell. I whirled around. "That's why you came over, isn't it?" New understanding dawned. "That's why we're here. You're not avoiding your girlfriend. You're trying to get information out of me."

When he shrugged, I knew I was right.

He kept picking up trash. "Would you have told me if I came out and asked?"

"No, and I'm not telling you now either. It's no one's business, and it's over with."

"Is it?"

I could only stare at him for a moment. There was something more to his tone. Mark was always the carefree, laidback one. He was actual friends with Logan—had been even before I started dating Mason and Mark's mom started with my dad. He'd never been like this, trying to pry into my business or having something akin to brotherly protectiveness in his voice.

I didn't know how to process this. "What are you doing here?"

He dropped his arms and gave up trying to work and talk at the same time. "I'm worried, okay? I know the type of trouble Mason and Logan get into, and I don't know." His jaw clenched as he was silent for a beat. "Maybe it's because you and I are actually like brother and sister. Maybe it's because my mom loves you so much. I worry. Okay? I just don't want anything to happen to you."

"Nothing does." But that wasn't true.

"You were put in the hospital by crazy chicks because of Mason." He looked over my face and neck. "I don't think it's a stretch to say those happened because of him, too."

My neck grew warm. I gritted my teeth. "Back off about this, Mark. You're going to ruin a relationship I was enjoying having with you."

My message was clear: Push me and I'll choose Mason. Every. Damn. Time.

After a moment he asked, "Did I tell you the crazy shit Cass wants me to do this summer?"

He'd dropped it. I should've been thankful, but I wasn't. Feeling a weird sense of disappointment mixed with wariness, I just shook my head. I shoved that away. Mark was a good brother, or he was trying to be. That was all. I couldn't get mad at him for doing what I'd do for him.

But as he launched into some story about Cass wanting him to join a walking club, I listened with a knot in my stomach. The previous conversation wasn't over. It had just been dropped, for now.

A few hours later, we heeded the worker's warning and made sure Keifer paid us. After he demanded to know who told us to request our money, he slapped some paperwork in front of us with a couple pens. "You might as well fill those out, if we're going to make this legal after all."

Mark and I shared a look.

Keifer noticed. "What? We're not completely illegal here." He tapped the papers. "I'll get what I owe you for today, but if you're serious about a job, come back tomorrow. Keep doing trash, and I'll find something better by the end of the week for you two." He paused, looking us over with suspicion. "I'm assuming you want to man a booth together?"

Mark lifted a hand. "I was hoping for the beer garden." That was true. That was the whole reason Mark suggested a job here.

Keifer laughed, but stared at me. It was like an idea had come to him, and he nodded. "Maybe. We'll see."

Mark frowned at me. I shrugged in response. I didn't know what that was about, but we left with money in our pockets.

We were nearing Mark's car when the worker we'd spoken to earlier called to us. He raised an arm and veered around some vehicles with the same lithe athleticism he'd showed earlier when he jumped into his booth.

"Hey! Wait up." Slowing as he neared us, he flashed his white teeth. "You two got paid?"

"We did."

I let Mark do the talking.

The guy bobbed his head up and down, seeming to mull something over. "Well, okay. Have a good night." He held a hand out in a wave, walking back to where he'd come from.

"That was weird," Mark said as we got in the car.

"Yeah."

But the guy wasn't on my mind. Mark's new protectiveness was. Mason would be waiting for me when I got home, but I didn't know if I wanted to tell him about this change. The job, yes. Mark's concern for me, no. Not yet, anyway.

# CHAPTER TEN
## MASON

The day had been…not as I'd expected. Quinn wasn't half bad when it came to offering ideas, and he no longer had that look he had in high school—like I had something he wanted and he hated me for it. I wasn't feeling the need to punch him at the end of the day. That lasted until we headed out to the parking lot and a girl with dark red hair greeted him, tipping her head back for a kiss.

I recognized her. Becky Sallaway, the chick who'd backstabbed Sam on more than a few occasions.

As they kissed, my phone started ringing. I turned my back on them, headed to my vehicle as I raised the phone. "Yeah?"

"You want to tell me why the fuck I'm getting messages that Sam's covered in bruises?"

I looked at the ID. "Funny. My phone says this is my brother calling, not Samantha's boyfriend."

"Fuck you."

I grunted, getting into the Escalade. "No, fuck you. You don't call and chew my ass out, like I'm supposed to report to you or something."

He groaned. "You're kidding me, right?! Why is Samantha looking like she got drop-kicked on her head, and why am I hearing this from Mark and not *you*?"

"Mark?"

"Yeah," Logan bit out. "You get why I'm a little pissed right now? I'm finding it out from Sam's stepbrother. What the hell is going on?"

"Nothing we can't handle."

He grew quiet for a moment. His voice was low when he spoke again. "Why are you shutting me out?"

"Because you're in Paris with Mom and with your girlfriend. I don't want you coming back early because you don't think I can handle things."

"That's not what—"

"That's exactly what you'd do." I sat back, the keys dangling in the starter.

"You don't have backup."

"I called Matteo in. He was heading home for a few weeks. He said he's happy to stay a while instead."

"Nate's not there."

"Nate will be here in two weeks."

"Then you're alone for those two weeks."

"Logan," I growled. I reached forward, starting the engine. "We're fine. We got into one sticky situation. Channing and his crew were there. They helped us out. We're fine. You think I'd let Sam be put in danger again?"

"Why was she put in danger in the first place?" he growled back.

Because she wanted to be somewhere her mother wasn't. Because she didn't want to feel afraid that the woman who gave birth to her might cross the street and potentially hurt her again. Because... I sighed to myself. Because maybe she just wanted to be normal and go to an event with her friend.

I said none of that.

"Because a situation got out of hand. I didn't read it right quickly enough. That's why."

"You weren't going to tell me—"

I was growing tired of this, real fast. "Stop it. You're acting like this is personal against you. It's not. I'm trying to be a decent brother. If you were here, you would've been there with us. You know that. I didn't tell you—I would've at some point—but I hadn't yet because I'm trying to let you enjoy your time away."

"Right," Logan grumbled. "Enjoy my time with Mom, you mean? It's like she's got a GPS strapped to Taylor's ass. Every time I get near her, Mom's coming into the room."

I relaxed, grinning now. "You're in the same hotel room as she is?"

"Mom got these big suites—you know, the type where it's a main living area with three bedrooms attached. She says I should respect her presence and 'refrain from inappropriate behavior.'" He snorted. "Her exact words. And what's worse is that Taylor is buying all her shit."

"Taylor's just trying to be nice. You're forgetting that Helen likes Taylor. She's not been given the ice treatment like Sam always has."

Logan swore under his breath. "That's just because of Analise. Mom'll get her stick out of her ass once Sam starts pushing out babies."

"Yeah. Maybe." I had other things to tell him, but I glanced out the window and saw one of those things approaching. This might be a good time to shelve Quinn for a longer phone call. "I gotta go," I told him. "I'll call you later."

Once Logan hung up, I turned the Escalade off and opened the door again. Adam had stopped a few feet away when he saw I was on the phone, but he closed the distance now.

"Uh, hey." The project partner who'd showed up at the country club eight hours earlier hadn't been cautious or reserved, yet he was exactly those two qualities now.

I narrowed my eyes. Whatever he was about to say, it was going to be on the personal level.

He jerked a thumb toward his truck where his girl was leaning. "Becky just got a text from Cass. I guess Mark showed up with Sam. They're talking about a barbeque. Would you want to—"

"Sam's there?"

He nodded.

"She's not planning on leaving?"

"Probably, but Mark's her ride, and he wants to stick around a while. I thought maybe—"

I waved him off. I didn't need to know any more. "Text me the directions. I have to pick someone up first."

"Oh." He blinked a few times. "Okay. Yeah, I can do that."

After picking up Matteo at Helen's house, we headed farther north in Fallen Crest. We lived on a good street, but this was another one, and Matteo whistled as he checked out the house.

"Is money just in the water or something? Is getting rich contagious here? Because shit, who do I kiss to get sick?"

I grinned, getting out and circling to his side. "Not these people." I filled him on the history with Quinn when I first picked him up.

"Why's Sam here again?" he asked, following me to the front door.

I didn't answer because I was wondering the same damned thing.

I rang the doorbell.

---

# SAMANTHA

I was having déjà vu from high school, except it was Matteo behind Mason and not Logan.

"Hey!" Mark approached them, his hand raised for a fist-bump. Mason frowned, but lifted his hand, and Mark threw his arm around my boyfriend's shoulders. "You'll never guess where Sam and I got a job today."

Mason's narrowed eyes moved in my direction. I shifted on my feet, tugging my shirt down. I'd been doing that since we arrived. It was my nervous habit—that and smoothing a hand over my stomach. I always tried to calm the nerves in there, but it never actually worked. I caught myself doing it again and cursed under my breath, letting my hand fall away.

Mason made his way to me, leaving Matteo and Mark to do their own fist-bumps. Matteo had met my stepbrother on a few visits, and the two had loved each other at first sight. Add Logan to their mix, and they were too much to take sometimes. Their bromance was on steroids.

"What..." Mason started, taking the chair next to me.

We had settled around tables surrounding Cass' pool.

"Mark said he just wanted to pick something up. That was an hour ago." I didn't share how that "something" had turned out to be his girlfriend. They'd been in a back bedroom until twenty minutes ago when Mark came out and told me Becky and Adam were coming over. I cast Mason a quizzical look. "I almost fell off the chair when Mark said you were coming. I was getting ready to run home when he told me that."

He groaned. "If I'd known that, I would've just come to pick you up."

I was about to ask what was stopping us from going now, but I caught his glance at Matteo. That was the problem. "He looks so happy to see Mark."

"Yeah."

"We can leave him here, come back later."

Mason gave me a halfhearted smile. "I can be an asshole, but that's a real douchebag move. I can't ditch my buddy here."

I refrained from reminding him how Matteo had ditched him at Channing's fight. Mason was aware of that, so if he was sticking around, there was a reason.

"What was Mark talking about before?"

"Oh." I rolled my eyes, ready to launch into the whole spiel when Becky and Adam came over. They'd arrived only five minutes earlier than Mason, so there'd been no awkward greetings. Yet. As Becky pressed a hand over her hair, trying to calm it, I saw how tightly she gripped Adam's other hand.

"Hey, Samantha." Becky's voice hitched, sounding breathless. She bit her lip fiercely. "Uh...how are you?" Her hand jerked up, pointing to me. "It's nice to see you here."

There was the old Becky. Awkward. Self-conscious. Tentative. The girl I saw a couple years ago hadn't resembled the girl who'd been my friend when so many turned their backs on me. She'd looked sophisticated with nice clothing, makeup, and her hair sleek. She'd seemed confident, too, and while physically she looked the same now, I felt some familiarity at seeing the Becky I used to know.

"Becky." I indicated their joined hands. "You guys seem to be doing well."

Her hand tightened around his. "Oh, yes. It's been wonderful." Her head tipped back, and she offered Adam a loving look. "Almost like a fairytale even."

Adam mirrored her look, a soft grin teasing his mouth, before he focused on us. "So are you two. I mean, since junior year in high school. That's a long time."

I glanced at Mason. He'd been watching the exchange with an unreadable mask, but I saw through it. He was thinking, *what the fuck is this?*

I almost laughed. "Yeah. We're doing good."

Mason frowned. "Why the fuck are we here, Quinn?"

There he was.

I laughed now.

The old Mason, the old Quinn.

For whatever reason, it settled me.

Adam coughed. "Nice, Mason."

"Sam thought she came here for a pit stop. We're both only here because we were told about the other. It seems like a setup. What's going on?"

Mark laughed uncomfortably as he migrated over with Matteo and Cass. "What's happening?"

Mason fixed him with a look, his eyebrows slightly raised, as if he were asking, *Are you serious?* "We're not friends with Quinn. Sam doesn't hang out with your girlfriend or this one any longer." He gestured toward Becky. "So why are we were?"

"No reason." Mark shrugged, resting his arm around Cass' shoulders. "I didn't mean to stay this long. Just got distracted. That's all."

I could hear Mason's thoughts. He was thinking this was bullshit, and I knew it was only a matter of time before that sentiment came out again, but not so nicely. Mason was being polite, so far.

I started to stand from my chair. "Well, then I think we're going to go. It was nice—"

"Wait."

Everyone turned to Adam. He rolled his shoulders back and, still holding Becky's hand, tugged her closer to the water. His cheeks pinked, and he pulled at his collar. "Okay. I can see it's time to come clean. Mark didn't set this up or anything, but I did kind of ask him to keep Sam here." He gestured to me. "I wasn't going to do this this way, but then I was told Mason and I were going to be working together and Mark said he was with Sam and…" He glanced down at Becky, a fond look coming over his face. "I thought 'what the hell.'" He put his arm around her shoulders, pulling her to his side. "I love you and I know you've been missing Sam over the years, so I threw caution to the wind and…"

"Adam." Becky touched his bicep. "What are you doing?"

A strangled laugh rasped from his throat, and the pink drained from his face. He coughed to clear his throat before dropping to a knee.

Oh.

My.

Go—he was going to propose.

Adam looked around, holding Becky's hand in front of him. "I'm sorry for the deception, but I knew you'd want Sam here for this."

He was…

He totally was.

He looked back to Becky, who had a hand pressed to her mouth. She began to tremble. Her eyes filled with tears.

"Rebecca Sullivan, you and I have had a whirlwind of friendship and then a relationship, but you've always been my *best* friend. You're always there for me, even when no one else is, and today, I'd like to ask you to be my partner for the rest of our lives."

"Adam." His name was a soft sigh. Tears streamed down her face, but she was glowing.

He pulled a small box from his pocket and opened it, showcasing a diamond ring. He held it out to her. "Will you marry me, Becky?"

"Yes. Yes! Oh, wow." She laughed and cried. She looked so happy as he slid the ring onto her finger and picked her up, whirling her around in a tight hug.

They kissed, and Becky could only look from her ring to Adam and back again. She seemed in a daze for a full minute before shaking her head and looking at us.

"I'm engaged, you guys!"

This was weird.

And awkward.

And uncomfortable.

Cass moved forward, holding Becky to her. "Congratulations!"

Mark congratulated Adam, as did Matteo. Mason held out his hand, giving Adam a quick nod of congratulations.

I looked around, but there was no one else. There should've been more people. Everyone seemed to turn to me. They were waiting for my congratulations, but all I could think was, "Why did you do that in front of us?"

"What?" Becky frowned.

Adam looked shocked.

"Just fucking congratulate them, Sam," Cass hissed.

I ignored her. "Why didn't you do this in front of your families?"

A pained look flashed in Adam's eyes, and I remembered how his dad had been a shithead the few times I saw him. But Becky... "Your parents," I whispered hoarsely. "This should've happened in front of them."

"You're being a bitch."

I ignored Cass again. Pain pressed in my chest, like someone was poking my lungs. I felt an impending doom. I shook my head. "Becky, I don't know... I mean, why?"

So many years. We'd been friends once. That ended, and now this?

Adam moved in front of Becky, shielding her from me. "I wanted you to be here for this. For her."

Becky rested a hand on his bicep again and stepped around in front of him. She clasped her hands in front of her and took a step closer, facing me directly.

"I was your friend once, Sam, and I'm the one who dropped the ball. I chose Adam over you when I should've chosen you first. I've always regretted that, and I think Adam's always known. A lot of time has passed, and I'm not asking for anything, but I'm glad Adam did this. I wanted it that way, and he knew it."

Her head bowed a moment before she gave me the shakiest, most scared and hopeful smile I'd ever seen on her. "Can you pretend to be my friend right now and congratulate me?" she whispered.

The wall I'd erected broke, and I pulled her into my arms, which she didn't seem to be expecting.

"Congratulations, Becky." She'd always loved him. "I am really happy for you. Really." I held her even tighter.

She hugged me back.

I couldn't remember the exact reason we weren't friends anymore. The pain and betrayal were like a faint fog over my memories. They were there, and I knew things had happened, but in this moment, one she'd remember for the rest of her life, I let myself feel that old friendship once again.

# CHAPTER ELEVEN

## SAMANTHA

"You were quiet on the ride home."

We had just entered our room. I sank down on the bed and curled in a ball, holding a pillow to my chest as I looked up at him. I had been quiet, content to just watch the scenery go by as Mason drove us. Matteo chose to stay behind. He wanted to party it up with Mark, and Mason and I couldn't blame him. There was a melancholy feel to us, or maybe it was just me.

I sighed. "It's hitting me that someone I used to love is engaged now."

"Adam?"

I frowned, then saw he was joking. "Becky." I laughed. "Asshole."

His eyes darkened, and for a moment I thought he was going to lay with me, but he turned for the closet. He pulled his shirt off and disappeared inside.

"That bugs you?" he called. "That she's engaged?"

I sat up, scooting my back against the headboard. I still held that pillow in front of me. "Maybe. I don't know why."

"Sam." He came back out, still with no shirt. I wasn't complaining. Mason was leaner than he'd been in high school, but more ripped. Almost every muscle in his chest and stomach stood out, and my eyes traced the V of his obliques, the way they disappeared under his light grey sweatpants.

"You're forgetting why Becky and you aren't friends anymore. Quinn was trying to break us up, and she chose his side. Now, it looks like she chose the right side for her since they're getting married, but that's not how it was back then. If you're beating yourself up over letting go of that friendship, stop. You can't be friends with someone who's not friends back."

He was right. I knew it, but I still felt a little hole inside where she used to be. "I don't know if it's Becky or my mom... I don't know what it is, but I feel off. I have since we came home for the summer."

He didn't say anything, but watched me with a knowing look mixed with concern. I wasn't saying anything new or surprising. Going somewhere Mason had enemies, then getting a job at the local carnival with Mark, and now being at Becky Sallaway's engagement—none of those were normal. The last was sprung on me, but I stayed even after I heard Becky and Adam were going to be there. I mean, it was Cass' house for fuck's sakes. Cass and I hated each other, but I still went.

I looked up and held Mason's gaze. "What's going on with me?"

His eyes clouded over, and he said almost as softly as I'd asked, "I don't know."

Dropping the shirt he'd been holding, he sat on the bed and he leaned down. His lips found mine, then he pulled back. His face was a few inches from mine and his eyes stared at my lips. "Whatever it is, we'll deal with it."

"Yeah?"

I was becoming breathless.

My body was starting to burn up.

Whatever I felt was beginning to fade, and a whole different pressing need was taking its place. Heat began to pool between my legs, spreading through me.

I closed my eyes, arching up against him, and groaned at the feel of him right there.

No matter what was going on with me, this would never cease. Ever.

His arm slid underneath my back and he moved me until I was in the middle of the bed. He lay on top of me, still holding most of his weight so he didn't crush me. He gazed down, his eyes molten with desire. His other hand lifted to my cheek and rested there, framing the side of my face.

He said, "Yeah. We'll figure it out."

That was enough. I turned my mind off.

We stared at each other for a moment, and then I lifted a hand and touched his lips. They were so perfectly formed. They only accentuated the strength in him somehow, but goddamn. I could feel all of his muscles as he rested on me. Mason was known as the fighter, the protector, the strong one. Sometimes I forgot how beautiful he was on the inside, too.

He smiled before he drew my finger into his mouth. His tongue swirled and rubbed against it gently.

I gasped and clamped my legs tight. The need for him was almost overwhelming now. My legs entwined around him, bringing him in full contact against me. Both of us gasped. I arched my back again, closing my eyes, just feeling him. His entire body rested more fully on me now, pinning me down.

My hand cradled the back of his neck, holding him prisoner.

I didn't want him to look away, to move away.

I wanted him inside of me.

His eyes darkened and as if reading my mind, he moved back to pull his pants off. After grabbing a condom, and pulling it on, he came back and settled between my legs.

My arms went back around him, like returning to their home.

"Sam," he murmured, tracing a finger down the side of my face. He tucked some hair behind my ear, and then I felt his lips against mine again.

Yes. Home.

That's what this was.

I groaned, my head falling back, and I felt his soft chuckle against my skin, but then he reached down and shifted, lifting my leg until I wound it around his waist. He dipped in, shifting, and I felt him at my entrance. He paused, then slid inside.

My eyes closed and I relished the feel of him in me.

He began moving, thrusting inside of me.

As he kept going, and he slid his hands up my arms to capture my hands, I opened my eyes. We were staring back at each other, watching each other. I could feel him reaching inside of me, searching, claiming me. Everything in my body yearned for him, yearned for more. I wanted more. I needed more.

The second he touched me, everything blared alive. I was awakened. Always.

In and out. Mason kept thrusting.

My fingers clamped down over his, sinking deep as his pace quickened.

"Mason," I gasped. Weak. His onslaught kept going, harder, faster. "I love you."

He groaned, climaxing, and his body clenched as he thrust into me a last time. It sent me hurdling over the edge, and I wrapped both arms around his neck, hanging on.

A moment later, he brushed a soft kiss on my forehead before he slipped out.

I still lay beneath him.

I didn't want to move.

I didn't want him to move, and eventually, we slept like that.

I woke later, but I was still in his arms. He was curled up behind me, and I went back to sleep again. All the doubts and questions would be there tomorrow.

# CHAPTER TWELVE

The rest of the week passed uneventfully.

Mark and I picked up trash at the carnival. Mason looked at me like I'd grown an alien head when I told him about our new job, but he didn't say anything against it.

He only nodded and kissed my forehead. "Logan will want to work with you when he gets back, even if he doesn't get paid."

And at the end of every shift, Mason picked me up. But today I texted that he wouldn't have to. When Mark and I checked in after lunch, Keifer announced we'd be manning booths today—two different booths.

"What? You think I'm a complete idiot?" he said to our disappointed faces. "No way am I letting the two of you fuck up. Don't know the ways, both of yas too green," he grunted, grabbing our red vests and exchanging them for carnival shirts. I got a blue one, and Mark got a black one. Keifer pointed at the shirts. "You rip those, and it's coming out of your paycheck. Got it? We ain't rich millionaires around here."

I was paired with the guy who told us to be sure we got paid that first day. He held out a hand, introducing himself. "I'm Petey."

I looked over his sun-streaked dark blond curls, bright blue eyes, matching bright smile with perfect white teeth, and lean build. He wore a matching blue carnival shirt, but his was bigger and ripped all over. A large gash went up the side, showing off how tan he was.

Keifer saw the gash, too, I could tell, but he only pressed his lips together. Petey smirked.

"Sam," I said as I shook his hand.

Keifer closed one eye, staring hard at Petey. I got a good whiff of chew as he exhaled. "You okay with her? Not going to mess this one up, are yas?"

Petey flashed a cocky grin and shrugged. "You're delusional, old man. I've never messed one up. Go on. Teach the other guy the ropes." He nodded to me. "I got this. She'll be fine."

Keifer didn't move, just continued to stare at Petey. Neither blinked. Neither moved. A full thirty seconds passed before Keifer broke, waving for Mark to follow him.

"If you do, we both know what's in store for you."

Petey just laughed. The sound seemed carefree, but as soon as Keifer was out of hearing distance, all smiles and charm dropped. A hard glint entered in his eyes, and he let out a soft sigh. Then he looked at me, and just like that, a switch flipped and the easygoing worker was back.

"You can tell me. You requested my booth, didn't you?" He winked.

"What? No."

"It's okay." He moved around me, jumping on the counter in one swift movement before hopping back down on the other side of me. "Come on. Follow me." He led me to the back of the booth and showed me some of the basic things I'd have to know in case the game stopped working. "Just in case I'm not around, you know, but I should be. This booth is my baby. But no worries. You won't be working here the whole time."

I followed him back to the front. "Where do you think I'll be put?"

"You're a townie. He'll put you somewhere he wants your local friends to come visit you." A waiting customer stood at the base of the rope ladder, and Petey scooped up the offered money. He gestured for him to start, and a second later, the customer was cursing. He'd already been flipped backward.

The man's friends cheered him on, making fun of him at the same time.

Petey leaned back in his seat, watching the whole thing. "You got a boyfriend?" he asked me.

"What?" How was that his business? "Yes, I do."

"Does he get into fights?"

"Why?"

"Because Keifer will want to know. If he doesn't, you'll go to the beer garden. Keifer will want all your friends to come in and get drunk. If your boy does fight, you'll be put in the swim tank."

Swim tank? I looked across the carnival. A large tank in the middle had a crowd of guys in front. They took turns throwing baseballs at the target, and each time one hit the bullseye, a girl in a bikini dropped into the water. I watched as she fell in and noticed how cold she looked. She trembled as she climbed back out.

My hands grew clammy and icy. I tucked them into my pockets.

"No, not there." Petey pointed farther down. "It's in the main. You'd just be swimming in there. It's a big pool-like place. People can pay for their kids to go swimming, or you might get some of the drunks in there, too."

My hands weren't as cold now. "Mark mentioned—"

"Sam?"

A female voice cut me off, and I looked up to see Becky, Adam, Cass, and another girl standing there. Becky held a polar bear to her chest, and Cass and the other girl each had a beer. Adam's eyebrows were raised.

"What are you doing here?" Becky asked.

I ignored her, asking Adam instead, "You're done working today?"

He nodded, his eyebrows still arched. "What are you doing here?"

"I'm working." I threw them a dark look before pulling out my phone. I held the phone up to Petey. If Mason was done with work, he could come and visit. "I need to text someone."

He nodded, pointing to the side. "Go to the back."

I slipped out and was texting Mason when Becky came around to the rear of the tent. "What are you doing?" I asked her.

"I could be asking you the same thing." She looked over her shoulder to the carnival. "What are you doing *here*, Samantha? Mark said you guys got jobs, but I didn't know it was at this place."

My phone buzzed a second later.

**Okay. I'll get Matteo. We'll come and walk around for a bit.**

I frowned. I wanted him here, but... I shook off the hesitation. I wanted him here. Only seeing him in the evenings was nice, but I still had to share him with Matteo, and Nate was coming at the end of next week. We never had gotten that living alone time. Logan would be here the week after that, and I assumed Taylor would come with him.

**I'm at the rope ladder booth. Love you.** I typed.

**Love you.**

I put my phone into my pocket and turned back to the booth. Becky was still standing there, holding that bear. She was biting her lip and I sighed. I crossed my arms over my chest. "What do you want, Becky? I mean, why are you doing this?"

"Doing what?"

"This." I pointed at her. "Standing back here. Pretending like you're scared or nervous, or whatever you're doing."

"I can't do all of that?"

"You're acting like we're friends."

"I..." She closed her mouth, moving back a step. "I didn't realize you were still like this."

"What? No." She was getting this wrong. "No, Becky. This is not me being a bitch. This is me reminding you how things have been for the past three and a half years. We haven't been friends, and it's awkward to find myself the guest of honor at your engagement. I mean, that's just weird."

"I didn't do that." Her neck grew red. Her cheeks would soon be matching. Her hands formed fists around that polar bear. "You can't get mad at me because Adam thought about all of that, but I'm glad he did."

A headache was forming. I gritted my teeth, knowing it'd be blinding me within an hour. "Look," I gentled my tone. "It was nice finding out that you wanted me at your engagement. That was..." I didn't have the words. I wasn't sure. There was still a tickle in my chest every time I thought about it. "But we're not friends. I hugged you. I congratulated you, but you're acting like we're friends again. I don't remember saying I was okay being friends with you again."

"Oh." She looked at the ground.

And I felt like an asshole, but you can't trick someone into being a friend. That's not how it works, or that's not how it worked with me.

"It is nice not having you or Adam as my enemy, though."

Her head lifted. Her eyes were bright with unshed tears. "Yeah?"

I nodded. I could give her that. "Mason said he and Adam are actually getting along. That's something." His exact words were that he 'didn't feel like knocking him unconscious every day,' but that was progress for Mason. I tried giving her a reassuring grin.

"Adam will like hearing that." Her bear looked to be in danger of decapitation. She squeezed him like she was a boa constrictor. "He was nervous when he got the assignment from his dad, said there'd be no way they could work together. But he's been saying the same, you know? He's impressed with Mason, said he has a brilliant head for business."

We were approaching unwelcome territory for me. Becky would start feeling all sorts of warm fuzzies, thinking thoughts about Mason and Adam becoming friends. That would lead to her wanting me and her to be friends, too, and I'd have to recycle everything I just said to her.

I began to inch around her, back into the booth.

"Well, fuck."

My eyes snapped up, and I recognized one of Jared Caldron's buddies.

"Caldron, look who's back here," he called.

Jared Caldron came to stand next to his friend, and I felt bathed in dirty and perverted mud. I fought against actually trembling; they'd get off on that. Instead, I moved past Becky and said under my breath, "Go around the back. Get Mark."

She wavered. "But—"

"Now!"

I blocked her retreat just as Caldron started toward me. His buddy was joined by another two, and I let out a breath.

"Where's your little friend going?" He leaned over to look beyond me, but Becky should've already been out of sight.

I still moved to block his view. "Where do you think?"

"Going for reinforcements?" He laughed, and a whiff of alcohol mixed with cigarettes and cotton candy coated my face. "Kade's not here. I would've seen him, and we've been over the entire place." He lifted an arm, holding onto one of the ropes used to set up the booth, and struck a cocky stance. He was literally leaning over me. His gaze lingered on the carnival shirt I wore. "You work here? That's... convenient."

He looked too smug. I fought against the urge to bring my knee up in a sharp jerk. Mason was coming, but I didn't know when he'd show. I needed to stall until Mark could get here, and I hoped Adam would join in. I wasn't holding my breath, though.

I moved back, moving away from the carnival midway. "Yeah. I work here. Why?"

"I pegged you for a stuck-up bitch. No rich priss works as a carnie."

"Really? How do you know? Spend a lot of time at carnivals?"

"Ha-ha." His eyes flashed. "I used to work at one that didn't stick around longer than two weeks." He pulled on the rope, testing how strong and tight it was. He gazed around the tent and the booth next to us. "I think this is a good company. They stay in one place for two months, too. I wish they'd been here when I needed a job back in school." His eyes raked over me.

I had that feeling of being covered in mud again. I'd need more than a few showers to feel like I'd cleaned off his filth.

His eyes darkened with lust. "Would've been nice if you were there, too. Maybe we wouldn't be on opposite sides like this." The lust dissipated quickly, anger coming back full force. His jaw clenched as he leaned closer. "But I know you're just slumming it here because you *are* a privileged bitch. I would've known it back then, too, and I would've fucked you, then tossed you to the trash. Kade wouldn't want to touch you, not after I ripped apart that pussy of yours."

I felt a low growl in the bottom of my throat, but I swallowed it. Time. I needed more of that. I just had to wait. Help would be coming.

All I said was, "Really?"

"Oh yeah."

He looked down my shirt, and I fought against the revulsion gathering in my stomach. It wanted to spew out all over him. I moved even farther back. I couldn't help myself. My body was on full alert, my mind screaming to get away from him.

"Where you going?"

"Hey! What's going on out here?"

I cringed. *Worst timing ever, Petey.* I didn't want him to get involved with this, too. He'd get hurt.

My co-worker stepped out of our booth, coming toward me.

"Hey, man." One of Caldron's friends stopped him, a hand placed on his shoulder.

Petey went still, his eyes narrowing. He looked at the hand, then at the guy it belonged to. "Get it off, or you're going to lose it."

"Hey." Caldron turned around to face Petey. He held his hands up, making his voice all friendly. "I know Sam here." He grabbed me, dragging me to his side and throwing his arm around my shoulder. I grimaced, but he kept on, "We've got a friend in common. We're just catching up. I wanted to tell her all about Budd, how he's doing in prison. Right, Sam?"

His eyes were on me.

Petey was watching.

Caldron's friends were waiting, too.

Stalling. That was what I was supposed to be doing. That was the smart thing to do. Being so close to Caldron already had me nauseous, but now that he was touching me, my senses were shutting down. My vision was tunneling. The edges were blurring, becoming black, and I could focus on only one pressing need: to get his fucking hands off of me.

I stopped thinking then, and I felt myself throwing off his arm, stomping on his foot, and swiftly turning to bring my knee up. It made contact, and he recoiled. I heard a roar, but it came from a distance. And then I stood there as Caldron sank to his knees.

There was something…

Wait.

Something… I needed to do something, but all I could do was stare down at him, seething. How dare he lay hands on me? I wanted to hit him once more, and I was bringing my knee up again, this time aiming right at his face, but he saw me. His face was contorted in pain, but he shoved me backward, a hand flying up to my face, and then I saw stars.

I swung around, falling, too.

After that, a tornado whirled inside of me. As Caldron struggled to get to his feet, his friends held Petey back. One of them looked like he'd been hit, but he was still in there, helping to keep my coworker restrained.

*Good for you, Petey*, I thought as a shadow fell over me.

I looked up, and Caldron was there, rage glittering in his eyes.

He raised a fist, and I knew this was it. He was going to beat me unconscious. And unlike the other times I'd been hurt, I didn't know if I'd come out of this one alive. Caldron looked like he wanted to murder me.

I felt myself pulling back. I didn't move, but my mind was leaving. It was retreating to a back area, somewhere I'd be safe. My eyes wanted to close, but I held on. I couldn't look away. If it was going to happen, if this was the end for me, I wanted this guy to see my eyes the whole time. I wanted him to see *me*.

His arm started to come down.

Then suddenly, he was gone.

Mason came out of nowhere, tackling Caldron and sending him slamming into his friends and Petey. Petey broke free, and then someone else rushed past me, right on Mason's heels.

I looked over. I was here. I was seeing this, but I wasn't here at the same time. I watched from above somehow. I swallowed, trying to stand up. I could come back. I could—I tried to tell myself it was safe now.

Mason reared back and rained punches on Caldron, one after another. Matteo was there fighting one of the other guys. Petey— *Petey?*—had tackled a third friend, and the fourth... I swung my head around; it felt so heavy. Mark was holding the fourth guy back, with Adam beside him.

"...ou okay?"

A voice sounded through the haze. I looked for that, too. Becky approached me, her hand stretched out. The closer she got, the clearer her voice was.

"You okay? Sam?" She touched me, but she still sounded at a distance.

I shook my head. I needed to clear it. Then with a snap, I was back.

"Sam?!" she yelled.

I held a hand out. "Stop."

People were yelling. Shouting. I could hear the deep thuds of punches being exchanged, and I gasped, feeling salt and dirt in my mouth. Mason was beating the shit out of Caldron. "Mason!" I rushed forward. "Stop!"

He was going to kill him.

*BOOM!*

I jerked back, and my head snapped around.

Keifer stood a few feet from the fighting with a gun in the air. He lowered it, pointing it at everyone. "Get out before I call the fucking cops!"

Mason scrambled off of Caldron, holding his hands up as he backpedaled to where I stood. Matteo came behind him, and Petey stood in the middle, wiping blood from his mouth. He rested his hands on his hips, his shirt ripped in half. One side was gone, and the other hung limply from his arm.

Caldron and his friends were slower getting to their feet.

"They started it," Caldron said, pointing at me. "You know what kind of a bitch you got working here?"

Keifer fired into the air again, his eyes bulging. "I don't give a damn. Get the fuck out of my carnival, or I'll let my boys finish the job." He got in Caldron's face, breathing down at him. "You got that?!"

"But—"

*"Get out! Now!"* Keifer motioned behind him, and five or six big guys started forward.

Caldron's eyes widened as those guys plucked him up. His friends, too. All of them were literally carried from the carnival.

Keifer waved his arms at the crowd that had gathered. "You all get going, too! Get back to the rides and games. This show's over, folks!" He turned, his sharp gaze landing on me. "You best start explaining, Missy, or you're out of a job."

# CHAPTER THIRTEEN

"Uh, it's like this, boss…"

Petey took over for me, and was explaining what happened, or trying to explain, in Keifer's office. The rest of us waited out in the hall. Adam, Becky, and Cass were standing, and Mason and Matteo sat next to me. Mark had been sent back to his booth once Keifer realized he'd only come over to help.

I sighed, standing up. Petey's explanation was sucking at some major levels.

Mason looked over. "What are you doing?"

I nodded at the opened door. "I need to do something. Petey's making it worse."

It was obvious Keifer wasn't buying the first excuse Petey had given him—that the guys attacked us for no reason.

Petey's hands were all over the air as I walked in behind him. "I was busy with some customers when I heard them. When I got there, the guy was already advancing on Sam. I don't know why they chose to have a problem with us," he said. "I mean, we didn't do anything, and Sam here, it looked like she'd had enough. She got fed up, you know? So yeah."

Keifer still didn't look like he was buying it, his eyes flat and a skeptical expression on his face. Or he was just pissed about it.

"Sam's a cool chick, boss," Petey added. "I'd keep her around for sure—all twisty and fierce."

"Okay." Keifer held a hand up, sitting forward in his desk chair. "Stop. You're not going to roll over on your co-worker. I got it. Now…" He transferred his no-nonsense gaze to me. "How about we get the real story, hmm?" He snapped his fingers, pointing to the chair next to where Petey stood.

I folded my hands on my lap. "Petey had nothing to do with those guys. He was trying to protect me."

"I'm aware. Petey hasn't been in a fight for an entire year."

"Yeah?" Petey grinned.

Keifer shot him a dark look. "I haven't caught him, I mean."

Petey laughed.

Keifer returned to me. "You were saying?"

"Those guys didn't come to the carnival for me, but now that they know I work here, or…" I coughed. "…used to work here, they'll be back. This is all my fault."

"Come on." Adam came inside, followed closely by Becky. Cass stayed out in the hall. "It was four on one. That's not fair, and it's not Sam's fault. You can't fire her, sir."

Keifer's eyebrows furrowed together. He leaned back in his chair, taking his time as he studied Adam. "And who the fuck are you?"

"Oh. Uh." Adam held his hand out. "I'm Adam Quinn. You might know my father, Steph—"

"Get that hand out of my face." Keifer stood up, looking at me. "This is what we're going to do. You are fir—"

"That'd be a mistake."

Mason spoke from the back of the office. He must've come in after me, and now leaned against the wall with his arms crossed over his chest. Everyone looked at him. It was like a sleeping panther had woken up, and everyone remembered they'd left the cage door open. Tension rippled through the air, and I glanced at Keifer. His eyes were locked on Mason. He didn't know Mason, but he knew this wasn't another Adam Quinn who'd tried to assert his dominance with a weak handshake. Mason was the real deal.

Keifer responded with a softer, "And you are?"

Mason shook his head. "My name doesn't matter."

"Then what does?"

"You have an opportunity here." Mason pointed to Adam and Becky, then to me. "If I were you, I'd be hiring townies for one reason and that's the draw they can have on the local community. That's why you hired Sam and Mark, right? You were eventually going to put them somewhere their friends would come and hang out? Spend their money on your food, games, booze."

"Maybe."

Keifer wasn't giving a lot away, but neither was Mason. He continued to lean against the wall. He rested one foot over the other, striking a casual pose.

"Those guys who attacked Sam aren't guys you want to side with," Mason said evenly.

"Who says I am?"

"They're the type that will come in, get drunk, and piss all over your place. Your carnival will get vandalized, and you know I'm right."

Keifer's eyes narrowed. "I wasn't going to let them back in."

"Firing Sam is the wrong decision."

Keifer's nostrils flared. "You already said. I'm still waiting to hear a good reason."

"Put her in the beer garden. That's where she and Mark wanted to work in the first place."

"Every goddamn employee works their way from the bottom up. I ain't putting any greenie in there. No new kid is going to pour my beer and fuck up my till. You got that?"

"So fast-forward the orientation," Mason shot back, standing straight now. His arms lowered to his side, but that only increased the tension in the room. His voice remained deceptively calm. "Put them in the beer garden. We'll come hang out. And if we're here, everyone else will come, too. Quinn's connected to the rich preppy group, and I'm connected to Roussou people. Put Sam somewhere we can be, to help protect her, and you'll double your normal sales."

"We do just fine on the weekends."

"I'm not talking weekends. I'm talking afternoons. If you do your homework, you know there's a good crowd at Manny's every night. That's our crowd. We'll bring them here instead."

I cursed inwardly. Heather would *love* that.

Keifer seemed to be thinking it over, his gaze skirting from me to Mason and back again. Finally, after a longer-than-necessary silence, he pointed to me. "This your boyfriend?"

"Yes."

"Were those guys after you because of him?"

How did he—

He smiled. "Four on one girl? It's always payback if that happens, sweetie."

I flushed, but glared at the same time. "My name's not sweetie. It's Samantha."

Mason came to stand next to me. "You can fire Sam. That's fine. She doesn't need this job. But she likes being here. Do what I'm suggesting and at the end of the summer, you can throw a big bash. Tell everyone Mason Kade is celebrating at your carnival before he returns to Cain U for his last year."

Petey's head whipped around, and Keifer went eerily still, almost glaring at Mason now. A vein popped out along the side of his jaw. "The football superstar? That kid?"

"Yeah," Mason said. "That kid."

Keifer jerked his head forward. "You that kid?"

"I'm that kid."

"Rumor's that your daddy's pretty rich, too."

"He is, and he's marrying Sam's mom. That's how we met, and that's why she doesn't need this job. You're the one losing out if you fire her."

"Now." Keifer barked out that word, leaning down to rest his hands on his desk. His jaw twitched. "I know that now, but the real question isn't whether I want to miss the chance at those extra sales. It's whether I want to deal with a bunch of spoiled pricks for the rest of the summer. You don't think we can draw in our own crowd? You don't think that's what we do for a goddamn living, *boy*?" He waved to the door, dismissing us. "Get the fuck out of here before I change my mind and have those guys carted back in."

Mason took my hand. "Fine." He led me out of the office. Adam and Becky trailed behind us. We found Matteo and Cass sitting on opposite ends of the bench outside. They stood when they saw us.

"What happened?" Matteo asked.

"Sam was fired."

Adam added to Mason's short explanation. "The guy's an idiot. He's losing a ton of money. He should've listened—"

Mason interrupted him. "Where were you?"

"What?" Adam took a step back.

"You were there. You could've helped her."

Adam's eyes widened. He looked at me, then Becky before turning back to Mason. He coughed. "I went to get Mark. I'm the one who told Becky to get security. She's the reason Petey even knew something was going on. We had no clue. They were behind the tent, and music was blaring. We couldn't hear."

That was bullshit. Petey might've been distracted because he was doing his job, but Adam would've noticed Caldron before he went between the tents.

"It's true," Mark said. "Adam came and got me. He's faster than Becky."

It felt off, but Adam's bases were covered. I had another issue to deal with. I dropped Mason's hand and rounded on him. "Did you do that on purpose?"

Everyone stilled. Again.

Matteo murmured behind us, "Fuck."

The only one who didn't seem surprised by my question was Mason. An unreadable mask fell over his face, and I knew he was guarding himself.

"Yes," he said.

"You knew my boss would be insulted by the way you talked to him. A kid telling him what to do—you knew that'd slam the door on me working here."

"Yes," he ground out a second time. "I'd do it again, too."

"Uh, guys." Matteo moved away from us, guiding Adam and the girls. "Maybe we should give them some space, huh?"

I was aware of them leaving, but my blood boiled. I couldn't look away from Mason. "Why? Why did you do that?"

"You know why."

Oh, no. I shook my head, shaking a finger in his face. "You don't do that. You don't soften your tone with me, like you're giving up this fight. You already sabotaged me in there. Don't back down now."

"I can't protect you here."

"You just made a whole argument that you could."

"I can't be here every single day."

"So? He could have me work at night, when you can be here."

"Every night?"

"Yes!"

"Every minute? Every time you have to take the garbage outside? Every time you forget something in your car and have to run to get it? I'm supposed to shadow you all of those times?"

"Yes!" Why was he fighting this? "We've had worse threats."

"Caldron's gone after you twice now. The first time I was right there. He's worse than Budd Broudou. He knows who you are. I can't trick this guy, and as much as I'd like to, I can't be with you at every moment. He's the type who will lie in wait, and he'll grab you the second I'm not around."

His arms were shaking, and he took a calming breath.

"Sam." He stepped forward, touching my arms gently. "This guy will hurt you."

I searched his eyes, trying to read his next move. "What are you going to do?"

"I'm going to hurt him first."

"You already did."

Mason didn't reply. Maybe that was the problem? Mason had already knocked him down, and Caldron just attacked again. If he kept coming, what could be done? I chewed on the inside of my cheek, keeping all those questions to myself. If I was thinking them now, I knew Mason had already processed them.

"What are you going to do?" I asked.

"I'm going to cut off his knees so the fucker can't walk."

I let out a shaky laugh. "That sounds like a good plan."

Mason chuckled, his eyes softening as he drew me against him. He folded his arms around me, and I felt his lips graze my forehead, tenderly, before he found my lips. I closed my eyes and let myself melt into that kiss until we heard the office door open.

"Well, kid, you talked me into keeping your girl around."

Mason tensed and lifted his head.

Keifer stood in his office doorway, arms crossed over his chest and a smug grin on his leathery face. Petey stood behind him, chewing on the inside of his cheek.

"You start in the beer garden tomorrow night," Keifer told me. "Eight o'clock sharp. Petey's going to be working with you." He turned, clapped Petey on the shoulder, and disappeared back inside.

Mason's plan had just backfired on him.

---

Every morning for the next week, I got up.

Every morning I went for an hour-long run, sometimes an hour and a half.

Every morning I stretched, then crossed the street to Malinda's house, and she met me with coffee on the porch.

Every morning we sat and stared at the gate two houses down.

And every morning that gate remained shut, so I would start another day with knots in my stomach, tense about the moment I'd see her.

At the end of each day, I finished my shift at the beer garden and slipped into bed with Mason. Then I'd wake the next morning, reach for my running shoes, and begin the process all over again.

# CHAPTER FOURTEEN
## MASON

"James is free to see you now."

I gave my dad's receptionist a cursory look as I passed by. He was the one who'd called me in, so yeah, he'd better be free. But the new girl seemed overwhelmed, despite her professional greeting.

"Mason."

My dad started to stand, but I shook my head and tossed some papers on his desk.

"What's this?" he asked.

"Those are the promotional ideas and plans Adam Quinn and I put together for the hotel's opening, and sorry, Dad..." I dropped into the seat across from him. "I hate to tell you this, but in all the time I've spent with him, I haven't gotten a whiff of anything illegal. He's annoyingly pleasant to work with, and happily in love with his woman. That's all I've got."

He frowned, leaning back with the papers in hand. He scanned them. "Nothing?"

"Nope." I leaned forward, resting my elbows on my knees. "But I don't know what you were expecting me to do. Quinn and I are not close." And remembering last night's fiasco at the carnival's beer garden, I added, "And that's never going to happen."

"Why not?" He dropped the papers back on his desk. His mouth flattened into a disapproving line. "I need something to get in with the mayor. You have to dig deeper on Quinn."

"I'm not a private investigator. You have an entire team of those at your beck and call. Use one of them."

"You don't think I haven't?" His voice rose.

So did mine. "I'm your son, not your whore."

His hand slapped the desk, and he pushed up from his chair. "You owe me, Mason. You and Logan both. My investigators haven't found anything, but that doesn't mean it's not there. Stephen Quinn dotes on his son."

I frowned. That wasn't what I remembered. "Are you sure? Sam saw an exchange between Quinn and his father a few years ago. There was no love between them, or that's how she described it."

He waved a hand in the air, dismissing the notion. "He had a heart attack last year. Apparently, he saw the light, and now he can't wait for his son to officially join his company. The boy is supposed to get married, too, as part of the deal."

"Wait. What'd you say?"

"What?"

"You said he's *supposed* to get married as part of a deal? A business deal?"

"I believe so. Why?"

"Because he just proposed to his girlfriend."

"Hmmm…"

My dad didn't look surprised.

"You don't think it's genuine?" That couldn't be. "I know when he gets laid. He comes to work whistling, and I could tell the two times they've had an argument. Those were the only two times I haven't wanted to punch him for being annoying. He's in love with Becky Sallaway."

"Where are you two working?"

"Why?" Sudden caution rose up.

"Because Maxine called and asked if you and Adam needed anything. She's under the impression you're done with your planning because you haven't been there for the last week."

I shrugged, leaning back. "We hit a snag, had to move our office somewhere else."

"Where else?"

"What do you care? We're getting the work done. We have three events confirmed, and yes, I've agreed to use my name for all three of them—plus a radio interview. Are you going to throw a fit because we're not planning where you want us to?"

"Yes," he barked. "Where are you working?"

"We're at the country club in the mornings." We were just somewhere else in the afternoons since Sam had to start working at two.

"And she said you guys leave at one thirty every day. Where do you go?"

"We're somewhere I can watch Sam. That's all."

My dad stared at me, and a full minute of silence passed before he asked, "Why do you have to watch Samantha?"

"Dad." I held a warning in my voice and started to stand up. "I'm not getting into it about Sam. That's my problem."

He rose with me, his head lowered like we were about to do battle. "She's the daughter of the woman I love. I know she's the woman you love, but I'm invested, too."

"Because of Analise?"

"Because you *both* love her—Logan, too. Now tell me what is going on."

*Should I?*

For the first time since I couldn't remember, I stared at my father and considered opening up. I wasn't forced to ask for a favor—not like two years ago when we needed help dealing with a guy going after Logan's girlfriend.

All the hatred and loathing I used to feel for my father was gone, and a small amount of respect had taken its place, but I still couldn't make myself say the words. I still didn't trust him enough.

He sighed, as if sensing my internal battle. "Mason, I know I was a fuck-up as a father. I let you raise yourself and your brother. I knew the effect my cheating had on your mother, and I still did it. I never stepped in and called her on her neglect, because that would've meant the reason for her neglect had to be discussed." He glanced away and stuffed his hands in his pockets. "I'm sorry." He looked back, raw pain on his face. "I know I've apologized before. I know I've tried to show you I'm a changed man, and I also know I can never force you to accept me back in your life. But you don't have to do any of that. You took this internship because of your business requirement. I get that, and I'm glad you're here. I wouldn't have it any other way. It would've hurt me if you'd gone to a different corporation. So, I don't know. Maybe you can just tell me what's going on because I love you? No tit for tat. No blackmail. Nothing. Just…I want to help if I can."

I studied him. He could be lying. He could use this against me in the future. If I was going to open up, so was he.

"When is Analise going to approach Sam?" I asked.

"What?" He tilted his head to the side. "What do you mean?"

"You know what I mean. She's here. She knows Sam is here. When's she going to make her move?"

He shook his head. "Analise promised Malinda a year ago that she'd step back. It's all on Sam's timeline. When and if she wants to talk to her, Analise is ready, but it's up to Sam. She said that to Malinda, and she meant it. Why?"

Because my girlfriend is running herself ragged, worried about when Analise will show up on our doorstep. Because she jumps every time someone knocks on the door. Because I'm tired of catching her looking out the window to see if she'll see Analise walking down the sidewalk.

I put my hands into my pockets and lifted a shoulder. "No reason. We were just wondering."

"You sure?"

"Yeah."

"Okay. Well, if you want to clue me in on why you have to watch Sam during the afternoon, I'd appreciate it." He held his hands up. "But I'm not going to force you." He waited a beat, a half-smile lifting the side of his mouth. "It's been nice having you work for me." He nodded to the stack of papers on his desk. "Thank you for all of that. I know the opening ceremony will be a huge success, and not because you're loaning out your name, but because of the work you've done. You and Adam Quinn."

I winced. "Don't give that guy any credit."

"Why? He's not doing his fair share?"

"No, because he is." I turned to leave and added over my shoulder, "That's what's annoying about him."

I heard my dad's chuckle as I left, and for once in a long time, I didn't hate the sound of it.

# CHAPTER FIFTEEN

## SAMANTHA

"If you wanted to work behind a bar, I could've pulled rank with Brandon. You didn't need to join my competitor."

It was late afternoon, and I was washing a glass when Heather slid onto the solitary barstool we had by the counter. It was there for the staff to rest while waiting for their orders to be filled. The rest of the customers had to come up, get their beers, and sit at one of the thirty picnic tables set up outside the beer garden's tent.

I lowered the glass and automatically reached for a beer. Sliding it across the counter to her, I said, "You know I'm sorry."

"I know." She took the beer. "And you already explained, but I gotta give you a hard time."

I shot her a rueful grin. "I feel like an asshole."

"As you should." She grinned back. "I'm just kidding. I have to give you some shit."

"But still…it's your business."

She shrugged. "It'll be fine. Your safety is more important, and it's not your fault that your boyfriend has enough clout in the community to pull people from one business to another." She closed her eyes, a soft smile on her face. "Oh, what it would be like to have a normal best friend with a normal boyfriend."

"Shut up." But I was laughing.

"For real, though…" She opened her eyes to look at me. "I just want you to be safe."

"I know, and I think I am." I glanced around the busy tables. Heather was right. The group that had been hanging out at Manny's moved with Mason to the beer garden. It wasn't just our peers—those who had stayed home after high school or the ones home only for the summer—but much of the rest of Fallen Crest as well. Channing had stopped in a few times, but he remained close to Manny's, so Heather wasn't hurting as much as she was teasing me about. I knew most of the Roussou crowd had taken Manny's as their new spot. Which had me thinking: "If Channing's running his own bar, why's he in Fallen Crest so much?"

"He's running it with his cousin. Channing takes the day hours, and Scratch has the evenings."

"He brings a lot of people over with him. Why don't they stay in Roussou and go to his bar?"

"Because Channing isn't there." She said it so simply. "And because his bar is geared to a rougher crowd. It's a hardcore biker bar."

"Really?"

She nodded. "It'll taper off in the winter months. He's over here because of me right now, and I'm here because of the summer hours. Then all the summer folk will head out, and Manny's will go back to normal. I can take a few more nights off." She rolled her eyes. "Plus, Channing's got his own pull now because of his fighting. I'm hoping he'll stop in the fall."

"Really?" I felt like a parrot.

"I'm not here to talk about my relationship and business," Heather announced. "I'm here to check in with you." She eyed the far table where Mason and Adam had set up camp, laptops, books, and notebooks spread out between them. "How's that going?"

"What do you mean? That Mason's here to protect me from Caldron? That he and Adam are working together here, or the fact that they're *working together*?"

"Any and all of that."

A customer came up, and I started to fill the order, but I couldn't help looking back to Mason's table. After Caldron's attack, the rest of the week had seemed almost boring. I worked at the beer garden every night, and after the first few passed with no incidents, Petey had relaxed. He realized I wasn't going to fuck things up for him, and the rest of the workers accepted me once they learned an increase in their tips came with me.

Even Keifer had stopped coming over and glaring at us every night. He still came in, but he only glared half the time. The other half he spent arguing with Petey or laughing with my coworkers. He hadn't checked in today. Yet. He would, and every time he did, he stared at Mason for a good ten minutes. Mason had stared back the first night, but when Keifer didn't do anything, Mason stopped paying attention. Or that was how it seemed to everyone else. I knew he was on full alert, and not just because of my boss. He was waiting for Caldron's next move. So far, nothing had happened.

So far.

It was going to happen, and I knew Mason was also counting down the hours until Nate arrived. He should be rolling into town at any moment.

"Things are okay," I told Heather.

"Really?" Her eyes found mine.

I shrugged, filling another order. "Well, I can say Mason will be relieved to have Nate here, too."

Heather waggled her eyebrows. "Where's the hottie Hawaiian?"

"You should know. He spends more time with you guys than with us."

That wasn't completely true. He'd stuck to Mason's side like glue for the first two days after Caldron's attack, then began heading to Roussou more and more after that. A certain blonde who had been wrapped around him on Channing's fight night kept calling. It didn't take a genius to figure out she was wrapping around him on a more consistent basis.

Heather snorted. "Right. He shows up for pussy, then after he gets his fill, he's off to find you guys." She turned to Mason's table. "He's not here, and I know he's not with Channing's crew. He must be at Tiffany's."

"That's her name?"

"Yeah. She's not bad, actually. But I don't think she realizes he's leaving for Cain U in a few weeks for football."

"Really?"

"She's not mentioned it, and I know her. If she knew her new boy-toy was a big footballer, that'd be the only thing she talked about." Heather grew pensive, her eyebrows dipping together. "Why didn't he go pro?"

"He stayed back to play one more year with Mason."

"Yeah?"

I nodded and left it at that. Matteo also had a girlfriend who'd broken his heart last year. She'd flown across the nation to pursue law at Columbia while he remained in California. He'd been heartbroken all over again when he realized he was single when Logan was not.

I filled three plastic cups with beer. "I think he's hoping he'll get drafted by the same team, but the chances of that are low. I don't think either is excited to be separated. They're going to enjoy their last year together on the team."

Heather seemed like she was going to respond, but then she was distracted as Becky, Cass, and three other girls walked through the beer garden to sit at Mason and Adam's table.

"What the fuck?" Heather murmured.

I waited, grinning. I knew what would happen next.

Mason didn't spare them a look, only jerked a thumb over his shoulder to the picnic table behind him. One by one the girls stood, all with varying scowls, and crossed to sit at that table instead. It happened almost every night when Becky and her friends arrived. They were always booted to their own table.

I shook my head. "You'd think they'd learn." They never did.

Heather didn't reply, and I looked over to see her and Becky in a heated stare. Becky was holding her own. I expected to see my old friend pale and shaking, but she wasn't. Her eyes were wide, her lips pressed in a determined line, and she was sitting straight up.

If she'd been my friend, I would've been proud.

But she wasn't.

"Sam."

I turned and headed to the opposite end of the counter where Petey waved me over.

"What's up?" I asked.

He placed five plastic cups in front of me, along with two filled beer pitchers. "Take these to those girls who just sat behind your boyfriend."

"No way." I crossed my arms over my chest. "I'm behind the counter, not on the other side, and they've not ordered. Since when do you give out free beer?"

"Look around. We're slower than normal. We need those girls to call their friends. Giving free booze to hot chicks helps with sales."

"You guys have been just fine with sales." Thanks to me. Thanks to Mason.

He nudged the cups closer to me. "I've been watching those girls. The redhead will stay as long as your boyfriend's buddy does. Once Mason and that guy finish working, they'll take off, and that means Mark's girlfriend will also want to leave. You're right. Our sales have been up, but they tripled the night those girls stayed, and you want to know why?" He moved closer. "Because they called their rich friends, who had no problem dropping hundreds of dollars on our beer. Your boy's been true to his word. He's brought people in, but that group, in particular, has no problem burning through cash." He tapped the pitcher. "Take the free beer to them, and try to smile as you do it."

I gave him a look. "Why me? Why don't you do it?"

"Because those are your people."

I snorted. Little did he know, but I picked up the pitcher and cups and moved out from behind the counter, making my way to them. Not a chance in hell was I smiling. I made sure my scowl was noticeable as I placed the beer on their table.

Cass rolled her eyes. "Service with a smile, Sam. Isn't that the motto?"

Becky was focused on Adam, but she looked around at the mention of my name. She stood, hurrying over to pick up a pitcher. "Sam doesn't have to do that. She's not a waitress." One of the other girls separated the cups, and Becky began to fill them. "This was free? Thank you, Sam."

"Oh, no." I pointed to Petey. "This was all him. He had me bring them over. I didn't want to give you guys free anything, but now that you have it, happy drinking. I hope you get drunk and puke all over your boyfriends' cars."

"I heard that." Mark came up behind me, his carnival uniform shirt in hand.

"Finished for the day?" I asked.

He nodded, his gaze guarded.

"Oh good. You can get drunk, too. Petey's orders."

Mark stared at me for a few beats. "What's wrong with you? You're being mean."

I opened my mouth. I so wasn...I was. My neck warmed, and I let out a silent sigh.

"I apologize to you, but not them." He knew who I meant. "Your girlfriend's been a bitch to me for years, and I have a hard time letting people back in once they've turned their back on me."

Without looking at the table, I went back to the counter. My eyes met Mason's for a fleeting moment, and I trailed a finger over his shoulders as I passed.

Heather gave me a knowing look when I returned to her, remarking, "That was entertainment. We need to schedule more of these outings."

"Fuck you." I laughed.

"Sam?"

I tensed, but turned around. If Becky'd had a hat, it would've been in her hands.

"What?" I readied myself.

"Can we talk?" Her eyes flitted to Heather, then she nodded away from the tables. "In private?"

"No."

I went back to working, grabbing a washcloth to wipe down the counter.

"Please?"

I kept working.

She kept standing there.

Ignoring. That was the best defense sometimes, but after a full minute where I cleaned three other counters, Becky was still there. The ignoring tactic wasn't working.

I tossed the rag into the sink and frowned. "What are you doing, Becky? I am not the Sam I was when we were friends. I am not passive. I don't take shit." My chest was getting tight. "I'm not nice anymore."

Heather jumped in, quietly, "Yes, you are."

"Not lately." I threw her a look. This wasn't her fight.

She held her hands up, leaning back on her stool.

Becky's shoulders lifted as she drew in a breath. "Are you done?"

"No!" I yelled, then came out from behind the counter. "Follow me." When we got behind the beer garden's tent, I turned around and crossed my arms over my chest. "What do you want?!"

"You're one of my moments."

"What?"

She looked down, and her voice quieted. "Adam asked me last year about my top five regrettable moments. You were one of them."

I could only stare at her. I knew what she was talking about, and my God, I was having a hard time holding myself back. I closed my eyes. My blood boiled, and I began counting to ten.

1

2

3

4—"Are you kidding me?!"

Becky shrank back.

"Do you know what I went through our junior year? Do you have any idea?!" I held up a hand, all my fingers spread out. "Five people turned on me that year. My mom. My dad. My two best friends. My boyfriend. All of them left me!" I held up one finger on my other hand. "You were my sixth. You were my salvation, until the guy you had a crush on made you choose. You chose him over me." My sixth finger curled in with the others. "You left me when I had no one."

"That year was when you started dating Mason—"

"And thank God I screwed him!" I registered movement from the corner of my eye, but I couldn't stop. Not now. Not anymore. "My family blew up that year, and yeah, I got another one. Mason and Logan became my family, and things have been just fine, but now you want back in?"

"Yes."

Her voice was meek.

I backed away, shaking my head.

Her face twisted. "I am sorry, Sam. I really am."

"But it's too late. I let you back in. I gave you a second chance, and you chose him over me. Again." I turned to go back, and Adam stood there, his gaze stricken. Cass, Mark, and so many others lined up behind him. I had to laugh. "You all came for the show? Well, sorry. Show's over." I moved forward, ready to bulldoze my way through, but they all moved aside. As I returned to my spot behind the counter, Mason waited for me. His eyes stopped me in my tracks, and that was when I knew.

I hadn't been yelling at Becky just now.

I'd been yelling at my mother.

# CHAPTER SIXTEEN

Petey stayed away. Thank God, but he was the only one.

I was still standing at the counter, unsure what to do, when Adam burst through the tent's opening.

"Thank you." His jaw clenched.

I looked up, feeling haunted. I didn't ask for what.

"She's been wanting your friendship back from the moment she knew she lost it. I've been telling her to let go. She wouldn't, though. She kept hoping and praying. That's why I worked it so you were at our engagement. She wanted that moment, because if there was ever a chance, I thought it would be there. You were at an event she'll remember for the rest of her life. You won't remember." He scoured Mason with a look. "I've no doubt you'll forget all about us when you move on to the big leagues, but she'll remember." He leaned over the counter, closer to me. "I helped take away some of that regret. She tried being your friend, and what'd you do in return? You spit on her. Fuck you, Samantha."

"Hey." Mason faced him squarely.

Heather still sat on her stool, watching me.

Adam's finger came down hard on the counter. "From this day forward, I want you to have nothing to do with Rebecca. You got that?!"

Heather grunted, rotating her barstool so she faced Adam as well. "Are you insane?" she murmured.

His eyes were heated and dilated, and the tips of his ears were pink. He threw her a look. "Excuse me?"

"You." Heather frowned at him. "Are *you* insane? That's what I'm asking."

"What?"

"What?" She mocked him in a huff before standing. "Who works here? Who came here? Who's continued to seek the other one out? Who's the one asking for friendship without doing a goddamn thing to earn it?"

She'd moved closer with each question. If she took another step forward, she would've been touching him. She angled her head up. She didn't give a shit how he stood over her, literally looking down.

"You have nothing to do with Sam," she told him. "Your girlfriend should have nothing to do with her. Not Sam. She's not done anything to deserve your treatment, and you better thank the assholes Mason's beat up in the last month because they're the only reason you aren't knocked unconscious right now."

She turned to Mason. "I get it. You have a monthly knockout quota or something?"

Mason didn't answer, but one side of his mouth lifted.

Adam skewered all of us with a look. "I should've known nothing's changed. Here I thought we were all moving past the bullshit from high school."

He turned to go, but Mason was right there, blocking him.

"What did you think we were doing?"

Adam's eyes narrowed. "What are you talking about?"

"You seem to have been under the impression we were friends?"

"Oh, please." Adam started to move around Mason, but Mason kept in front of him. Adam let out a sigh, lifting his arms in a helpless gesture. "What do you want? Yes, I was the idiot. I'm now realizing there were no friendship promises made."

"You just assumed?"

Mason was stone cold, no reaction or emotion showing on his face. His chiseled jawline was firm, and his eyes were almost dead. Even though I'd been writhing underneath him this morning, another sensual shiver slid down my spine. It was eerie, but I wanted him so damned much in this moment.

"Yes. I just assumed. Happy now?" Adam spat.

Becky and Cass came to the beer garden's tent entrance, and Adam looked over Mason's shoulder. "I'm coming. I just had to grab something."

Becky's face was wet from tears, and Cass had a hand on her shoulder.

I felt kicked in the stomach, and the fight left me.

Becky had been a good friend, in her way. She'd never stabbed me in the back. It was time I moved past it. I came out from behind the counter. "Becky—" I started.

Her eyes widened while Cass' narrowed. "Stop right there," Cass said. "You've done enough damage. Thank you."

Ignoring her, I asked Becky, "Can we talk? Please."

Her head jerked in a nod, and she wiped the tears from her face.

I headed for a far table. It was empty, and I didn't know anyone sitting at the neighboring tables. Becky sat across from me, her movements cautious and slow. I noticed and wrung my hands together on my lap.

She folded her hands, laying them on the table in front of her. Her shoulders seemed to shrink in size. "What else is there to say?"

"Your timing sucks."

A harsh laugh came from her. "Don't hold back, Sam. Please."

"My mom is back in town. Did you know that?"

Her head had been lowered. She raised it now, her eyes finding mine. I tried not to wince at the compassion that flooded her gaze. Tried. Guilt coated my insides, and I failed.

"She came back last year, but I've been avoiding her since then."

"That's why you stayed at Cain last summer?"

I nodded. "And why I've barely been here for holidays. All of it was because of her."

"But you're here for the entire summer now?"

I nodded again. "And so is she."

"Has she said anything to you?"

"No." Maybe the joke was on me? "That's the funny part. I saw her SUV and knew she was in it, but that's been all. Every day I'm waiting for her to show, like she's going to pounce on me or something." I raked a hand over my face. "I'm wound up tight, and you're the one who got it. I'm sorry for that."

"For that?" A soft frown marred her features. "But not…"

"But not for the rest. You can't trick someone into being friends with you, especially if there's bad blood. I suddenly found myself at your engagement, but I didn't ask to be there. I was put on the spot to congratulate you, and I did mean it, but now you guys are here, and you're coming at me like we've been friends this whole time. If you really want to be friends again—"

She leaned forward. "I do. I really do."

"—then you need to ask if we can. And you need to respect my answer, whatever it is."

"Oh." Her gaze fell to the table again.

"It's not that I don't want to."

"Yeah?" She looked up again, hope in her eyes. She began to smile.

"It's that I need time."

"Oh." The smile fell away.

She began to get up, so I covered her hands with mine. "I was stabbed in the back by so many people in high school, it caused some damage inside me. I've only been able to trust Mason, Logan, and Heather for the last few years." I squeezed her hands gently. "But more people have shown me I could trust them, and that doesn't mean I can't make some room for you, too."

Ice ran through my veins. The more I talked, the more fear spread through me.

"I just need time. That's all."

She nodded, and her tears fell on our hands. "I can give that to you. Thank you, Samantha."

She left, and a moment later, Mason and Heather came and sat with me.

"Did I just make a mistake?" I asked.

Mason didn't reply. He just held my hand under the table.

Heather shrugged. "Fuck if I know. She was your friend in school."

I sighed and over my shoulder I heard, "Uh…is this a bad time to announce my awesome arrival?"

I turned to see Nate coming over with Matteo. Both wore crooked grins. Nate spread his arms out.

"Come on, you guys. I know you want to line up to hug this motherfucker here. Don't be shy. My awesomeness is contagious." He winked.

Mason got up, shaking his head. "You were just on the phone with Logan, weren't you?"

"Hell yeah, my Mason motherfucker. Come here, you gorgeous son of a bitch."

The two clasped each other in a bear hug. Heather and I hugged him after, then moved back so Mason, Matteo, and Nate could converge, and a second later, they were laughing like giggling girlfriends.

Watching them, seeing the love between Mason and Nate, I couldn't help but remember how Nate had messed up. He'd treated me badly at moments in high school, had sided with his fraternity against Mason in the beginning, and I knew he'd done other things, but Mason always forgave him. I asked him once why he did that, and his answer had been simple: "Because he was there for me at my lowest."

Becky had been there at my lowest.

Maybe actual forgiveness was the right thing to do, and as my gut approved that decision, the tightness in my chest eased.

# CHAPTER SEVENTEEN

I felt Mason ease into the room.

My back was turned as I stared out the window, but I knew I was right when I heard the door click closed.

"You okay?" he asked.

I had no reason not to be, but I wasn't.

"I'm trying to remember why we hated Becky and Adam so much in high school. I can't remember." I turned around, hugging myself. "I felt the anger. It was this surge. It was overwhelming. Mason, I haven't felt like that since my mom, since I moved in with you and Logan in the first place. I..." What was going on with me?

"We're older. The wounds are still there, but I get it." He shrugged. "I've been having a hard time remembering why I loathed Quinn so much, too. I mean, I remember when he tried to take you from me, but the guy's been easy to work with. I'm glad he got in your face tonight. It was a good reminder. That's the guy I hated." He sat on the edge of the bed. "I wanted to hit him."

"Yeah." I moved to sit with him. He leaned back, his hands finding my legs and helping me settle astride him. "What are you doing in here? Nate's back."

"And he's talking to Matteo."

One of his hands moved under my shirt. I felt its heat on my back, and I shivered.

He leaned closer to me. "I wanted to check on you anyway." His mouth nuzzled under my jawline. His breath tickled me and warmed me at the same time.

I closed my eyes, already feeling the sensations of being too close to Mason wreaking havoc over me. My body warmed, and those flutters begin building in my stomach. I was a little breathless as I tipped my head forward, my lips searching for his.

This.

He answered, his lips finding mine.

The kiss was a gentle touch, a mere graze, and then he applied more pressure.

My need was building, and I sunk lower on his lap. His hands moved around my ribcage, sliding up and slipping under my bra. He cupped my breast, his fingers resting just next to my nipple. I wanted him to touch it, rub against it, flick it. He waited, our kiss deepening. I opened my mouth, and his tongue touched mine just as his fingers brushed over my nipple.

I surged in his lap, molding myself almost completely to him. He was teasing me. I moaned, just wanting more. I would always want more.

"Sam." He pulled back, but kept his hand on my breast. The other went to my hip, and he pushed me down so I could feel him through his pants. Why were we still clothed?

"Hmmm?" I reached for his lips again. I just wanted them on mine.

He tensed when my mouth met his again, and he growled, "Fuck it."

His free hand dipped into my pants, and ten minutes later, Mason was above me.

I wrapped my arms around his neck, feeling him everywhere, and as he thrust into me, I knew all the talking was done.

## MASON

I slipped from the room after Sam fell asleep. When I entered the kitchen, Nate was waiting with a beer in hand for me.

"Matteo took off. Something about a chick waiting for him?"

"He's got a girl in Roussou." I took the beer from him, gesturing for us to head outside.

He nodded, and once outside, we sat around the bonfire cage even though there was no fire. It was just the two of us, drinking beer in complete darkness.

That was when Nate asked, like I knew he would, "So what's going on?"

I told him about my arrangement with my dad and about Caldron.

He let that sink in for a minute. "And your plan?"

"I can't find anything on Adam because I don't know what to press him with. I was thinking of taking a road trip to see if we can find something."

"Road trip?"

"Way I'm thinking, if I was doing something illegal, I wouldn't want it in my office."

"Or at home," Nate added, taking a drag from his beer.

"Both places that could get raided."

"You'd put it somewhere off the grid."

"Like a cabin."

Nate was thinking just what I was.

"Does Adam have a cabin?" he asked.

"Becky mentioned a cabin on the ocean up north." I used the exact words I'd overheard one night in the beer garden, making air quotes. "'A big white house in the middle of nowhere.' They talked about having us up there. Don't know if they meant it or not."

Nate grinned. "We have an address?"

I matched his grin. "I have an idea where it is."

He leaned forward, held his beer up, and clinked it with mine. "Well, then, let's add burglary to our resume. Lord knows we don't have enough bad shit on there."

I leaned back, taking a long drag from my beer. "It's nice to have you back."

He held my gaze. "It's nice to be back."

Matteo was great to have around. He'd helped in that fight, but he wasn't Nate, and he wasn't Logan. He wasn't the guy I asked to do something illegal if it meant helping out someone I loved. And I wasn't doing this for my father. I was doing this for Sam. If Becky was back in her life, then Adam was, too. And I didn't care how much in love he claimed to be. If he'd had a hard-on for Sam in high school, it'd come back around again.

I wanted something on the son of a bitch if that happened.

"When do we go?" Nate asked. He looked like he might be ready now.

I finished my beer and tossed the empty bottle in the bonfire cage. "When Logan gets back."

# CHAPTER EIGHTEEN

The next day, Petey eyed me our entire shift. After the thirtieth stare, I put down the washcloth I'd been using on the counter and turned around. "What?"

"What?" He jumped back. He'd been two feet from me.

"Either Keifer told you to keep an eye on me and you took that in the literal sense, or you want to say something. What is it?"

"Why are you here?"

I frowned. "What do you mean?"

"Your boyfriend is Mason Kade. Even I've heard about his football reputation, and he's here, working some rich internship for his daddy." He pointed at me. "And I heard what he said about you. You don't need this job, but you don't act like one of those rich, stuck-up bitches. Why are you here?"

"Because I needed a job."

He moved forward, leaning against the counter next to me. "But that's the thing." He turned to rest his back against the counter so he could watch the beer garden and me at the same time. "I asked around. You usually work with your best friend at Manny's. You're not there this summer."

"What do you want me to say?"

"The truth?"

I paused, checking to see if that was sarcastic. It wasn't. "Besides wanting to do something else, Heather's boyfriend is involved in underground fighting. Some of Mason's enemies are, too, and word would get out if I was working at Manny's. They could find me there."

"That Caldron guy and his goons?"

I nodded.

"But they already know you're here."

"They aren't Mason's only enemies."

"Why are you paying for what he did?"

I shook my head. "I'm not paying for it. They could hurt me to get to Mason."

"They're pussies then."

"That Caldron guy is mad because I helped put his best friend in prison. He would've raped someone if I hadn't." I left out the part where Mason had orchestrated the whole situation so someone else was in that predicament, not me.

"File a restraining order."

"What?"

A group of bikers came up to the counter. Our conversation paused until their orders were filled and they moved to sit at one of the picnic tables.

Petey jumped up on the counter next to me, swinging his legs. "If someone's trying to hurt you, why don't you go the legal route? Me?" He touched his chest. "No way. We don't work that way here, but you could. I'm not getting why you don't."

I shrugged, feeling that same damned tightness in my chest again. "We've always taken care of our problems ourselves."

"Except the time you got that guy's best friend put in prison?"

"Except that time."

A slow grin stretched on his face, and he nodded, approving. "I think you guys are carnies at heart."

"What?"

"Carnies at heart. We deal with our own. That's how you guys operate."

I shrugged. "You haven't even met Logan yet."

"Who's he?"

I opened my mouth, but how could I possibly explain? He had no idea. I just smiled instead.

# CHAPTER NINETEEN
## MASON

"What are we doing?"

"Sshhh!" Both Matteo and Nate replied to Adam's question. I was in the driver's seat, and I kept my eyes on the road, but I knew Nate had twisted around. I could only imagine Matteo delivering his own glare next to Adam in the backseat.

The answer to his question wasn't going to grab a burger, which is what I'd told him when we left the country club. Nate and Matteo had arrived, ready for our first errand, and we'd been leaving under the guise of going to get food when Adam decided a burger sounded good to him, too. Hence the uninvited guest.

"You know that guy who attacked Sam at the carnival?"

"Yeah." His answer was slow, cautious.

"We're dealing with him."

"What?" He jerked upright, grabbing my seat. "What do you mean 'dealing with'?"

Nate twisted around again. "What do you think we mean?"

"I don't know." Adam sat back, his eyes darting all over the car.

"We're not going to kill him or anything," Matteo said.

There was silence for a beat.

"You're new to this group," Adam said.

Nate barked out a laugh. "And you're not? You weren't even invited, Quinn."

"I was told you were going for a burger, not about to commit a crime."

"You're right." I positioned the rearview mirror so I could see him. "Next time we're about to make a drop on some guy, I'll make sure to lead with that. And again, you weren't invited, Quinn."

"Maybe next time let me know that." He sat back in a huff.

I fought against rolling my eyes. "Fucking relax, okay? We're not going to do anything illegal. We're just going to try to find out where this guy works and lives. That's all."

"And Mason didn't fight you coming, because this guy would've hurt your fiancée, too," Nate added. "Another day, another night, another place, she could've been caught up in this mess as much as Sam."

"Yeah, but Sam—"

I stopped at an intersection and looked in the mirror at him. "What?" I had a hunch what he was going to say, but I wanted him to say it.

He clamped his mouth shut, literally squirming in the backseat.

"Remember you have some balls," I told him. "Finish what you were going to say."

He looked away, his jaw clenching. "I was going to say that Sam's in this because of you. Becky wouldn't be put in this situation. Driving around and finding where this guy lives and works isn't something I would be doing."

"You're right." The light turned green, and I moved forward. "You'd have your daddy find all the answers and deal with it himself."

"I wouldn't." His gaze jumped back to mine.

I raised an eyebrow. "You sure?"

I felt Nate watching me. There'd been a few occasions when I was forced to go to my own father, but this wasn't one of them. I wanted to deal with Caldron on my own.

Adam shrugged, turning back to look out the window. "I don't put my women in jeopardy. That's what I do."

I stopped the vehicle and had Adam outside in two seconds flat. He was up against the Escalade, my hand to his throat, before any of us comprehended what I'd just done. Even I blinked a few times before I realized it.

Nate pulled me off, pushing me a few feet away while Matteo stepped in front of Adam, a hand to his shoulder like he was holding him back. Adam didn't move, though. He only stood there, a dazed look on his face. When he finally realized what had happened, he surged forward.

Matteo held him back easily, grunting, "Dude. Chill. You'd get your ass wiped, and you know it."

"What the fuck?" Adam yelled around Matteo.

My blood was pumping, and I started for him without thinking. Nate shouldered me back, saying under his breath, "Mason, calm down."

"He's blaming me for Sam."

"And he's right."

"What?" I turned on Nate, but he was right and even as I registered that, I felt a pit in my stomach. "That fucker *is* right."

He pushed me farther away, far enough so we could talk without Quinn overhearing. "Stop it. I know you're feeling guilty right now, but it's whatever. You are who you are. Sam knew that before she fell in love with you."

"But Taylor…"

"And Taylor knew who Logan was before she fell for him, too." He clapped me on the shoulder. "You guys don't like to get pushed around. It is what it is. Don't let some asshole like Quinn get in your head. He might not put his girl in danger, but you know what he does do? He cheats. He's not this perfect do-gooder like he's acting. He's just another slick business guy like his dad, and some of those guys cheat on their wives. He's going to hurt his woman in ways that Sam will never even think about. He went after Sam for upsetting Becky. He got involved in girl business. You wouldn't do that."

"I got involved when Kate was going after Sam."

"Because that was your ex targeting your woman. Not the same thing. He doesn't have a relationship with Sam. They aren't even friends."

I sighed. "I just want to find Caldron and beat the shit out of him."

"But you're not going to." Nate's words were a statement, with just a hint of question.

"No," I told him. "We're going to ask around, find out where he works and lives, and go from there."

"Then let's do that."

"I was planning on heading to Channing's bar before Quinn pissed me off."

"Get used to it. I assumed you brought him with to try to get close to him?"

I nodded. "I could've told him to get lost, but yeah."

"You're not thinking of being friends with him, are you?"

"No, but if he's around us, he'll relax. We can get a better window into how he really is." A guy shows you his real self when you push him out of his comfort zone. Nate was still looking at me weird. "What?"

"What if it doesn't work? What if we actually have to pretend to be friends with him?"

I grinned and clapped him on the shoulder. "Then it's your turn up to bat. There's no way in hell he'll buy that Logan or I suddenly want to be friends with him."

"What about Matteo?"

"He won't be here long enough, and the less dirt I can put on his hands, the better." We watched the two. Matteo still had Quinn blocked and up against my Escalade. Quinn stuffed his hands in his pockets and glared at me.

Nate shuddered. "Let's just find something at that cabin. I don't want to have to go through that."

"Come on." We were only a block away. Locking my Escalade with the push of a button, I called, "Our first stop's just over there. Follow us."

---

Channing's bar was dark inside, lit with neon signs. Swanky and dirty somehow described the interior, and also the few guys bellied up to the bar. We'd passed some Harleys in the parking lot, but I already knew Channing's bar had become a biker bar, so I wasn't surprised to see the leather on each guy—top of the line stuff. They turned to watch us. I couldn't blame them. We didn't look much like them, with our preppy clothes, but they didn't scare me.

I nodded to the bartender. "Channing here?"

She scanned us, her top lip curving in a sneer. "Who's asking?"

But Channing had already heard me. He came to his opened office door, which was set off to the side of the bar counter. "Ka—" He began, then seemed to remember who was in his bar and corrected himself. "Mason! What's up?"

"Can I talk to you?" I pointed to his office.

"Sure. Yeah." He turned to the bartender. "Ang, can you get the rest of the guys whatever they want? On the house."

Surprise lit her face. "Sure thing."

I followed him back into his office and leaned against the far wall as he closed the door. I opened my mouth to speak, but he held up a finger, hitting the switch on a large fan set in the corner. When the sound filled the room, I sat down in one of the chairs across from his desk. "So you don't just use that when it gets hot in here?"

He shook his head, taking his seat. "Those guys aren't dumb out there. If they hear something that could help their club, they'll use it."

"They're one-percenters?" I didn't mean the kind my dad was.

"Yeah."

"Good to know." They were the one percent of motorcycle clubs that did illegal shit.

He leaned forward, resting his arms on his desk. "What are you doing here?"

"I texted Brandon, asked him if you were at Manny's."

"He said I wasn't."

I nodded. "So I guessed you'd be here."

"Okay. What's going on, though? Sam okay?"

"Caldron saw Sam at the carnival. He tried to hurt her again."

"You serious?" He wiped his hand over his face. "Wait. Sam was at the carnival?"

"Your girlfriend hasn't told you? Sam and Mark got jobs there."

"What?" His eyebrows shot up. "Mark's her stepbrother, right?"

I nodded.

"What the fuck is she doing working there?"

I didn't want to get into it, so I just said, "Change of scenery. It was mostly Mark's idea, but that's why I'm here. I need to know where Caldron works and his address."

"Oh." He reached for a pen and paper. "That's no problem. He lives on a place a few miles outside Roussou. It's an abandoned farm, but his house is mostly known for partying and drugs." He wrote down the address and slid it over to me. "And he works in Fallen Crest, actually."

"Where?"

"For your dad, his landscaping business over there."

"You serious? My dad?"

"Sure am. He comes here at night sometimes." He pointed to his closed door. "And keep his name quiet when you leave the office. Those guys are sometimes his friends, other times his enemies, depending on whether he owes them money or not."

"Will do, but this just got a lot easier now that I know he works for my dad."

"You're going to get him fired?"

"The opposite." I smirked, standing up.

He followed me to the door. "You're going to promote him?"

"Something like that."

I reached for the door.

"Wait." I looked over to see him frowning. "You'll owe your dad then. I know you don't like that."

I opened the door this time, looking at where Adam was sitting. He and Nate were at a far table, while Matteo had bellied up right alongside the bikers. My eyes were only for Quinn, though. "I'll have to find something else to make us even."

He followed my gaze, understanding in his voice. "I was wondering about the newbie. Keeping him close?"

"Something like that," I said again, giving him a quick nod. "Thanks for this. I owe you."

"No, no." He shook his head. "Sam came to my fight because Heather really wanted her there. If anything, this is just me making *us* even. You wouldn't have this problem if you hadn't been forced to come that night."

"Still, thank you."

"Be smart, whatever you're going to do." The guys at the bar glanced over, and Channing lowered his voice. "You've got a lot going for you. I wouldn't want anything to jeopardize that."

I knew what he meant, but as long as I had family here, as long as Sam wanted to come back and see her family, I'd have to deal with Caldron.

"I know," I told him. "Thanks again."

I stepped out, giving Nate the nod. "Let's go."

He and Quinn followed, the latter being only too eager, but Matteo still had a full beer in hand.

"Matteo," I called.

"What?" He saw us at the door. "Hold on." Holding a hand in the air, he tipped his head back and chugged the entire bottle. He finished with his new friends cheering him on and grinned, patting the two closest to him on the back. "That's how we do it where I'm from. I'll see you guys later! It was nice meeting you all."

Nate leaned close, his voice quiet so Adam couldn't hear behind us. "He's like a big Mastiff. Friendly to everyone and the size of a real-life boulder."

I laughed. "Why do you think I love playing with him on the team?"

"I get it. I hated him freshman year, thought he was replacing me. I love the guy now."

I did, too, but he wasn't Logan. I was ready for my brother to come home.

# CHAPTER TWENTY
## SAMANTHA

I was finishing my shift by taking the garbage out at midnight when I felt someone behind me. Dropping the bag, I whirled around. I didn't know if I was going to launch myself at them or run, but my knees were bent and ready to do one or the other.

I did neither.

It was Kate.

I felt the old disdain automatically rise up. Mason's psycho ex-fuck buddy. I wouldn't have recognized her except for the cold hatred in her eyes. She'd filled out, gaining a few pounds since high school, and she wore a low-cut red corset. Her blond hair was pulled back in two French braids, and she wore heavy makeup with raccoon-style eyes and bright red lips. Glitter on her lipstick matched the glitter spread over her chest. She took me in as I stared right back at her.

"Holy shit," I breathed.

"What's Mason up to?"

And we were right down to business. Good to know. "Uh…" I cocked my head to the side. "Even if I did know, I wouldn't tell you."

"He went into Channing's bar. My boyfriend was there. What would Channing and Mason have to talk about?"

"You mean besides the fact that their girlfriends are best friends?" I shook my head, mocking her. "Because we are. Heather Jax. Me." I linked my hands and showed her my entwined fingers. "Like this. Tighter than your vagina ever was."

"Nice." She rolled her eyes, smacking her gum. "Same old annoying-as-fuck Samantha Strattan."

"Yeah. That's what I am. Annoying."

A second eye roll. "Has Mason picked up some of Logan's sarcasm, too? Because if so, he's not the guy I fell for in school."

"Oh, no." Well… "He might've picked up some of Logan's sarcasm, but he's definitely not the guy you fell for in school. That was just a guy using you for sex. The guy he is now is way better. Better standards. Better girlfriend. Better everything, really. Better future, too." I forced a smile, knowing she'd see the hard edges. "You'd never have a shot with him now."

"I stand corrected." She snapped. "You're a bigger bitch than you used to be. Too bad I didn't get you worse than I did in that bathroom."

I sucked in a breath. This bitch didn't just go there… My hand formed a fist, and I thought about swinging. I might've, except Mark stepped out from the shadows behind her. She didn't seem to notice he was there, but his presence brought me back to reality. Mason and I were here for the summer. We were moving on in a couple months. And everything I'd said was true. Mason had a much better future.

Mark circled around her, his hands stuffed in his pockets. His confused gaze switched from me to her as he came to stand next to me.

"Who are you?" he asked.

I let some control back in, smoothing my fingers out.

"Who are you?" Kate countered.

I didn't want to hear some jab about whether I was going to screw this stepbrother, too, so I said quickly, "He works here. He's a friend."

"Really?" She skimmed him up and down, interest softening her mouth into a seductive smile. "How good of a friend?"

"You've got no shot with me."

"A good, loyal friend."

"Hmmm." Her features flattened. "Whatever then, but I meant what I said. Mason needs to keep out of Roussou, Sam."

"Why are you here warning me about this?"

"Because I still care about Mason. I think I always will. It's not his fault he has piss-poor taste in women, but it is his fault if he keeps poking his head around Channing's bar."

I felt Mark's gaze on me. I could feel him wondering what the hell she was talking about. I ignored him. "Channing's a friend."

"And Mason has enemies who hang around with Channing. Enemies he doesn't even know about."

Oh. That wasn't good.

"Just warn him for me?" she added. "I'd hate to see that fine, rich ass six feet under, if you get my drift."

"Are you kidding me?"

"*Yeah.*" Now her sarcasm was thick. "I'm here as a big prank, because I've been hoping to seek you out for the last three years. You know, for the fun of it." Her gaze intensified. "I mean it. This is for Mason's safety." She gave Mark another long, considering look, and let out a soft sound before she turned and left.

"What was that about?" Mark asked after a moment.

"I have no idea." But I was going to find out. "What are you doing here? I thought you finished earlier."

"I did, but Mom called. Thought I'd give you the heads-up in person."

"Oh." That didn't sound good. "What is it?"

"She's doing a pool party at the country club, and everyone is invited."

"Everyone?" The hairs on the back of my neck stood up.

"Everyone. Cass, Quinn, Becky, Amelia. Even Peter is going to be there."

"Why would Malinda do that?"

"Because it's my birthday." He threw an arm around my shoulder, pulling me tight. "I want my stepsister there, so buck up, Sam. We've got another shindig to look forward to."

I groaned. I almost would've taken more Kate over this event. Almost.

Mark walked me to my car after I clocked out. He followed me home until I turned left toward Helen's house and he kept going. I texted him after I parked.

**Thanks for following me home.**

He buzzed back a moment later. **No problem. Mason was going to come, but I told him I'd do it.**

I found Nate and Matteo taking shots in the kitchen when I went inside. They waved, lifting their glasses in the air.

*"It's Sam!! Samantha is hoooooome!"* Matteo bellowed.

"Hey guys." I waved back. "Mason?"

Nate pointed to the hallway. "Bedroom. He's changing. He was going to join us until you got here."

"Yeah, well, here I am."

Matteo cupped his hands around his mouth, calling out in an announcer-style voice, "And she is off, folks. Like a racehorse running the race of her life. Veering down the hallway, past the other rooms, closing in on the bedroom, she is nearing home. She's nearly across the threshold. That victor's crown is just waiting for her—"

"If you don't stop likening me to a racehorse, I'll come back there and turn you from a stud to a gelding, Matteo," I yelled to him.

I heard a smattering of laughter before he called back, "Noted, and I love you, Sam."

I could hear Nate still laughing. A second later Matteo said something more, and Nate's laugh got louder, but instead of going back, I went into the bedroom.

I had someone else's ass to kick.

Mason was coming out of the bathroom, wearing sweats that hung low on his hips. He had a shirt in hand and was about to pull it over his head. I grabbed it and tossed it to the floor.

"What's up?"

I shut the door, crossing my arms over my chest. "What were you doing in Roussou today?"

"How did you know that?" He scowled. "Mark?"

"Did Mark know?"

"No, but Matteo could've told him."

Okay. I didn't have to ream my stepbrother out. "I heard it from Kate."

"Kate?" His scowl lessened to a frown. He began rubbing at his forehead.

"Yeah. Your ex-booty call found me when I was taking the garbage out."

His shoulders tightened. "Did Caldron send her?"

"No."

"So how'd she know?"

"She said one of the guys who saw you in Channing's bar was her boyfriend."

"What else did she say?"

"That there's someone close to Channing you and he can't trust. Whoever that is talks to Caldron."

"Kate said all this?" He pointed at me. "To you?"

"I know." I crossed the room and lay on the bed, where he joined me. "Imagine my shock. She still cares about you."

"I want to know who's been talking to Caldron." He leaned forward, his back muscles bunching as he rested his elbows on his knees.

I fought the urge to run my hand over them. If I did, this interrogation would soon change tones, and I didn't want that to happen. Not yet. I sat up and moved over so I was half-facing him, one leg pulled up to rest on the bed, my other foot still on the ground.

"What were you doing in Roussou?"

"I wanted to find out where Caldron lives and works."

"And?"

He was still thinking, wondering who the traitor was in Channing's crew.

I sighed, giving in and tracing a finger up his back. "It could be anyone. You don't know all of Channing's friends."

"True." He relaxed slightly, reaching up and catching my hand. He laced our fingers together, using his hold to tug me closer. I shifted so my leg went around him. He pulled my other leg over his knee, and I only had to lean forward half an inch to rest on him, hugging him from the side. His hand moved to my knee, and he began tracing up and down the inside of my thigh. "He works for my dad. I'm going to see if he'll promote him."

"What?" I started to pull away.

He caught my hand, keeping me in place. He shot me a sideways look. "The requirements will be that he has to protect you, not hurt you. One move against us, and he's out of a job."

"You think that'll work?"

Mason shrugged. "If it doesn't, we'll figure something else out. I know where he lives, and it's no gated community."

"You'd do something to his home?"

Mason moved so he could see me squarely and touched the side of my face. His thumb rubbed over my cheek. "Do you not realize the lengths I'll go for you?" he asked softly.

A pocket of air caught and held in my throat.

He leaned forward, his forehead resting on mine. "I scare even myself, Sam. There's nothing I won't do for you."

And his lips lowered to mine.

# CHAPTER TWENTY-ONE

It was Saturday, and I wasn't working. Petey had told me he wanted his regular staff on. They were complaining about not getting their usual amount of tips. He'd had a weird look on his face, his features all twisted up, but when I didn't argue, the weirdness left him.

And this meant I had an entire afternoon just for running. I'd been skipping lately, which seemed to appease Mason. He always reached for me when he woke in the mornings, and the last few days, I'd been there.

Those had been good mornings indeed.

This morning had been no exception. He reached for me, and it wasn't long before he was sliding inside. I knew this was always the best way to start a day. Always. No exceptions.

My theory had been reinforced when we went to the kitchen and saw the haggard set of Nate and Matteo's shoulders.

I pointed at Nate's face. "You actually look green."

He moaned, lurching for the sink. Grabbing hold of the counter, he waited, but nothing came out. He was only dry heaving.

"Oh my God. Never challenge Matteo to a shot contest. And if he challenges you, just let him have the victory." He gave Matteo a dark look where he lay across the island counter, his butt on a barstool.

His mouth moved against the granite. "I still don't think you won."

"Oh, God." Nate held his head over the sink again. "It comes in waves. I have air, and then nausea. Air, then nausea. It won't go away."

Mason moved behind me, putting the coffee into the machine. I held the empty pot, unsure if I wanted to use the sink.

"That could be contaminated just by you being there," I noted.

"What?" Nate saw what was in my hand. "Oh." He moved back. "Go for it, quick. I might spew at any moment."

I filled it quickly and poured the water in the machine as I pressed *brew*. It started to churn, and I stepped away. "If you guys are so hung over, why are you up?"

Both pointed to Mason.

I looked up at him. He grinned. "I have today off. I made them promise to get up and go golfing with me, no matter how much they drank last night. They promised."

"You're going golfing?"

He nodded.

"Were you drinking last night?"

"It's not really the actual act of golfing that's of interest. It's more about *who else* is going to be there." His eyes locked on mine, waiting for me to figure it out.

Mason had two enemies, at least that we were dealing with right now. One was not the golfing type, but the other…

"Ah. I got it." Adam or his father was going to be on that golf course. "And that reminds me, Malinda is throwing a BBQ at the country club today. She reserved the pool and everything."

Nate and Matteo groaned.

Even Mason grimaced. "You're going to make me go to that?"

"If I have to go, my posse has to go."

"We're your posse?" Nate was grinning at me, or trying. The pallor of his skin made him look like the Joker.

"Mason is, and you're his, so same thing. I need backup."

Nate glanced to Mason. "Quinn will be at the party. That's different than what we have planned for today. That's *socializing*." He said it like that was a bad word.

"I think Quinn senior, too." Wait. I didn't know that. "Well, maybe not. I don't know, but it's at the country club. It's Saturday. I wouldn't be surprised if he shows up."

Matteo sat up, clutching his stomach, and asked, "Why do we care about Adam's dad?"

Mason, Nate, and I shared a look before Nate coughed. "Uh…We don't. Why would you think that?"

Matteo lifted his head in confusion. "What? But you guys just said—"

Mason moved forward, reaching behind me for the filled coffee pot. "He was an ass to Sam one time in school. That's all."

"Oh." Matteo looked to me. "Sorry, Sam. I'm sure he won't be anymore. He's probably ecstatic about his son's engagement." He smiled, and a dimple showed in his cheek. "It's kind of sweet, if you think about it. One rich family falling in love with another rich family. They can make babies who are even richer. It's like you guys all know how to seek each other out, really stick it to the poor folk. Don't want them contaminating the breeding well."

This wasn't normal Matteo, and I glanced at Mason. I wasn't sure how to respond.

"Becky and Adam met in high school," Mason said. "It was a private school, but I didn't go there. Sam transferred out for her last year and a half of school. And you ain't poor anymore, Matteo. You've got NFL teams eyeing you. Your parents might not have a lot of money, but that doesn't mean they would contaminate anything. They made the best fucking lineman I'll always want running next to me. No money, no breeding, no private schools could produce someone like you, and I'm thankful."

Matteo couldn't speak at first. His Adam's apple bobbed. "Thank you, Mason," he croaked out, blinking rapidly. "You didn't go to a rich private school?"

Mason smirked. "Fuck, no. Can you imagine that? We probably would've burned the building down."

Nate's head snapped toward Mason at the mention of burning.

Matteo laughed, his massive shoulders bouncing. "That's true. Man, I really miss your little brother. When's he getting back?"

"A few weeks." Mason clapped a hand to Matteo's shoulder. "I think we're all missing him."

After that, a solemn feeling lingered over the group. I felt it even as they left to go golfing, and I couldn't shake it away as I headed across the street to Malinda's house. She called while the guys were getting ready to leave and offered me a ride to the country club.

I was dressed in a running outfit, but the tank top could pass for a social event. That was the hope anyway. I had running shorts on underneath a flowy skirt, and my shoes were cute enough that they still went with the outfit. My running music and earbuds were tucked away in one of my pockets, along with my phone.

I knocked on Malinda's door. "Hello?" I called, going inside.

"Sam, honey." Malinda moved across the hallway from the kitchen to the dining room, packages in hand.

I followed and saw twenty gift bags sitting on her table. "What's going on?"

"It's an impromptu wedding shower for Becky and Adam." She stuffed the packages in her hands into the gift bags. She motioned to a pile of them on the counter behind me. "Can you help me out? Each bag gets one of those."

"What are they?" I could see long, rectangular boxes wrapped in white tissue paper.

"Bracelets. Each bag gets a set of jewelry. I've got the earrings and necklaces in all of them. I just need to get the bracelets in the rest."

I went to work, and when I got to the end I saw another row of smaller bags placed on the table, too. "Who are these for?"

"Those are done. Those are for the guys."

I counted another twenty and began feeling sick to my stomach. "Who all is going to be at this party?"

She stopped, straightening from one of the bags, and frowned at me. "I thought Mark told you?"

"He said you reserved the pool for his birthday party at the country club."

"Was that it?"

"And that his friends were going to be there."

"Oh." She turned to the bags again. "Well, yeah. It's partly a birthday party for Mark and also a wedding shower for Adam and

Becky. I'm surprised he didn't tell you that part. Aren't you good with her again? I thought Mark said something about that."

"I guess I am…" But all of those people from high school? I was back at the beginning of my junior year again. Analise had just left my dad. Jessica and Lydia had turned on me. The Academy Elite only wanted to use me to get to Mason and Logan. All those old feelings twisted and churned inside me, like a thunderstorm trying to strike its way out.

"What?" Malinda's voice suddenly sounded panicky. She rushed to my side. "Samantha, are you okay?" She felt my forehead. "You don't feel feverish. What's wrong?" She held my shoulders and peered into my eyes. "Are you really not okay with this? Mark assured me you would be. I won't make you go if it's a situation you aren't comfortable with."

I heard the caring in her tone.

I heard the love.

I heard the warmth.

Relief had me swaying on my feet. She wasn't Analise. She wasn't Lydia or Jessica. She wasn't turning on me like they had.

I nodded, my neck feeling loose and my head unusually heavy. "I'm fine. Mason, Nate, and Matteo are going to be there. I'm fine."

"Are you sure?"

"I really am fine." Feeling a little steadier, I put my hands over hers on my shoulders and squeezed. "I've just been feeling old anxiety that I thought I'd left a long time ago. That's all." I grinned, trying to reassure her. "Apparently, I still have some baggage to work through."

"Oh, honey." She pulled me in for a hug, rubbing my back. "You'll get there. You have people who love you and support you. No matter what. If you need anything, you tell me. I'll drop anything I'm doing for you. Okay?" Malinda leaned back, holding my shoulders again.

I nodded. "I know."

And I did, which is why I helped her carry all the gift bags out to the SUV. We were just finishing up, and Malinda ran inside to make sure she'd gotten everything out, when I noticed someone standing at the end of the driveway.

I looked up, and froze.

Analise stood there, looking like I did without the flowing skirt. She wore leggings with earbuds in her ears. She seemed frozen in place, too, except one hand reached up to take out one of her earbuds. She let it go and slowly looked to face me squarely.

"Okay! Everything's ready. Are you?"

I heard my stepmom's voice. Bright. Cheery. Then the door closed, and her footsteps came across the pavement.

She stopped. "Oh."

I couldn't look away from Analise, who still hadn't moved.

"Okay!" Malinda clapped her hands together. I heard the forced note in her voice. She came up behind me, touching my arm and guiding me to the vehicle. "You get in here, Sam. And—" She shut the door, moving around to the driver's side. There was no misstep, no hesitation. She didn't look down the driveway as she climbed inside and started the engine. "Ready to go? It'll be a fun event."

She reversed down the driveway, having enough room to turn around before driving out onto the street. As we turned the front of the SUV to face out, my heart felt like it was crawling out of me, but there was no Analise anymore.

We drove out, paused at the street, and as Malinda turned left she grabbed my hand and squeezed it.

"She was out for a walk, sweetheart. That's going to happen. We'll just, uh—we'll have to start getting used to it."

The sentiment sounded sane.

My mom lived on the same block as we did. Of course I'd run into her, but... As we drove down the street, I couldn't stop myself from looking for her. The gate to the Kade mansion was closed. She wasn't behind us on the sidewalk, or on any sidewalk I could see as we left our little community.

She was gone.

# CHAPTER TWENTY-TWO

There was laughing, squealing, and hugging. Way too much hugging.

Once I helped Malinda unload everything to the pool's veranda, I had to make an escape. I went to hide in a far corner of the country club's lobby, waiting for Mason, Nate, and Matteo to show. Mason's text said they had one hole to finish, but shouldn't be too long. As far as I was concerned, any more time was too long.

Where I was sitting, people had to walk past me to the pool area, but there were a bunch of bushes and potted trees hiding me. So I could see them; they couldn't see me.

It seemed to be a Fallen Crest Academy reunion, but only for those who hated me. Miranda arrived, actually hanging on to Peter's arm. Then Amelia arrived, along with more members of the Elite squad, the nickname their group acquired at school. They'd been the top of the social system. After that came a lot who I couldn't remember, and then I thought I'd die because Jessica and Lydia came in, too.

I shrank in my seat as I watched my two ex-best friends waltz past like they came here every weekend. Though maybe they did. I had no idea.

"What are you doing?"

I turned and looked, but I couldn't believe it. "Jeff?"

My first boyfriend—the guy who'd cheated on me with one of the ex-best friends who'd just walked past—now stood at my side, his face twisted in confusion. His hair was spiked up, and he wore shades with a trendy T-shirt and ripped skinny jeans. I got over my initial shock and just took the sight of him in.

"You still look like a preppy rocker wannabe," I said. "What are you doing here? You weren't friends with this group in school."

"And you were?" He paused. "Wait. You kinda were, then you weren't. I've not been enemies with them. You were. I should be asking you that question." He winked, smirking. "But are you kidding me? The invite got posted on social media. Hell yes, I'm coming." He plopped down next to me and hunched his shoulders, slumping down in his seat, too. "Who you hiding from?"

I hit him. "Not funny. You're going to give me away."

He took his sunglasses off to look at me. "Sam, you're clear as day when you first walk into the lobby. Every person who's come this way has seen you."

I felt the blood drain from my face. "Are you serious?"

He nodded, looking like he was trying not to laugh. "Really, though..." He leaned close, lowering his voice. "Who are you hiding from?"

"You!" I thrust a hand out, then pointed to the pool area. "All of them. They're all FCA people."

"So?" He shrugged, getting comfortable and throwing a leg up over his arm rest. "The invite said it's Becky and Adam's first wedding shower. Which, by the way, their parents are pissed that your stepmom is throwing the party."

I scrunched up my nose. "It's also for Mark's birthday."

"When's his birthday?"

"Uh..." I had no clue. I lied, "This weekend." I should've known.

He rolled his eyes, putting his sunglasses back on. "You're lying. I can still tell."

I hit him again. "I'm not."

"Ouch!" He rubbed his arm. "You hit Mason like that?"

"He doesn't deserve it."

"Hey. Is it true? You guys are warring with Roussou again?" He whistled under his breath. "Blast from the past. I feel like we're back in high school again. What are they planning? Car bombs? They going to burn down a bar or something this time?"

Why all the references to burning? I winced. "No. Nothing like that."

"What?" Jeff narrowed his eyes. I could just see through the darkened lenses. "Oh, shit. Mason's going the grown-up route now? What? He's going to pay for them to go away or something?" He groaned. "That's so lame."

I narrowed my eyes right back. "You're lame. You never answered me before. What are you doing here?"

"I'm friends with Becky."

I gave him a look.

"I was kind of friends with her," he amended. He dropped his leg and leaned across the break between the chairs. "Look, the invite went out on Adam's Instagram. He said anyone could come, so if you're thinking only their actual friends are going to be here, you need to get a clue. Anyone still in Fallen Crest this summer is heading here. It's the perfect excuse to scope out the country club. Plus, it might be everyone's last attempt to get in good with Adam Quinn." He glanced back to where everyone was congregating.

Get in good with—I hadn't heard that right, had I?

"What are you talking about?"

His eyes slid back to mine. "You haven't heard?"

"What are you talking about?"

"Quinn's going into politics. He made the announcement at graduation. Weren't you there? Everyone's been watching him. He went pre-law, now he's gotten into Harvard Law, and after that he's going political. I thought you knew."

I had no clue. But I wasn't completely shocked. "Becky's going to be a political wife?"

Jeff laughed. "Yep. I've no doubt she's got dreams of being a first lady one day."

Jeff's revelations punched me in the chest, but even so, I had to admit it felt right. Of course Adam would go into politics.

I shook my head. "All that power. All that control."

"All that pussy," Jeff added. "Becky's in for a rude awakening, but that's on her. Like she doesn't know what Quinn is really like."

"Things are different," I told him. "Adam's happy with Becky."

Jeff started laughing.

I shot him a warning look. "I mean it."

"Okay." He patted my knee before he stood up. "You keep thinking that. I'm going to head in there to get the free food before it's all gone."

He'd been gone less than thirty seconds before I heard Mason ask from behind me, "Was that your ex-shit bag I just saw talking to you?"

I ignored Mason's question. He knew Jeff and I were fine. He wasn't pissed about him anyway. Instead, I stood and said, "Adam's going into politics. Did you know that?"

Nate and Matteo had come with Mason, and both had different reactions. A proud smile bloomed on Matteo's face while Nate just started laughing.

And laughing.

And laughing some more.

Mason nudged him. "Shut up."

"It's just…" He shook his head, trying to stop. "*Of course* he's going into politics. Fuck. That makes so much sense."

"That's what I thought, too." I nodded.

"Why is that a bad thing?" Matteo asked.

"You're seeing him be a good guy right now," Mason explained.

"He's not always been a good guy," Nate added.

"Nor will he be in the future," Mason concluded.

He watched me as he spoke, and I saw a flicker of emotion there. I wanted to ask if they'd found out anything on their golfing adventure, but Matteo was here. Mason didn't want him affected by our battles, so I held my tongue. I'd ask later.

We all stood and looked across the club's lobby. Just on the other side of some glass doors was the pool veranda, already filled with people from my old school. No one spoke, but Mason started forward. I followed, as did Nate and Matteo. We followed our leader into what I was beginning to think of as enemy territory once again.

As we reached the last door that separated us from them, their conversations began to stop. It felt like one by one, everyone was turning to watch us enter.

I couldn't blame them.

Mason reached behind him, and I slipped my hand into his.

Mason and Logan were gods to them. There were legendary rumors and stories about the Kade brothers, and even though Mason and Logan had gone to public school, I knew first-hand how much everyone had wanted to be like them or be with them. Even now, eyes widened, mouths opened, and people were almost gawking at Mason.

This was his football celebrity. They would've had something akin to this reaction before, but it was more now.

Nate leaned close, whispering, "I forget about his football status, you know?"

I nodded. "I know what you mean."

A part of the crowd shifted, and Adam appeared first, with Becky in hand, followed by Mark. My stepbrother stayed back as Adam approached with his hand held out.

"Mason, glad you stopped by."

Mason frowned, looking at him with narrowed eyes. He didn't move to shake his hand. Unease slithered down my spine. This felt staged. Something about Adam's approach seemed off. He had an odd look in his gaze.

I looked at Becky, saw the fear there, and knew whatever Adam was hoping to accomplish, it wasn't good. I stepped forward, intentionally bumping Adam's hand aside.

"What are you talking about? My stepmother is throwing this party, remember? You're acting like we weren't invited." I leaned closer, but made sure everyone could hear my words. "It's more the other way around, Adam. Something like your engagement."

I felt bad seeing the hurt flood Becky's face, but knew the others would speculate about what I meant. That was what I wanted. We weren't beneath Adam. He wasn't going to push us that way.

An unreadable mask came over his face, but I didn't care about him. I stepped toward Becky. "Can I talk to you?"

Her eyebrows pulled in before she nodded. "Okay."

I led the way back to the front lobby, but I didn't stop. I kept going, veering into an empty conference room.

"Sam? What's going on?"

I moved around her, shutting the door. "Is it true that Adam's going into politics?"

"What?" She hugged herself before her mouth set in a determined line. "How is that any of your business?"

But she knew what I was going to say. Just like she'd known the whole time.

I nodded. "So he is."

"Why are you asking?"

"Tell me one thing. Was it your idea for me to be at your engagement party?" I waited a beat, watching the questions flit across her features. "Or Adam's?"

"It was mine." She looked away. "I might've mentioned it a few times."

That told me everything I needed to know. "Becky, don't marry him."

I reached for her hands, but she pulled them away.

"How dare you?" She took a step back.

"I dare because you knew this is what I would say. That's why you wanted to reconcile. He wanted me, Becs. Not you. He plotted to get me, over and over again. That's why Mason hates him. And now this, your engagement, him going into politics—you wanted me back in your life because I'm the only one who'll tell you the truth."

She turned away, still hugging herself, but she made no move to leave. She was listening to me, and I had to think it was because I was saying what she wanted to hear.

I softened my voice. "He's going to cheat on you."

She sniffled. "How do you know?"

"Because *you* know." There were windows in the room that looked out over the pool. Adam wasn't watching us, but he kept glancing at the doors that led to the lobby. I noticed Jessica and Lydia next to him. Jessica reached for his hand, and he turned toward her.

It was a flashback for me; only instead of Adam, it had been Jeff.

I couldn't help myself. "Is he already cheating on you?"

140

"What?!" She whirled around, saw what I was watching, and shook her head. "No." She sounded a little stronger now. Her small shoulders rolled back, and she lifted her head higher. "But she's been trying. I'll admit that much."

"He's not sleeping with her?"

She shook her head, standing next to me. "I installed a program on the computer so I can monitor all his emails and social media pages."

Um. Holy shit? I felt my jaw falling.

"She's been private messaging him, but so far he's not responded. He's just been polite, as he's been with all of them." Her gaze lingered on Lydia before moving on to Miranda and Amelia. It stayed the longest on Amelia.

"She's the one you're worried about?" I felt so proud of her. I couldn't explain why, but it was like my little sister had grown up before my eyes.

"Yeah. She's the one he shares the most with."

"They were friends in school."

"Not that great of friends. It changed a year ago. They worked on a project together at college. It's been…different since then."

"What about Miranda? She dated him."

"She's in love with Peter." Becky shook her head. "I used to worry about her, but she only talks about how great Peter's been in their messages. She asks about me, too. Amelia's never brought me up."

"That says a lot."

"I know."

"You just needed me to say it, didn't you?"

She let out a deep breath, her eyes downcast. "I needed someone to say it. I've felt horrible thinking it, but yeah. I needed someone else to voice the same concern. I'll be fine now. It's like you gave me permission to doubt the man I love."

"You're going to still marry him, aren't you?"

She turned away from the window, looking me square in the eyes. Her gaze held mine steadily. "Yes. I'm not going in blind, and I do love him. I always did. I chose him over you. I turned my back on a good friend, and I've felt regret ever since. Marrying him is a small way of making it right. I know that probably doesn't make sense, but he can provide me with a good life until we divorce, if that's what happens."

"You're going to keep monitoring him?"

"Oh yeah. If he leaves me, he won't know what hit him. I'll have years of evidence."

I reached out and took her hand. This time, I meant it when I said, "I'm glad I have your friendship again."

She squeezed my hand so tightly. "Me, too."

# CHAPTER TWENTY-THREE

We were heading back to the pool when Malinda stopped us as we crossed the lobby. "Hi, Becky, honey." She touched my hand, still beaming at Becky. "Congratulations on your upcoming nuptials. I'm so happy for you and Adam." She looked at me. "Sam, can I have a minute with you?"

"Uh, sure."

Becky hugged Malinda before she went back outside, and my stepmother pulled me in the opposite direction Becky and I had just come from.

"What's going on?" I asked her.

She didn't answer, just increased her pace. She wound back outside, but we took a hidden path behind the pool. Palm trees and shrubbery blocked us from view. I heard raised voices, but couldn't place them until we rounded a corner.

Standing in a small group outside an entrance to the country club's tennis courts, with a bunch of golf carts behind them, were James Kade, Steven Quinn, Adam, and Mason. There was no sign of Matteo or Nate.

I leaned forward. "What's going on?"

She wrapped an arm around my shoulders and whispered. "Your father is coming to help with the situation, but I thought it was a good idea to have a woman present. I can't stay. I have to get back to the party or someone will start wondering if something's wrong." And on that note, she pressed a kiss to my forehead, then hurried back.

I approached, hearing Mr. Quinn yell, "It's my son's engagement party. I can enter if I want to."

Oh, goodness. He was drunk. He flung an arm in the air and would've hit Mason if he hadn't ducked. Instead, Mason caught it, twisting it around Adam's dad's back and pulling it tight.

Ignoring Mr. Quinn's yelp of pain, he said quietly, "All of Adam's friends are celebrating over there, and yes, it's your son's party, but you're drunk, sir. I don't think you want their memory of Adam's party to be about your drunken antics. Or do you?"

He bucked against Mason's hold. "You're just jealous. Your future's been mapped out since before you were born, and you can't stand how happy Adam is."

I didn't move closer. I wasn't sure if I was the best female presence for this job.

Mason shot Adam, who looked exasperated, a dubious look.

"Dad." Adam reached out, touching his dad's shoulder. "That's not the case, and you know it. Yes, I'm very happy with Becky, but Mason's happy with Samantha."

"Samantha." Mr. Quinn gurgled out my name. "That's the girl, Adam. You should've been with her. I like your little Becky, but she doesn't have the breeding Sam Strattan does."

I wasn't hearing this. There was no way.

"Dad!" Adam barked out.

Mason's eyes took on a murderous glint, but he didn't say anything. He continued to hold Mr. Quinn's arm behind his back.

"Steven," James waded in. "You had too much whiskey playing golf. Let your son call a car for you and go home. Sleep this off."

"Oh, yes. Breeding." Mr. Quinn's smile turned into a leer. "You know what I'm talking about, James. I bet she's like Analise in the sack—"

*No. No. No.*

I was rooted in place. I couldn't leave. I couldn't even lift my hand to cover my ears. So I closed my eyes.

"Steven!" James yelled.

"Dad!" Adam screamed at the same time.

"Hot...writhing..." Quinn's tone was warm, gushing, and I felt sick again. He kept going. "She can buck you like a wild mustang, if you know what I me—"

My eyes flew open as I heard a punch.

Quinn would've fallen if Mason hadn't been holding him up. After a second punch from James, Mason let go. Adam grabbed his father, and Mason moved to shove his own father back.

"Dad," he said. "Stop."

"When did you sleep with her?" James strained against Mason's hold. "When?!"

Quinn looked oddly calm. He wiped his mouth and looked at the blood on his hand. Then he laughed. "Wow. I can't believe—James, you punched me."

"When did you sleep with Analise?"

Adam held his dad back, but he didn't need to. Steven Quinn wasn't moving. Adam looked over his shoulder, his eyes closed in pain at James' question.

"Not when she was with you," Quinn said.

I heard another set of footsteps behind me. I knew those steps. I'd been listening to them all my life, and I reached out when the man who raised me drew near.

"Dad," I said, my voice a hoarse whisper. "Don't."

"It was when she was with Strattan," Steven continued. "She was with almost all of us. You had to have known, James."

James was shaking. If Mason hadn't been holding him back, he would've been on Adam's dad again. Adam and Mason looked strained and tense, alert for any other attacks. No one was paying my dad or me any attention.

"I don't care if it was when she was with David. You don't talk about her like that!" James yelled.

My dad turned and left, as silently as he'd come.

I looked back, and Mason met my gaze. When he saw David's retreating back, he nodded. That was all the permission I needed. I hightailed it out of there, hurrying after my dad. I ran across Nate on my way, and ignoring what he started to say, I pointed to where I'd come from.

"Mason needs your help. I gotta handle something of my own."

"But—"

I was already gone.

I found my dad in the parking lot, weaving through the vehicles to find his. He wasn't even waiting for the valet. "Dad! Wait."

He was close to his truck when he turned around, keys in his hand. "Honey, I'm okay."

I searched his face, unsure if that was true or not. I saw some strain, but for the most part, he looked like his usual loving self.

I swallowed a knot in my throat. "Are you sure?"

"I made my peace with what your mother did long ago. I left because that fight isn't mine anymore. Whatever Analise did in the past, it's in the past. I have you, and I have Malinda. That's all I need."

"And Mark."

"And Mark." He nodded. "You're right. I'm proud to have him as a son."

David Strattan wasn't my biological father, but he was my dad in every other sense of the word. I realized now that neither of his children was biological.

I frowned. "Dad…" Could I ask what I wanted to ask? Was it even my business?

"Sam?"

"Can Malinda still have children?"

"Oh, Sam." He pulled me in for a hug. "I know what you're thinking, and I don't need children of my own. Your stepmom and I have talked about children, but if we decided to have them, we wouldn't go the biological route. We'd adopt. She went through menopause early. She can't have any more children."

"I'm so sorry."

He shook his head. "It's not for you to worry about. It's not even for you to think about. There was a time I wanted my own child, but I had you, and those were the days when I worried whether Analise would even let me keep you as a daughter. You were enough for me. Then I was lucky and got Malinda and Mark, too. I have a daughter and a son, and two more stepchildren with Mason and Logan—four if you count Nate and Matteo. I'm very blessed."

"Are you sure?"

"I am." He hugged me again. "You should go make sure Mason's okay. Steven's a nasty drunk. I have no doubt he'll start ribbing Mason about you. That's what he does. He searches for a person's weakness and pushes on it. He already knows Mason and James' weaknesses: the women they love. That was another reason I left. If Quinn had started in about you, I don't know what I would've done."

"Oh." Well, fuck. New alarms sounded in me. "Yeah, I should head back then."

But when I got there, the two fathers were gone. Adam and Mason remained, and Nate right next to them.

I approached, unsure if I was still needed. "Everything okay now?"

"Sam." Adam's chest rose with his head. The regret in his eyes mixed with anger. "I'm sorry for what my dad said. I didn't know you heard any of that until Nate came out, but he was drunk. No. That's no excuse. He… I know you think I was coming at you guys earlier, but I wasn't."

"Jeff said you're going into politics," I said.

"I'm hoping, but with my dad how he is…" He motioned in the direction Steven Quinn must've gone. "I don't know if that's a possibility. I'm getting ready to take over the family company if he doesn't stop drinking, and you never know. Maybe he'll end up going to rehab, too." His eyebrows pushed together. "Where's the one your mom went to again? We might need a good referral."

"Is that what you think?"

"Hmmm?" His head tilted. With his hands in his pockets, his body half-turned away from me, it came off like he was distracted.

Was he? Was that why he was asking for the wrong information?

"My mom wasn't a drunk. Is that what you think?"

"I'm sorry. What?" He turned to face me, his hands still in his pockets.

Adam knew my mom wasn't a drunk. I said, "You just asked where my mom went to rehab, like your father would go there for his drinking." I waited. Would he realize his mistake? "You were there, Adam. I talked to you about her. I confided in you."

And I waited.

Then I saw it. Realization filtered over his face, followed by regret, and then sympathy. "Sam, I'm so—"

I waved that off, shaking my head. "Sorry. I know. I heard you. My mom wasn't a drunk and a junkie. She wasn't an addict at all. She has a mental disorder, and she went to intensive therapy for it. I could tell you where she went, but I don't think that's where you'd want to send your dad, if you're actually going to send him somewhere."

I'd had enough. Things were fine here. Adam was off in his own head, plotting or planning something. I wasn't sure why Mason and Nate were still here, but I didn't care. I started to head back. I needed to hug Becky one more time, and then I was ready to leave.

"I wasn't lying about my dad."

Adam's voice stopped me. I turned around again.

"And I do remember your mom," he said, his eyes boring into mine. "I'm distracted right now because I do want to go to law school and into politics. I don't want to stay here and take over my dad's company, so right now when I asked about the wrong type of rehab, I was wondering if somehow my mom could take over instead. Or one of my sisters. Would that be fair to even ask that? Molly is the next oldest, but she's just graduating high school. I don't think that's a fair burden to place on her shoulders. And then I wondered if that would affect Becky's decision to marry me. If she'd be okay if we stayed in Fallen Crest for the rest of our lives, if she truly said yes to me because she loves me."

Stark pain looked back at me.

"So please take my apology because I do mean it," he finished.

I jerked my head in a stiff nod. I didn't trust him regarding Becky, but I could recognize another child in pain over a parent. "Becky agreed to marry you. She doesn't care what you end up doing. Believe that."

"Thank you, Sam. I will."

As I turned to go, I heard a voice I hadn't heard for almost two weeks.

"Uh, yeah…"

I was already starting to smile.

Logan came around the back entrance, hand in hand with Taylor. He pointed behind him. "Just saw Dad helping this asshole's pops into the car, and they both reeked of booze." He dropped Taylor's hand and held up his arms. "Come to me, my big brother. The better-looking Kade is back in town!"

My family was back together again.

# CHAPTER TWENTY-FOUR

Mason hugged Logan, then Nate, and I was last.

After setting me back on my feet, Logan skewered Adam with a look. "What's that motherfucker doing here?"

I let Mason answer that and moved to hug Taylor. "Hey. How was the trip?"

"Good." She waved to Nate and Mason, a little shy.

She was the closest to me, but even we weren't super close. She and Logan had been together for almost a year now, but since she was from Cain, she liked to stick close to her friends there. Logan slept more at her house during the year than ours, which had caused some tension between him and Mason.

Taylor raked a hand through her dark blond hair. "We got to the house, but no one was there, so Logan used a GPS tracker thing he has installed on Mason's phone. When he realized you guys were here, he got really quiet. Is this a bad place?" She looked around. "I gotta say, this is somewhere my dad would hang out."

"It's not really the place. It's the people."

"Sallaway or Sullivan?" we heard Logan saying. "I remember taking one off your hands more than a few times. Not that one? Tate."

Adam shook his head. "Nice, Logan. Yeah. It's just great to have you back."

Nate ignored Adam. "It's Becky, Sam's old friend."

Logan looked at me. "Old friend, right? Don't tell me that's changed, too."

"Uh, it was old until about thirty minutes ago. It got genuine again."

"It did?" Adam asked.

I ignored him. "Don't knock it until you meet her again, Logan. She's changed."

"Not a backstabber any more?"

More like just a smarter backstabber, but I shrugged.

Logan turned to face his brother. "What the fuck is going on? You stopped taking my calls a week ago."

"You stopped calling."

Logan thought about that, tilting his head to the side. "Oh yeah. I think my battery died, and I lost the charger by the Eiffel Tower." He winked at Taylor. "Plus, I've been a bit preoccupied. You know, hanging out with your coach." He turned back to Mason. "We're the best of friends now, Mase. I call him Big Poppa Bear."

"Right." Mason's tone was doubtful.

"And he calls me his little baby bear. We spoon porridge together, sleep in each other's beds, and even tried snuggling on his big daddy chair one time." He grinned, staring off into the distance. "Such good memories. I'm the best daughter's boyfriend ever."

Taylor frowned. "You had a beer together. That was it."

"Yeah, but while we enjoyed our Corona, I knew what he was thinking. I was thinking the same. We synced, Taylor. You can't take that away from us. Me and your dad, we have a bond you'll never understand."

"One where you're Goldilocks?" She smiled. "That's not a bond I want. I'm good with the one I have. You might have heard about it; it's called reality."

Mason and Nate grinned, and Logan pretended to pull an arrow from his chest. He held it up. "Look at that. It went in through the front." He smirked at Adam. "Not the back, like someone I don't want to know here."

"You're a fucking asshole."

Logan's chest puffed up. He was so proud of himself. "Ah, name calling. Another trip down memory lane. That's so *high school.*" He winked.

Mason caught my eye, a meaningful look there, and I got the message. He was still trying to investigate Adam. If he came to his defense, Logan would be all over that like a bloodhound. Whereas if I stopped things, that'd make more sense. I cleared my throat, moving forward. "Okay. Enough with the pissing on each other."

"He started it," Adam sneered.

"Adam, go back to your engagement party." I looked to Logan, whose eyes lit up at the mention of party. "And Logan, you stay away because Malinda is hosting. It's not one to crash and start a scene. It's for Mark's birthday, too."

The eager light faded from him, and his shoulders almost slumped. "Fine, but where's Matteo? I thought he was here, too."

"He's probably hitting on some of *my* friends." Adam started off. "I'll send him out if I see him," he called back over his shoulder.

Once he was gone, all humor fled Logan. "What the fuck, Mason? For real. What the fuck?"

"It's more complicated than it seems."

"I'd hope so." Logan looked at me. "Are you actually friends with her again?"

I nodded. "I wasn't lying. It became genuine thirty minutes ago when I learned she has a monitoring program installed on Adam's computer. She can get into his email and social media pages."

"Wait. What?" Mason asked.

I looked at him. "Yeah. Why?"

"Your new friend has a *spying* program on his computer?"

"Oh." *Spying.* What he was doing. "She had it installed to catch him if he starts cheating, but—"

"Can we get access to it? Is she watching his business emails?" Mason asked.

I lifted a shoulder. "I have no clue. I think she's been mainly focused on his messages with other female friends."

"Sam, we need to get into that program. That'll help a lot."

Logan held his hand up. "Okay. I've been gone a month. What the hell is going on?"

*"Logan!"*

We could hear Matteo yelling as he came down the pathway, heading right for us. He still hadn't seen us, though.

Mason dropped his voice low. "He doesn't know."

"What?!" Logan said.

"He's a good guy," Mason added, just as Matteo came around the corner. "I don't want him involved."

*"Dude!"*

Logan cursed under his breath. "You're an asshole, Mase. God, I love you." Then a cocky smirk came over his face and he held his arms out. "What's up, my fellow SBC-er motherfucker?"

Matteo swept Logan up in a bear hug and shook him. "Holy crap. It's good to see you." He pounded Logan's back. "My soul brotha connection."

As the two professed their love for each other, I drifted over to Mason. His hand came to my hip and around my back as he pulled me against his side. Even now, I could feel some of the tension leaving him.

I studied Taylor a moment. Things were changing. That was a fact, but this dynamic—Mason, me, Logan, even Nate, and now Taylor—that wasn't going anywhere.

# CHAPTER TWENTY-FIVE

Mason didn't waste any time.

I was given the task of taking Taylor out on the town that night, which meant I'd be taking her to Heather's. Matteo was given clearance to spend the night with his girl, and once he left, Mason, Logan, and Nate took off as well. I wouldn't have thought anything about what they were doing, except all three were dressed in black, and Mason had grabbed some ski masks. I watched as he put them in his bag.

I didn't ask. I didn't want to know. When Mason kissed me goodbye, I just whispered as we hugged, "Be safe."

"Always."

That was debatable, but I said the same to Logan and Nate after hugging each of them, too.

"You know nothing," Logan replied. "Taylor knows nothing. Have fun tonight."

"Yep." I patted his arm. "That's the plan." What we would do, I had no idea, but I knew I needed to keep her away as long as they were gone to keep her from asking questions. I texted Heather my mission before we left.

**Heading over. We need to keep busy until I hear from the guys later.**

Her response came five minutes later. **No clue what you're talking about, but don't want to know. I got a party we can go to.**

When we walked into Manny's, she was behind the counter.

"Does this party have Caldron on the guest list? Kate? Matteo?" I asked.

She'd been reaching for some menus, but paused. "I didn't know there were stipulations. No Matteo?"

I shook my head.

She shrugged. "I'm just teasing. No way he'll be at this party." She looked past my shoulder. "Hey, Taylor."

Taylor waved, staying a good distance behind me. "Hey."

The past flirting that'd gone down between Logan and Heather hadn't been an issue for Taylor, or so Logan said. But I couldn't help but wonder if some of that had been swept under the rug.

Taylor moved closer, glancing around the place. "So Logan said Roussou people were the enemy." She looked at a table where three girls wore Roussou football jerseys.

I grinned at Heather as I replied, "Not all."

"Hmm..." Heather grunted. "Technically I'm Fallen Crest."

"But your boyfriend is not." I winked at her.

Her smile turned smug. "And he's just as amazing as the rest of us."

I added for Taylor's benefit, "I'm pretty sure the party we're going to tonight is a Roussou crowd?"

Heather moved out from behind the counter, taking a bunch of menus to some incoming customers.

"Considering the Kades have dropped the ball on throwing kickass parties," she said as she returned, "I'd say the Roussou crowd is the only type of party you want to attend nowadays."

"It's safe for us?" Taylor asked.

She nodded. "Completely." She held up her house key. "Make yourselves comfortable. I'll be there in twenty minutes."

I snatched it up. "By comfortable, you mean start drinking?"

She pretended to be confused. "Is there any other meaning for that word?"

Taylor and I moved around another incoming wave of customers and headed down the side alley to Heather's house.

# MASON

Logan popped his head up in between the front two seats. "How far is this place?" He'd agreed to ride in the back because Nate had the GPS ready to go.

"We don't have an exact address, just an idea where it will be."

"That's fucked up. We could be driving for hours."

We hadn't been. We were an hour north of home, but as Nate said something else to Logan, I turned onto the shore road. Sam had said the cabin was located on this highway, and this area matched Becky's description—not many houses, so a lot of trees and rocky cliffs. Nate and Logan were still going back and forth when I stopped the vehicle at the end of a driveway. I could see the tops of a white mansion, and the name on the mailbox said Quinn.

"We're here?" Logan asked.

"I'm taking a wild guess, but yeah."

"Do we know how we're getting in?" Nate asked once we were parked. The house was three stories, with a wraparound porch. Logan and I shared a look as we got out and stood in front of the place. It was a cabin. Yeah, it was big and sprawling, but it was still a cabin. The paint was a little worn. I could see a few spider webs on the porch. The place wasn't kept up, and I'd bet there was no state-of-the-art security system in place either.

Logan hopped up on the porch and rattled the door. "It's locked." He glanced back at me.

I gestured around to the back. "Check all the doors. They might have one unlocked—or even a window."

And we were in luck. The door to the attached garage had been left unlocked, but inside was another door that opened into the house, and that one *was* locked.

Logan started laughing.

"What?"

He stepped carefully on a rug. "Are you kidding me?" He knelt down and felt under it, pulling out a key. "Fuckers literally left it under the rug. That's almost as bad as keeping it in one of those fake rocks."

He unlocked the door, and we went inside. We filtered into the kitchen, and Logan clapped his hands. "Okay, my genius brother. Where do we start?"

Nate flicked on a light over the stove. "They have electricity."

"So if they have a computer, we can turn it on."

"Let's hope they don't use a password," Logan added.

I clapped him on the shoulder. "Maybe we'll get lucky again and they'll have their password written down somewhere."

"Fuck. They probably will. But for serious, though." He looked at me. "What are we looking for?"

"Anything that looks illegal?" I wasn't sure what we were looking for, or if it would even be at this place. I just wanted something in hand to exchange for the favor I needed to ask my dad. I'd need his help dealing with Caldron, and I didn't want to owe him. "Just look through their files."

"Got it." Logan nodded. "We're thinking of what we would do if we were doing something illegal, like keep incriminating files as a backup in case something happens? Something like that?"

"Would you keep that in your house or office?"

"Where the authorities would go first?" Logan shook his head. "No way, and thinking of that, we need to start using Dad's old place again. There are lots of good hiding spots for our future illegal endeavors."

Nate had been rifling through one of the cupboards, but he stopped to grin at us. "Are we future white-collar criminals?"

"Everyone needs to have aspirations."

Ignoring the joking, I moved down a side hallway and opened a door. "I found the office."

"Just remember, Mase," Logan called from the kitchen. "*Bigstick* is a perfectly acceptable password. Just because you use it, doesn't mean others won't."

"Fuck you," I called back, but was smiling as I turned on the computer and sat down. When the password screen came up, I rolled my eyes, and typed it in. "Apparently, Steven Quinn doesn't have a big stick. It's not the password."

"Rocket man?" Logan suggested.

Nate added, "Pornstar?"

I typed in *Bigstud*. And nothing. "Screw it," I muttered, shuffling through some of the papers on the desk. Inside the drawer, I found one word scribbled down. K45it()rd. It was set apart from all the other notes, and typing that in, I got through.

Logan and Nate were still throwing out ideas. *Big Johnson. Big Willy. Womb broom. Yogurt slinger. Taco whisperer.* I let them go, and stopped listening.

Mr. Quinn kept a lot of business files on this computer. I looked through everything that seemed related to Fallen Crest, something about business holdings in Roussou, and a whole ton of files about the country club. I was still reading and skimming through them when Logan said my name.

"What?" I looked up.

"You've been in here for an hour."

"I have?"

"Yeah. Thanks for letting us know you got in." He came around to stand behind me.

"Sorry. I didn't think you were actually trying to help with the password ideas."

"Yeah, maybe not." He tapped my shoulder. "So which one worked? It was yogurt slinger, wasn't it?"

"Nope." I clicked on another file titled *Payables*. "It was taco whisperer."

"I knew it! What a dirty mind Quinn has." Logan chuckled. "I bet Quinn junior is just as dirty. Gotta be, if he's going into politics."

"Hey!" Nate came into the room, frowning. "You got in and didn't tell us?"

"It was on a need-to-know basis, Nate, and you didn't need to know."

I tuned them out. Logan was going to needle at Nate, which he'd been doing since he got back, and Nate was going to ignore him at first, then shoot insults back or get pissed. That had been their dynamic since we were kids.

"You find anything yet?" Logan asked.

"What?" I looked up, distracted. I'd been staring at a screen of names and numbers, but none of it was making sense. "No." I pulled out a flash drive and began saving everything. "I'll just save as much as I can. We can look through it later. Can you guys check any back rooms or the basement for paper files?"

The two shared a look and shrugged.

Maybe coming here had been reaching, but I knew a bit more about Quinn's business than I had before.

An hour later, we were heading back when Logan read his text messages. "Uh, guys?"

"What?" Nate leaned forward, now the one sitting in the back.

Logan looked up at me, cringing slightly. "We need to head to Roussou."

"Why?"

I'd told Sam to take Taylor out, and knowing Sam, that meant she'd find Heather. I already had an idea of what he was going to say when I heard him.

"They're at Channing's house, and Taylor just texted. Caldron's there."

I pressed the accelerator. If we got picked up by a cop, I didn't care. I needed one to follow me to Channing's and keep me from killing Caldron, because that was how I felt at the moment.

I gripped the steering wheel, my knuckles whitening, and we didn't talk until I braked outside Channing's place.

I was running for the house not even a second later, with Logan right behind me.

# CHAPTER TWENTY-SIX

Everything started out fine. It was fun, even.

Taylor and I finished a bottle of wine by the time Heather joined us, and all she did was pack a bunch more in a box, and then we were in the car. The party was at Channing's, as his little sister was gone for the weekend. It was actually in the building behind their house, which was a safe distance away from any nosy neighbors. We were in the kitchen making margaritas when the first of Channing's friends came in.

Big, muscular—a few I recognized from Channing's fight.

They all nodded to us, and seemed to know who I was. I didn't remember their names, but I could tell they were good people. Heather greeted each of them by name, hugging all of them. There was respect in the way they talked to her, respect in how they nodded, acknowledging me. None of them stood and leered at Taylor, who stuck to the background. I couldn't blame her for that. These guys looked rough. Some arrived on motorcycles. Some wore leather cuts and bandanas. Others looked more like us, in jeans and T-shirts, the way Mason and Logan dressed, but when you mixed all of them together, even I was a little intimidated.

The margaritas turned into shots, and that turned into a game by the bonfire in Channing's backyard. I think maybe it was the sound— the laughter, shrieks, the sounds of more and more motorcycles joining the party, or maybe even the music. Hip hop blared, and suddenly, the party Heather had told me we'd be fine at went from a medium-sized gathering of people she trusted to a large party, and I knew she didn't trust all of the new arrivals.

On more than a few occasions, I saw her freeze up, her eyes glued to someone walking into the backyard. That was when I started checking the time, checking my phone for messages. There were none. That meant Mason was still looking, but I noticed Taylor on her phone.

"Are you texting Logan?" I asked.

She nodded, not looking up. "I'm starting to get the creeps."

I was, too, and I was torn. I didn't want to interrupt Mason, but this was becoming a dangerous place for us to be.

I touched Heather's arm. "How about we go inside?"

She looked around. "Yeah. We can go to the basement."

We found Channing down there, playing pool with his friends. Some of the knots loosened in my stomach, as it reminded me of when Logan and Mason would play pool with their friends. For a moment, I forgot about the people outside. No one was tense in here. It was all jokes, stories being shared, and a good-natured game of pool.

Heather went behind the bar, and we bellied up. A few other girls came over, along with two guys named Moose and Chad. Heather introduced them as two of Channing's best friends. Moose was huge, with a bald head and gentle brown eyes. Tattoos covered the sides of his skull and the back of his neck, like their other friend from the fight night. Chad wasn't as muscular as Moose, but he was taller and a little leaner. He had a full head of red curls, green eyes, and the beginnings of a small beard. They positioned themselves between us and the rest of the room, and I knew they'd been sent by Channing to be our protection. I didn't remember Chad from the fight event, but I did remember Moose. He'd made a point of coming over and shaking Mason's hand that night.

A little while later we were laughing at something Moose said about Chad. It was funny and lighthearted, nothing important, but it was the moment before all hell broke loose.

We were laughing.

About some joke.

And none of us were scared, but then things changed.

I heard the voice behind me.

"This is where the real party is at."

Chills went down my spine.

Jared Caldron had walked into the room with an entire group following him. I stopped counting once I got to ten guys behind him, and I nudged Taylor back around the corner so he couldn't see us.

Heather grabbed my arm and yanked me down under the bar. I hauled Taylor with me, and we huddled at Heather's feet. She stood, rolling her shoulders back. She tried to appear casual, but her knee was shaking.

Moose and Chad took position at the bar's opening. If anyone wanted to get to us, they'd have to go through them.

Above me, I heard Channing say, "It's a private party, Caldron. You need to go."

"Go? Are you serious?" Caldron laughed. So did his guys. "We walked right in. Been out there for twenty minutes. Thanks for the free booze, by the way."

I closed my eyes, but not just from fear. I needed to sense as much going on in the room as possible.

"Leave, Caldron."

"And what would you do if I said no?"

"I'd say we're going to make you."

Heather's knees began hitting the cupboard underneath the bar. I looked up, but she seemed completely unaware.

"You?" Caldron snorted in disbelief. "Half your crew is wasted outside. My guys are blocking the doors. They got no clue what's going on in here."

"Because there's no way one person in here can't call or text. Yep. You're right. We're screwed," Heather bit out.

Her knee was banging hard into the shelf now. I reached up and stopped it. She glanced down and shifted her stance. Taylor looked at me. I shrugged.

"Shut it, Jax, or I'll be spending a lot of down time at your old man's place. I'm sure you'd love that, wouldn't you?"

She flipped him off.

He laughed. "You got fight; I'll give you that. She's got fight, Monroe. I'd bet she's real good in bed, huh?"

"You're going to shut it right about now." Channing's voice was a low warning.

"You've already made that threat, and nothing. No follow up. I'm still here."

Caldron's voice was as equally low, a challenge in itself. I could imagine him spreading his arms out, as if to say, *Here I am, come get me.* But as I listened, there were no sounds of scuffling or physical contact.

I waited, my heart in my throat.

I noticed Taylor on her phone, punching the letters and numbers furiously. She was biting her lip. She took a breath, and her lip started trembling until she bit down again, stopping it.

She was going to be bleeding soon.

"Caldron." Channing's voice sounded closer, like he'd shifted toward the bar. "I said stop."

"I know you did." Caldron was closer, too.

He was coming toward us. Heather tapped my legs. Her hand slipped under the bar, and she motioned for me to move aside. I did, as much as I could. As soon as there was enough space, she moved in, now trying to be a human shield so he couldn't look down and see us hunched there.

It was useless. Caldron was coming. I could hear his movements. People were beginning to push each other. A few girls said, "Watch it!" and "Hey! I'm standing here."

They were looking for us.

I felt it in my gut. Someone came, saw us, and texted him we were there. And now we were trapped like animals in this basement. The only way out was through Caldron and his goons. I positioned myself with hands flat on the floor on either side of my legs—almost in a runner's starting position, except I would jump up and not forward.

Taylor's phone flashed. She held it up, and I read Logan's text.

**Here. Now.**

The fighting was about to start, and if Mason and Logan ran in, someone could blame them. That couldn't happen, because this had a really good chance of being broken up by the authorities. If anyone was going to take the blame, I'd make sure it was Caldron.

My heart still in my throat, I took a quick breath and pushed upright.

"Sam!" Heather hissed, her eyes wide.

My eyes met Caldron's, and I knew I was right. He wasn't surprised to see me. A smirk tugged at his lip. He looked way too smug.

"Who was it?" I asked.

"Who was who?"

"Who told you we were here."

"We?" He made a point of looking around. "Who's 'we'?"

Taylor was about to stand up. I touched the top of her head and pushed her back down. He didn't know Logan was here, though he would shortly, but he really didn't need to know about Logan's girlfriend. She'd just be one more target for him.

I smiled at him, cold. "Don't read into that. I like to refer to myself and my awesomeness as two separate people. You know, because I'm that awesome."

He shook his head. "You're pretty cocky, considering I finally got you."

Channing stepped forward, along with the rest of his guys. Moose and Chad left the bar's opening and joined their group of friends, who began to form a wall.

Heather hissed next to me, under her breath, "What are you doing?"

"Making sure he starts the fight, and not us."

She cleared her throat. "Let me do this then."

I looked sideways at her as she launched herself up over the bar, using her height advantage to jump to the front of the line. She came to stand next to Channing, her hand on his arm. He glanced down at it, then at her. She passed along some kind of message with that touch, but I couldn't decipher it from where we stood.

"Caldron." She smiled at him, folding her arms over her chest. "I don't even know why you're here. You're wasted space. You were back in high school. You still are today. All you do is walk around with your buddies, acting like a tough guy, but you never back it up. You've been in two fights against Mason Kade, and he laid you out both times." She gestured to Channing. "You've been puffing your chest out since we graduated and making all sorts of threats toward my boyfriend. But I think I know what's going on."

He frowned at her.

She leaned forward, dropping her voice to a whisper, though everyone could hear. "It's okay if you're a pussy. Or if you're *the* pussy, if you know what I me—"

His face turned red and in an instant he was throwing the first punch. Heather didn't finish her sentence before Channing yanked her behind him. He ducked under Caldron's arm, then rounded up with an uppercut.

After that, it was on.

I heard screaming, yelling, and people crying out in pain, but for a moment before any of that, there'd been total silence. After Caldron lashed out, everyone needed time to comprehend that the brawl was on, and in that second, I heard my own gasp for breath. It sounded deafening to my ears, and I knew—I would remember that gasp for the rest of my life.

Chad yanked Taylor and me backward, pulling us out of the bar and off to the side down a hallway. Moose went with us, bringing up the rear and pushing away others who tried to get to me. So far, no one was trying for Taylor. I looked back to find Heather, but I couldn't see her. There was just a mass of people fighting.

"Come on." Chad shoved open a door, and we saw an egress window. He pulled out the screen and climbed out, then ripped through the covering. He lifted Taylor and tossed her out onto the lawn. I was next, falling half on top of Taylor. We rolled to our feet quickly, and Chad and Moose climbed out behind us.

"Let's go." Chad pointed to the cars and started running, holding Taylor's arm.

I began running with them, following Moose. They could get Taylor to safety, but I had to go back to find Mason and Logan. I knew they were here; Mason's black Escalade was parked on the lawn. Moose fell back, glancing at me.

I waved him on. "I'm right behind you."

He nodded, and the three of them ran faster.

I couldn't wait any longer. I turned and sprinted back for the house.

"Sam!" Taylor yelled after me.

I kept going, shouting over my shoulder, "Mason and Logan are here. I have to!"

I heard a smattering of curses and knew at least one person was coming after me. An arm wrapped around my waist, and I was suddenly in the air.

"No!" I began fighting. I needed to get free.

"Fuck's sakes. You're insane." It was Chad. He grunted, evading my legs. "Okay, okay. I'll go with you if you stop hitting m—" My elbow smacked his chin.

"Oh." I cringed. "I'm sorry."

"Stop, okay? Stop."

I nodded, waiting till my feet were on the ground. He set me down and backed away with his hands in the air. "I'm not going to stop you, but I have to go with you. Okay? I have to. Channing told me to protect you."

I nodded again. "They're my family."

"I get that." He glanced at the house. The fighting had spilled out to the yard. He cursed, then yanked off his sweatshirt. He held it out to me. "Put that on." As I did, he pulled the hood forward. "Maybe this will help camouflage you a bit."

I pulled my hair forward, too, and started running ahead. Chad caught up and ran next to me, and we began shouldering our way back inside.

There were more screams, more shouts, more everything.

I could smell blood in the air. Blood and sweat.

Then everything slowed down, and I watched my nightmare come to life. I couldn't get to Mason and Logan. They were going to be hurt, and I couldn't do anything to stop it. I was pushing, pulling, and clawing my way through, and still I couldn't see them.

Then, suddenly, there was a clearing in the crowd.

I saw Mason and began to yell his name—

*Bang!*

*Bang!*

*Bang!*

Three shots rang out.

# CHAPTER TWENTY-SEVEN
## MASON

*"Mason!"*

I turned, hearing my name, and there was Sam. She stood in the back, next to a guy I recognized as one of Channing's friends. The guy I was holding threw a punch, and I caught his arm. Twisting it backward, I heard a satisfying pop and knew he'd be useless for the rest of the night. I clipped him across the face, just enough to daze him, and shoved him into another group of Caldron's friends. Logan was exchanging punches next to me.

When we heard the gun, we both froze a moment, but it seemed to have come from a ways away, so we kept going. That was when I heard Sam yelling for me, and seeing her now, I grabbed Logan and yanked him with me.

"Hey!" He snarled until he realized it was me. "What are you doing?"

I pointed. "It's Sam. Let's go."

We took off, back the way we'd just come. Some guys tried to rush us, but we dodged and punched, or evaded and caught them, tossing them to the side.

"What about Channing?" Logan asked as we went.

"Channing's fine. Caldron wants our heads on a platter, not Channing's. We have to get Sam and Taylor to safety."

Then we were out, and Sam began running ahead of us. The guy with her helped push our way through. Logan and I joined him to encircle Sam and form a barrier. She could just run and not have to worry about fighting.

I reached out once, my hand sliding over hers. I couldn't help myself. I needed to reassure myself she was safe. She was, and her hand squeezed mine as we kept running.

"Taylor." Logan spotted his girlfriend ahead, waiting inside my Escalade.

I recognized Moose with her and glanced around. No Nate. I stopped. "Wait."

"What?"

Logan hurried forward, climbing inside my vehicle and hugging his girlfriend. Sam and the guy who'd been helping her stayed back with me. Once Moose saw Taylor was fine, he headed over to us.

I looked at Sam. "Nate's not here."

"Was he in there with you?" the guy asked.

I shook my head. "The fighting was already happening. Two guys were shoving each other when we went in through the basement door. I looked back, but it was only Logan with me. I don't remember Nate at all. I thought he went in with us?"

Sam slipped her hand in mine, but I was already looking back.

I had to go in again.

"Wait." The guy touched my shoulder. "Let me and Moose go in. I'll text Channing and Heather, let them know you guys are good, but we're searching for Nate. Monson, right? That's his last name?"

I nodded, scanning the house. People were beginning to run out, heading for their cars. Some were just running down the sidewalk.

"Hey!" Logan shouted from the vehicle, waving his phone in the air. "It's Matteo. He and Nate are headed back to the house. They're safe."

"Matteo?" Sam asked.

I didn't care. That was enough for me. I swung back around, my hand out. "Thank you for watching Sam and Logan's girl."

The guy shook my hand, a strong, steady grip. "No problem. I know you're good with Channing. That makes you good with me. I'm Chad, by the way." He nodded to Moose. "And this is—"

"Moose." I held my hand out to him, too. "Thank you. I remember you from the fight night. Thank you for helping then."

"Oh yeah."

Another strong handshake.

"We should go. Cops are going to show up." Chad started to head for the street, and Moose went with him. "I'll be in touch with Channing," he added before they left. "We need to find out who got shot, if anyone."

A guy running past us stopped. His chest heaved for breath, and he raked a hand through his hair. "It was two bikers from rival clubs. They saw each other, and one pulled a gun."

"Are you serious?" Chad frowned.

The guy started to run off, but Chad grabbed him and hauled him back. The guy nodded. "Yeah." His eyes were wild. "I saw it myself. I was smoking up."

The sound of sirens had him jerking around to see where they were coming from. "I gotta go." He pawed at Chad's hand. "If they arrest me, they got more than just fighting on me, if you know what I mean. Let me go, man!"

Chad released him, and the guy scrambled, darting through people and disappearing into the crowd.

Sam pulled on my hand. "Let's all go. We're all okay."

I heard the urgency in her voice and pressed a quick kiss to her forehead. Nodding to Chad and Moose again, we went our separate ways. Sam settled into the front seat and pulled out her phone as I started the engine.

Her phone buzzed a moment later as I turned down the street, and she let out a long sigh. "Thank God. Heather's fine. She said she'll call later." She lifted relieved eyes to mine, giving me a shaky smile. "She's okay. Everyone's fine."

# SAMANTHA

Everyone was fine.

I kept telling myself this on the drive home, but had something been different, everyone might *not* have been fine. Someone could've been hurt. People I loved were somewhere that a gun was shot. A different person, maybe a different time, or even a different place, and we might not have been driving home with everyone. I couldn't shake that thought, and maybe everyone else had it, too, but I didn't want to sit around, have some drinks, and bullshit the night away. I didn't want to hear Logan's jokes or even sit in Mason's stoic silence. I wanted touch, and I wanted to remember we were alive.

As if sensing my needs, Mason took my hand once we were home. Nothing was spoken, but we went to our room, which was exactly what I needed. My hands were on him the second the door shut. His mouth was on mine. He pressed me into the door, and the need was deep. It was primal. It was now.

I needed Mason now.

We made love like we were never going to be able to touch again.

I arched underneath him as he slid inside of me, but even that wasn't enough. I needed more, and Mason began to thrust. Deeper and deeper. He kept a hand on my waist to anchor me, but I wanted his hands all over me. I wanted his mouth everywhere. I needed so much more than what he was giving, and as if sensing that, he pulled out. My eyes snapped to his. What was he doing?

He turned me over, and I gasped, pressing an arm against the headboard. My hand wrapped over its edge, because I was going to have to hold on. I felt him behind me, and then he was inside.

I was alive.

I was awake.

God, this was exactly what I'd been yearning for.

He set the pace. It was a medium rhythm at first, something I would normally love and gasp for, but I groaned. My head fell back. His hands caught some of my hair, and he wrapped it around his hand. Yes! My breasts began to graze the headboard. He pulled my head back, just slightly, but I shifted back farther, pressing into him as he thrust inside of me. I met him hard as he kept moving. I could feel him. My walls tightened around him.

More. Still more.

I needed to feel pain. Maybe. Maybe it would help remind me we were alive even though someone had been shot tonight.

I looked back. I wanted him to see the hunger in me, and as he did, his eyes darkened. He began going harder.

Still more. Still harder.

"Mason!"

His hand flexed on my ass, and he slammed into me.

This was what I wanted—rough, savage. I wanted it so many different ways, so many different positions, and so many different times. I wanted to remember we weren't dead. None of us. That gunshot hadn't been intended for any of us.

We pounded this truth into my body, into my brain, and after we were both spent, I curled up next to him.

I still wanted that feeling out of my head—the moment I'd heard the gunshot and couldn't get to Mason. But as his arms encircled me and his hand caressed my breast, I knew I'd never be free of it.

I could've lost one of my own tonight.

# CHAPTER TWENTY-EIGHT

I slid from the bed a few hours later.

Mason was sleeping, and he rolled over as I moved. The arm that had been holding me now lay empty on the bed, his hand and fingers pointing toward me as if asking me to come back. I couldn't.

I had a nightmare, and hearing those three gunshots all over again had woken me. I'd been trembling in bed, and I still was as I dressed for a run and laced up my sneakers. I grabbed my phone and earbuds and stepped into the hallway, but my hands weren't strong enough to press them into my ears. They kept falling out.

I cursed under my breath, and I felt a hand on my elbow. I almost screamed, but it was Taylor. She looked haggard and pale, and as she caught my earbud and pressed it into my ear for me, I caught a whiff of throw-up on her breath.

After both earbuds were in place, she stepped back. We looked at each other. I didn't ask if she was sick, and she didn't ask why I was going running. We understood each other perfectly.

I slipped out the door, and I glanced back to see her going to the kitchen. I had no doubt she'd be sitting at the kitchen table with a cup of coffee untouched in front of her when I came back.

But I couldn't think about that. This need to cry, to rage, to laugh— it bubbled inside of me, and I only wanted to suppress it.

I started off down the driveway and turned onto the sidewalk.

I didn't want to warm up this time. I started out hard, and I knew I would keep the same pace until I collapsed somewhere.

I didn't want to feel this morning.

# LOGAN

I woke alone, and after going to the bathroom, I knew where Taylor would be. I could smell the coffee, and sure enough, there she was—perched in a seat at the kitchen table, her coffee getting cold in front of her. One of her arms rested on her knee, her hand touching her face like she was trying not to cry as she looked out the window.

I waited a full thirty seconds, but she never moved.

"Can't sleep?" It was meant to sound casual, but it came out like a bad joke. I winced, sitting down across from her.

She looked over, the agony in her eyes centered right on me. I felt like there was a damned hot poker stuck in my chest, burning me from the inside out.

"Are you fucking serious?" she asked, anger and exhaustion lacing her words.

"I'm sorry. I didn't mean that the way it came out. I just—"

"Just what?"

I suddenly placed the weird smell from the bathroom. "You threw up." I fell back against my chair.

"I sure did."

And then even more dots connected for me. I silently cursed my stupidity. "Your mom."

"The entire time I kept trying not to think about it." She looked back out the window, her words softening. "I wasn't in the house tonight, but I heard that gun. Three shots. Three times someone pulled that trigger."

I knew where this was going, but I couldn't stop it, even though I wanted to. I couldn't take away her past, no matter how much it haunted her. I was helpless except to sit and listen, so I did.

"I ran into Sam earlier," she said, still looking outside. "She was going for a run. I know she runs. I know you said that's what she does to cope, but I didn't get it. I mean, I get it. I've been at the house when she left to go for a run and when she came back. I know how long she goes for sometimes, but it wasn't till this morning that I really understood it." She looked back to me now. "She looked as haunted as I feel. She's going to run until she doesn't feel, just like I threw up, but it never matters. The feelings always come back. Maybe I should try it her way. I bet she doesn't feel for a couple hours after she's exhausted."

"What Sam does—" I leaned forward, making sure I was speaking gently. "—isn't healthy. She's just trying to run from the feelings."

"Literally." Taylor laughed, shaking her head. "But that's not what she's doing. She's not trying to hide from her stuff. She's trying to control it, suppress it so she can get a handle on it. That's all she's doing."

"Look." I spread my hands on the table. I itched to go to her, pick her up, kiss her until she could only feel me, but I did none of that. "I don't know what's bothering Sam right now, but—"

"It doesn't take a rocket scientist!" Taylor's eyes jerked over my shoulder, and I knew my brother was there.

"She left your bed for the same reason I'm sitting here," she said to him. "She's scared to death of losing you guys. She lost everything before, and you two picked up her pieces. She can't go back. I'm not sitting here worried I'll lose someone to a gunman. I'm sitting here because I already did. My mom died, and I was right back there in that hospital tonight when I closed my eyes."

She stood, her eyes blazing at both of us. "I'll get over my stuff. It's called PTSD, but that doesn't change the fact that you both could've been killed tonight."

"Taylor," I started, standing up. Mason was right next to me, but he didn't say a word. His hands were in his sweatpants pockets, and he wasn't wearing a shirt.

"I am angry, Logan, and I have every right to be angry. You're not children anymore. You're not pissed off because your dad's a cheating whore and getting a divorce. You're going to be a junior in college. Mason, you're a senior. You're both too fucking old to be doing this shit."

"Taylo—"

"You were somewhere a *gun was at!*" Her hands were in fists, pressing down on the table so much I worried she'd break a knuckle. "You have serious enemies, and not even the typical douchebag jock who's pissed because you stole his girlfriend. You have someone going after you because you helped put his best friend in prison! That's *insane!* What are you two doing?!" She looked at us a moment before she kept yelling. "Be normal! Be boring even! At least you'll be alive then!"

Then just as quickly as she'd blown up, she quieted. Her head hung down, and her shoulders rose and fell twice as she took two deep breaths.

She reached for her coffee cup. "I will be fine. I will get over this, and I will move on. I know we're going back to Cain in a month, and when you're there, life is steady. I've been around long enough to know that my stuff was your last dramatic hiccup there, but being back here?" She shook her head, her hand curling tightly around her cup. "It is scary being here with you guys. If you both are smart, you'll leave and never come back to Fallen Crest again. Visits. Holidays. Those short-term intervals are fine, but living here?" She drew in a shallow breath, closing her eyes. "You guys are going to get yourselves killed. If you don't do it for me, do it for Sam. You're her lifeline. Don't *ever* cut that string."

Taylor dumped out her cold coffee and left the kitchen.

On a typical day I'd have a sarcastic drop-the-mic comment ready to go. Today I swallowed it, pushed past Mason, and followed my girlfriend back to bed. I climbed in and hugged her to me.

I held on to her as hard as I could.

# SAMANTHA

I was still running, and it was going on an hour and a half now. My legs were getting weaker, but the storm raged on inside of me. It was churning, twisting, and lashing out. I had to keep going until some of it faded. I couldn't deal if it wouldn't, but as I cleared a valley, I suddenly slowed.

Mason's black Escalade was parked next to the running path. I was high up in the hills, with Fallen Crest long behind me, so seeing another person at all was surprising. Having it be Mason was even more so.

Dressed in a black hooded sweatshirt and black sweatpants, he leaned against the seat, his door open. His hair was wet, his eyes shadowed as he watched me come toward him. He took my breath away.

"Hey," I managed, my breathing erratic. I rested my hands on my hips. "What are you doing up here?" I looked around. The road he'd driven on was narrow. Barely any cars made their way up here. "How'd you know I came this way?"

"Because you went running to suppress something. I knew it was bad, and you always take this route if it's really bad."

"Oh." A warm feeling flooded me, covering some of the tension inside.

He stood. "Taylor chewed Logan and me out after you left."

"She did?"

He nodded. "She said we need to grow up." He shrugged. "I'm pretty sure the undertone was that I'm a tool for not being sensitive to your worries."

"My worries?"

I felt like I was still running. My chest tightened. My breath pressed against it, trying to get free.

He moved closer, almost within touching distance. "Your life fell apart. Logan and I picked up your pieces, and she said you're worried the same thing will happen all over again." His eyes looked into me. "Is that true? Do you think something's going to happen to me or Logan?"

I shrugged. "I was worried about that, still am, but that's not all that's going on with me."

"Then what is?"

"I…" I could only stare at him. Memories of when we first met, that whole year, flashed in my mind. It was too much, but I felt a pressure in me. It was pushing harder and harder. I didn't know what that was, but it was uncomfortable, and I couldn't get rid of it. Finally I just gave in, bending over. "I have no idea."

"Your mom?"

"Probably." I rested my hands on my knees and looked up at him. "Does that make me crazy? She hasn't even done anything. I saw a car she was in, and I saw her walking one morning, but she's in here." I straightened and pointed to my head. "She's like a fucking worm. She got in here, and I feel her wiggling around. I want her out, Mason, but she won't go."

"Maybe you should go see her."

"What?" I stopped. He couldn't have suggested that, not him.

He leaned back against his seat, resting an arm on his open door. "She's here. You know it. She knows it. The wedding is only a month away."

I sucked in my breath. I'd forgotten about the wedding. "Am I supposed to go to that?" Or worse— "Am I supposed to help with that?"

He looked ready to say something, then thought better of it.

"What?"

He held his hands up in the air. "It's not that I was keeping this from you; I just heard it once, and I forgot to say something because I figured you knew."

"Mason," I warned, keeping my eyes locked on him. "Tell me. Now."

He groaned. "I thought Malinda said something to you. Honest to God, that's why I didn't say anything the one time I thought about it. But she's been helping your mom with the wedding."

"What?"

"Fuck. I'm sorry, Sam. I really am. I honestly thought you knew."

Had Malinda said something? Maybe. "She talks to my mom, and she's been on this whole kick to spy on other weddings. It makes sense."

He softened his voice. "Is that what all this is about?"

"What do you mean?"

His eyes softened, and he moved toward me. His hand touched the underside of my chin, and he lifted my head so I was looking up at him. His thumb rubbed over my cheek in a loving caress.

"You went to Channing's fight without me. You're working at a carnival. Now you're running like you used to. Is this all about your mom, and now the gun incident last night, or is there something else going on?"

Was there something else? I felt that storm in me, pressing to get out, rising up, exploding. I shook my head. I couldn't even talk about it. "If I knew, I would tell you."

"Okay." He pulled me to his chest, cradling my head there. His lips brushed my forehead. He smoothed a hand down my hair, rubbing over my back in comfort. "You don't have to push it. When you know, I'm here."

I closed my eyes and rested.

# CHAPTER TWENTY-NINE

Logan was waiting outside when we pulled into the driveway at home.

"He texted. He wanted to talk to you," Mason told me as he parked.

"Hey—" Logan started as we got out of the Escalade to head inside.

Mason went on ahead, and I held a hand up, stopping Logan. "If you're here to apologize or reassure me you're not going anywhere, you don't have to."

He frowned, raking a hand through his hair and grabbing a fistful. "Really?" He gestured behind him. "It's just that Taylor reamed us out, and I thought maybe—"

"I didn't go running because I was worried about losing you and Mason." I cocked my head to the side. "Well, I did, but it wasn't *all* about that."

"Yeah?"

I nodded. "Some of it's about my mom, and there's other stuff. I'll be fine. I promise. I'm not mad at you, if that's what you thought."

"I know you aren't, but I still feel bad."

I grinned. "So Taylor reamed you out?"

He laughed, his hand falling from his hair. His shoulders seemed to loosen. "Yeah, and Mason came out shirtless in the middle of it. Another time and place, and I would've been all over him for doing that. I think he came out to find you."

I tried to hold in my grin. "And he found your girlfriend instead."

"Good thing I'm Logan Kade. I mean, come on. If I wasn't the #sexmachine, I might've felt a little self-conscious." His eyes grew thoughtful. "I'd never noticed how ripped he is. I think he needs to cut back on some of his training. He's lean cuisine now. Does it hurt? When you're bumping and grinding against him? Do all those hard muscles give you road rash or something?"

I clapped him on the shoulder, turning for the house. "Stop while you're ahead."

"But—"

"Stop, Logan."

"Okay." He sighed, reaching around me and opening the door.

Nate, Matteo, and Mark waited for us inside. No Taylor, and no Mason.

"Where's my boyfriend?" I asked.

"Getting some water," Matteo reported.

"Where's *my* other half?" Logan asked.

Nate grinned. "If she's smart, heading back to Cain without you."

Logan scowled. "Not funny, Nate. Not funny."

Nate laughed. "I think she's downstairs watching TV or something."

"So what's going on?" Logan asked, sitting down. His hand rested along the back of the couch. "What's Malinda Junior doing here?"

Mark sneered at him. "So funny, Logan."

Logan shrugged. "You never call. You never email. I don't get letters from you. What's going on? It's like we're not even brothers anymore."

"I'm Sam's brother, not yours."

"Means the same thing."

"And you read your own mail? I thought that's why you got a girlfriend. So she could go through all your mail and fan letters."

The joking suddenly stopped, and Logan leaned forward. "You want to say that again?"

Mark's lips formed a line. "You haven't been around all summer, and the first time I'm seeing you, you're giving me shit about not talking to you? I've been here. Where've you been?"

Mason came back from the kitchen, but paused behind Mark.

"I know you were with your girlfriend, but fuck, man," Mark continued. "All you care about is your brother, Sam, and now your girlfriend. From what I've been hearing, you haven't been such a good friend to Nate, much less Matteo."

Nate looked confused.

Matteo shot him a look. "I'm the lowest on the totem pole? Is that what he's saying?"

Logan ignored them both and shot to his feet. "You want to be penpals now? I was joking. That's what I do. But fuck, man, if you really want to have Dr. Phil phone calls, just call me. If I'm not fighting or having sex, I'll pick up."

"No." Mark shook his head. "That's not what I'm saying—"

"You sore because I didn't stay for your bday pool party? Well, I'm sorry about that, but we had things to deal with."

"That's what I'm talking about." Mark pointed at him, snapping his fingers. He gestured to Mason, too, seeing him behind him. "You, too. I heard about the party last night—that there was some biker feud and someone pulled a gun. I got a text from Matteo asking me what was going on, and I had no idea. He couldn't get ahold of you two."

Mason and Logan looked at Matteo, who shrugged and lifted his hands. "I didn't know what to do. I was with Tiffany last night. She got a text about a big party at Channing's, and we were headed there. We'd almost gotten there when we heard the gun. A huge crowd came running down the street after that." He indicated Nate. "I saw this one running and picked him up."

Nate grimaced.

"Yeah," Matteo added. "We came back here, but no one was around. I knew you guys were here because the two Escalades were in the drive. But I didn't want to turn creeper and look in the bedrooms."

I flushed, knowing what Matteo would've seen if he had.

Mason looked at him. "You brought that girl here? To this house?"

"Yeah." He looked at Logan, then me. "Was I not supposed to?"

I met Mason's gaze. Kate had said someone was talking. Could it be her?

"You met her at Channing's fight?" I asked him.

"Yeah." Everyone looked at me as Matteo continued. "She was hanging with some of her friends."

"Who are her friends?" Mason asked.

"What?"

"Who are her friends?"

Matteo slowly stood. "Look, if you have a problem with her, I won't bring her around."

"Have you?"

"What?" Matteo ran a hand over his face, suddenly looking tired.

Mason asked again, "Have you been bringing her here?"

"Once or twice. Not a lot. I've been at her place."

"She has her own place?"

"She's got roommates."

Oh, fucking hell. I closed my eyes, cursing in my head. This was the leak. "Would one of those girls be named Kate?"

"Yeah," Matteo confirmed. "How'd you know?"

"And does Kate's boyfriend hang out at the house sometimes when you're there?"

"Yeah, he's a big mofo. Some of his buddies were at that bar the other day, too. That's why I said hello..." He trailed off, suddenly seeing angry faces around him.

Mason turned away. I hung my head, but Logan shot to his feet. "Are you fucking serious? You've been hanging with our enemies?"

"I didn't know they were your enemies. I swear!" Matteo moved around Logan. "Mason, I didn't know. I'm being honest."

"What is going on?" Mark sat down, his gaze jumping around the room.

Mason said to Matteo, ignoring my stepbrother, "There's a shit ton of history here. You're always so happy. I didn't want to rain on your parade. We've got enemies around these parts, and if you get involved, it can make you paranoid. You seemed like you were having a good time."

"There's no way he would've known about Kate," I offered.

"Who's Kate? Other than Tiffany's roommate," Matteo asked.

Mark snorted. "Some chick that went psycho on Sam a while back."

"What?!"

I shook my head. "It wasn't out of nowhere. She and Mason used to have a thing, before me."

Matteo turned to Mason. "You dated her?"

"I used to fuck her." His lips thinned. "Unfortunately."

"She and her friends thought they were in an actual girl gang and jumped Sam," Logan said. "They put her in the hospital one night."

"Oh. Wow." Matteo's voice grew quiet. "I'm sorry, Sam. I had no idea Kate was like that."

"You guys were told someone was snitching?" Nate asked Mason and me.

I nodded. "Kate found me at the carnival one night. She said we needed to be wary, that someone in the inner circle was talking." I looked back at Matteo. "You had no way of knowing, so don't feel bad."

"He didn't really know anything, right?" Logan asked Mason.

"Not really."

Matteo frowned, scratching his head. "Yeah, you guys talk in riddles sometimes. I think I've gotten used to it, but now I'm starting to realize it's just all code for things. Look, don't tell me anything. I'll stop seeing Tiffany. We're not serious. We were just having fun until I go back to school and football."

Nate and Logan seemed satisfied with that. Both leaned back on the couches, stretching their feet out.

Mark kept looking from person to person, and after a moment he threw his hands up in the air. "Am I the only one pissed right now?"

Matteo said nothing, just sat between Logan and Nate on the couch. Mason moved to stand next to me and touched the small of my back, his hand shifting under my shirt to rest against my skin.

"Why are you mad, Mark?" he asked.

"Because—" he sputtered. "I want to know what's going on."

"We can't tell you." Logan disentangled his arm from the back of the couch and leaned forward.

"Why not?"

"Because you're friends with Quinn," Logan explained.

"But *he's* working with Adam." Mark pointed to Mason.

"Doesn't mean I'm friends with him."

"He thinks you are."

Mason frowned, his hand pressing harder against my back. He tugged me against him. "What do you mean?"

"He thinks you guys are all copacetic. Becky, too. They were asking what was going on last night, since everyone knew you were at that party."

That didn't sound right. "Becky asked, too?" I said.

He looked at me. "Well, I mean…" He lifted a shoulder. "She was there, and Adam was asking me. She didn't tell him to be quiet or anything. I just took it to mean she agreed with him."

Becky loved Adam, but she understood we weren't friends with him. That made me feel like something else was going on, but it wasn't something I could get from Mark. When Mason and Logan fell quiet and remained that way, I knew what they were doing. Mark might be friends with Logan, and friendly-ish with Mason, but he was *my* stepbrother. He was mine to handle.

I moved forward. "Mark, are you asking because you were worried about me, or because Adam asked you to find out what was going on?"

"He—" Mark stopped again. He gripped the back of his neck. "Adam didn't really ask in so many words, not like he wanted me to find out. But it still pissed me off. I had no clue what was going on, and then I heard there were gunshots at a party you were at? Yeah, I guess I got mad." He glared at Logan, then Mason. "She's not just yours. She's mine, too. My sister. My family. You can't keep putting her in danger all the time."

I didn't look up at Mason. I didn't dare because he was either ready to rip Mark's head off, or—I didn't want to know. I stepped toward my stepbrother. "Mark, it's not like that."

"Yes, it is, Sam. It has been for a long time."

He was coming after Mason. There was no way things would end fine now. I saw Logan stand to come to his brother's defense. You attack one, you attack all. That was our motto. But this was my stepbrother.

I held my hands out, as if to help silence him. "Mark, it's not like that. I swear."

"It has been, Sam! You can't argue that. Those girls putting you in the hospital. Didn't you guys deal with a drug dealer the other year? How is that safe for Sam? And Sebastian? I mean, there's a pattern, and you guys can't deny it. Over and over again my sister is in danger. And this year, a guy tried to hurt her at the carnival, the fucking carnival. We gotta go to work tomorrow, and I'll be worried the entire time that someone's grabbing her or worse, just like that Broudou guy tried."

I felt Mason right behind me. Logan had moved forward to stand on his other side. I saw Nate rising out of the corner of my eye. This was *so* not good.

Mark opened his mouth to keep going, and there was so much he could say.

I closed my eyes. The list was long, but then I felt that storm inside of me again—it was pressing and pressing, trying to get free, until suddenly I yelled out, "It's not them!"

There was a moment of silence.

"You can't say it's not them, Sam. I know—"

"It's me."

I opened my eyes, knowing everything was right there. He could see the pain, the yearning, the rage. All of it was showing, and I couldn't do a damned thing to hide it.

"This summer, it's been me, Mark. I went to that fighting event without Mason. I shouldn't have gone, and I should've left right away. I didn't. I'm the one who put him in danger. And getting a job at a carnival, where someone from Roussou could easily find me? It was your idea, but I sure went for it. All summer I've been lost. I was thinking of psychology, but it didn't feel right. Not completely. All the other majors I thought of didn't fit either, so I don't have one. I have no clue what I want to do with my life. Mason's got two career paths he's getting ready for. Logan is doing communications, and everyone knows he'll be amazing at whatever he ends up doing with it."

"I will?"

"Heather is running Manny's, and she's going to marry Channing."

Mason looked down at me. I saw the movement from the corner of my eye, but I couldn't bring myself to look at him. Shame flooded me as my words spilled out. "Even Becky and Adam know what they're doing with their lives. They're getting married. He's either going to take over his dad's company or go to law school. And she's going with him."

One by one, I was removing the knots inside me. I tossed them out until there were just two left. They were the biggest of all, and I moved away so Mason wasn't touching me. It didn't feel right to let him comfort me as I said this.

My voice dropped to a hoarse whisper. "And my mom's getting married this summer. I'm not avoiding her because she wants back in. I'm avoiding her because…" Here it was. The first boulder was her, but the second was what she represented. "…She's getting married, and I think the whole thing is a crock of shit."

Her.

Marriage.

All of it.

I didn't want to get married.

That was the last boulder sitting on my chest, but I couldn't say it. I couldn't tell Mason because I knew it was something he wanted.

I didn't believe in marriage anymore. It was one more thing my mother had destroyed for me.

"Excuse me." I left. I didn't know where I was going, but I couldn't stay here. The truth was going to spill from me, and I wouldn't risk it. I could lose Mason that way.

"Sam!"

He followed me outside, but I turned and held my hands out. "No. Let me go."

I still couldn't look at him, but his voice sounded closer when he said, "Sam, what's going on?"

It was me. I was the monster here. It was all me.

"Just…let me go, for now." I started forward again. "I need some time."

And before he could grab me or change my mind, I took off.

I didn't stick to the sidewalk or the roads. I cut through back paths, and when I came to a crossroads, I ran away from any place I'd ever been before.

# CHAPTER THIRTY

I ran and walked for hours.

I went all over. I was close to Roussou at one point before I circled back to the east end of Fallen Crest. I didn't go to anyone else. It wasn't right to talk about this feeling with anyone other than Mason, but I wasn't ready to talk to him about it.

For once I was in a position where I couldn't go to him and know everything would be fine, no matter what. It might not be. This could be a game changer.

My stomach rumbled, and spotting a grocery store, I went inside. I needed water and some kind of sustenance. I still had a few miles to cover before I was home. I'd have to rest the rest of the night and tomorrow morning to recover before going in to work.

I wanted to dart in and out. I wanted it to be quick. I knew I smelled, so I decided to just grab some energy gel packets. I wouldn't have to wait for my stomach to digest them.

I moved toward the right aisle, and that was when I saw her.

I had to laugh.

I'd been avoiding Analise for so long, but this was the moment we would really cross paths: in the freaking grocery store. My aisle was next to hers, but there she was, holding a bag of coffee. No one else was in the aisle, and she hadn't looked up. I could still go.

But I must've made a sound because even as that thought flitted through my mind, she looked over.

She dropped her bag of coffee. "Oh."

A lump formed in my throat.

It wasn't surprise, or fear, or pain that flashed across her face. She didn't pale. Whatever was going on with her face, I was *not* seeing those things, because that didn't make sense. My mom was evil. She was a bitch. She was the monster who wanted to take Mason's future away, not this woman who seemed to shrink in size the longer I stood there, staring at her.

She hadn't seemed like this before, when I saw her walking. She'd looked like a ghost then, an eerie figment of my imagination. This woman was real. I could see emotions inside of her.

"Stop it." I couldn't take it.

Seeing her as a real person was too much.

She'd bent down to pick up the bag, and paused when she heard me. She looked up, suspended there a moment, before she snatched it. Straightening, she frowned at me. Her gaze grew clouded, and she dropped her eyes to the coffee.

I expected a scathing comment.

I braced myself, ready.

Nothing.

She wouldn't tear her gaze from that damned coffee bag.

I couldn't handle this. I strode forward and took the bag from her. "You're not going to say anything?"

She swallowed, looking at me, but not really. I felt like she was looking through me, searching for something behind me even.

She still said nothing.

I ground my teeth together. I deserved a response. "Mom!"

Her eyes welled up and she gasped. "Samantha." Her hand covered her mouth. The tears rolled down. "I..." She reached out, but I backed away. "I, I'm sorry. I never thought I'd hear you say that again."

*What? Mom?*

Emotions swirled through me, but one thing stood out: the fact that I was feeling them. I wasn't numbing myself. I wasn't turning on the robot-Sam. I wasn't even feeling the itch to run. This was...new.

I didn't like it.

I put the coffee back on the shelf. I didn't know what to say.

Apparently, she didn't either because she just watched me back away, one step at a time. It was so fucking surreal, this moment. We'd barely spoken, but I felt like I'd just run another gauntlet.

I was exhausted. Feeling my own eyes tearing up, I turned and left.

---

It wasn't dark, but it was close to dusk when a pair of headlights pulled into the park area where I was resting. I knew it was Mason. I didn't move from the picnic table where I sat. I just looked up as he turned off the Escalade and came over. God, even now, my mouth watered for him.

He was dressed in dark grey pants, the kind he wore after a workout. They were lightweight and soft to the touch. He'd pulled on a Cain University T-shirt, and as the wind swept over us, it pressed the shirt against his chest. I could see every ridge, dip, and valley in those stomach muscles, and I was already yearning for the next time he'd be holding me.

That feeling was never going away

Mason was it for me. He was the real deal, and I wasn't going to find anyone else like him again. But marriage—even the idea of it sent chills through my blood.

He didn't say anything. He only sat next to me at the picnic table, his knee lightly pressed into mine. That was his greeting. It was small, but intimate.

I sighed softly, hanging my head.

His hand rested on my back, and he began rubbing circles.

"You okay?"

That was all he asked. No demands about where I'd gone or why I went. No lectures about how he'd worried about me.

Even more shame bloomed in me, but I nodded. "I think so."

He continued to rub my back, up and down now.

"I saw my mom again."

"Where?"

"Grocery store." I lifted my head, turning to look at him. "I went in to grab some energy gel so I'd have enough strength to make it back home, and there she was." I snorted. "Buying coffee. I don't remember her drinking coffee before. It was tea—or wine."

Mason smiled lightly. "I thought she liked bourbon."

"I think she did." I shook my head, exhaustion, shame, and sadness washing over me. Also gratefulness. I reached for Mason's hand, and our fingers laced together. "Thank you."

He squeezed my hand. "For what?"

"For coming to get me. I don't think I had enough in me to get home to you."

"Well." His top lip curved up. "You forgot the gel packets." He leaned forward, lightly nipping my shoulder. "Makes sense."

I laughed, some of my sadness fading, but not all of it. I was suddenly even more exhausted than before. "You know what I mean."

He lifted his head and brushed my hair back from my face. He cupped my cheek and turned my face so I was looking right at him.

"I'll always come for you," he said softly. "You never have to thank me for that."

My throat swelled, and a tear slipped from my eye. He caught it, brushing it away with his thumb, and leaned forward. His lips brushed mine, so softly, so gently. I closed my eyes, welcoming his tender touch. Then he applied pressure, and I opened my mouth. The same feelings as always surged up in me, pushing the exhaustion, sadness, and shame to the side. I was starving for his touch, just like I'd been last night, but this was slightly different.

I wasn't reassuring myself that he was fine. I was reassuring myself that I would be fine. Whatever my issues about marriage, everything would be worked out. It had to be.

Mason got up from the picnic table and picked me up. We kept kissing, and my legs wrapped around his waist as he carried me to the Escalade. When we got back to the house, he parked in the garage, a place that was always empty. We didn't make it inside the house. There were too many people in there.

Mason locked the garage door and the side door so no one could interrupt us. Then he caught my hand, tugged me to an inflated pool bed, and for a few hours, we were completely alone—no brothers, no best friends, no parents. Just him and me.

# CHAPTER THIRTY-ONE

It was close to three in the morning when we tried sneaking inside.

Mason and I were tiptoeing in when the kitchen light turned on. Logan stood in the hallway that led to the bedrooms and raised an eyebrow.

"Where have you two been?" He pointed to the front of the house. "I know you didn't just get here, because I didn't see any headlights."

Mason straightened up, holding my hand behind his back. "What we were doing and where we were is none of your business."

Logan crossed his arms over his chest. "I was worried."

"I texted you that we were fine."

"Sam runs off, literally, and you take off four hours later to pick her up. I get one text from you an hour ago saying you were fine." Logan shook his head, *tsk*ing at us. "Not cool, bro. I'm a part of your relationship. I don't get where you think I'm not. It's not just the two of you. There are other people to consider—"

"Do you really want me to say all this same shit about you and Taylor?"

Logan grinned, his arms dropping. "Touché." He saluted. "Hope the two of you made sweet, sweet love wherever you were. I'm off to bed."

"Since you're up..." Mason stopped him, crossing to the fridge and opening it. He pulled out some leftover pizza and tossed a water bottle to me. "Cop a squat. We've got some stuff to talk about."

Logan looked back over his shoulder, a yearning look on his face. "I could wake Taylor up right now. You know how good middle of the night sex can be, right? You're aware of what you're making me miss?"

"Sit down." Mason motioned to the kitchen table. "It's not like you can't wake her up when we're done."

"True." Logan grabbed the pizza box, pulling out a few pieces and putting them on a plate. He warmed them in the microwave before sitting down.

My stomach growled, loudly.

Mason smiled. "Hungry?"

I groaned, opening my water. "I don't know if I dare eat. I could get cramps."

He warmed a couple pieces for me before doing his own plate. Logan waved his pizza at me. "Don't say my brother never feeds you."

I frowned. "When would I ever say that?"

He shrugged, biting off half of his slice. "You never know."

"Is everyone else asleep?" Mason asked.

"Matteo broke it off with that chick, and he came back a while ago. We all had a few beers together before he passed out in his room downstairs. Taylor went to bed a little before that, and Nate knocked off the same time as Matteo. Me, I've been up and waiting for you two lovebirds to stop doing the mating dance in the garage." He winked, wiggling his eyebrows. "Didn't think I'd figured it out, did you?"

"It's the only place we could've been if we'd already arrived. You checked the pool house, didn't you?"

"Yeah." Logan picked up his second piece. "I saw you pull up, and I went searching when you didn't come in. I knew you guys wanted privacy, but my inner Harriet the Spy was nagging me. I got curious." He frowned to himself. "Just now remembered we have a garage. Why don't we ever use the garage?"

"Because it's only three slots wide. We could park six cars in there, but someone would always have to be moving their car out of the way. It'd be too much of a hassle."

"Thank God Mom's got a huge-ass driveway." Logan looked at the pizza on my plate and nudged it closer to me. "The only way it gets to your stomach is if you eat it, Sam."

"I know, dumbass."

He smirked. "You're calling me the dumbass when you're the one who needs to be reminded how to eat. Put it in and chew—unless it's Mason's dick. Don't chew then. Please, don't chew. I don't want to take my brother to the emergency room for that."

"Logan." Mason glared. "Stop talking about my dick."

"What else is there to talk about? You haven't brought up what you wanted to talk about, and I keep thinking about what I could be doing with my dick while I'm sitting here waiting."

Logan spoke as if that made perfect sense. I shook my head and picked up my pizza. He was right. I needed something in my stomach. I'd done too much physical activity over the last twenty-four hours.

As if both had been waiting for me to start eating, as soon as I took my first bite, Mason said, "We need to figure out what to do about Caldron."

"What do you mean?" Logan was all business now.

"I wanted something on Quinn first before asking Dad to help deal with Caldron." Mason grimaced. "That didn't happen."

"Yet," Logan corrected. "It didn't happen yet. We can still trade it in when we find something. What were you going to ask Dad to do?"

"Promote him."

"Say what?" Logan pretended to clean his ear out. "I heard that wrong, right?"

"We have to deal with things differently. Your girlfriend's right. We can't keep doing the shit we're doing. My football career is another reason besides Sam's safety—well, our safety, too. I get caught doing anything, I could not have a football career. One video, and I'm fucked."

"Yeah." Logan sighed. "Those were the good old days, when we didn't give a shit. Growing up sucks. Okay. So you want to promote him?"

"He'll have more incentive not to do anything then. If he goes after any of us, but Sam most of all, he loses the extra money he will have been making."

"It's a good idea, but do you really want Caldron to have more responsibility? What factory does he work at?"

"I think he's at one of dad's landscaping companies. Manual labor."

"Got you." Logan nodded, his forehead wrinkling. "He could go up a notch and still not have access to anything real that could hurt Dad. So the question is, how are you going to proposition Dad to do this for us?" His eyes slid to mine. "Last time he countered by making us be his groomsmen."

"I know." Mason sighed.

"What?" I looked between the two.

Mason frowned, and it only deepened as he pushed his empty plate away. "You might have to agree to do something for him again."

Logan jumped in, "But that'll go away once we use whatever we find on Quinn. We'll leverage that against what James will want you to do. The favors will all be wiped clean."

Yeah. That sounded great. It sounded logical even, but James Kade was a millionaire businessman, if not a billionaire. If he wanted something, I had a hard time imagining him taking it off the table once Mason and Logan found whatever they could on Steven Quinn.

But I nodded. I ate the rest of my pizza. I said and did what they wanted me to, but I had my doubts.

"When's this going down?" Logan asked as we all stood, done for the night.

Mason looked to me. "You're working a shift tomorrow night—well, later today?"

I nodded. "I have Tuesday and Wednesday off. I'm working next weekend, though."

"Dad asked me to give him an update on Wednesday, so if you two show up with me, he won't be prepared. That'll be the best time."

Logan clapped his hands together. "Wednesday it is. Mission 'to deal with Caldron and bamboozle James Kade' is in progress." He pretended to rub his hands in an evil manner, snickering.

Mason shook his head. "Don't do that, and don't say *bamboozle* again."

"Why not?" Logan followed us down the hallway. "I like it. It reminds me of boobies. Who doesn't like boobies?"

"Don't." Mason shot him a look as we reached our room.

Logan had stopped at his door and shrugged, grinning. "You're the boss. But wait. Do you know what you're the boss of?"

"Don't—" Mason started.

"Of boobies!" Logan laughed, heading inside his room.

We laughed, too. For once, I was thankful for the long run I'd taken, for seeing my mom, and for knowing the plan against James Kade. Because once I hit that pillow, I fell asleep immediately, my worries about marriage forgotten—at least for now.

# CHAPTER THIRTY-TWO

A few days later, James Kade sat behind his desk, squared off against Mason, Logan, and myself. Logan and I sat in the chairs, and Mason stood to the side. At the moment, however, James Kade only had eyes for his eldest son.

He leaned back in his chair, his fingers tented. "Let's hear it. What's the reason you brought an audience to this meeting, Mason?"

Mason dropped a file on the desk.

"And what's this?" James leaned forward, bringing it in front of him.

"That's a file on one of your employees."

"Jared Caldron?" James skimmed through the papers. "He's a laborer for my landscaping company." His eyes lifted back to Mason. "Why am I reading about him?"

"Because he was best friends with Budd Broudou in high school, and what you don't know is that we had a hand in getting Broudou sent to prison."

James didn't seem to react. His face remained passive for a full fifteen seconds before he shot to his feet, sending his chair flying into the bookshelves behind him. "What did you do?"

I stood up. "They didn't do anything. I mean, not really."

Mason said over me, "She's lying for me. I did do something."

Logan stood up, too. Everyone paused and looked at him, and he held up his hands. "I wanted to fit in. Everyone's standing."

Mason cursed, rolling his eyes.

James' attention went right back to Mason. "You're going to explain everything to me."

"Budd Broudou and his brother were our rivals in high school. They did shitty things to us. We retaliated—"

"Of course you did. Why would my sons ever *not* get revenge?"

Mason kept going, ignoring his father's sarcasm. "Brett turned to our side—or kind of on our side."

I felt Mason's eyes linger on me.

"And Budd got pissed. He said he'd been waiting for me to get a girlfriend so he could destroy something I cared about."

"Oh, God." James swung his gaze to me. "Samantha…"

"So I pretended to be dating someone else."

"What?"

"For a weekend, I was with someone else."

"You cheated on Sam?"

I'd been staring at the desk, reliving the past, but looked back up now. "No," I said fiercely. "He did not cheat on me."

Logan slid his hands into his pockets. "He set up his ex to take the fall for Sam."

"I didn't enjoy touching someone else, but I had to, and I had to do it where Budd Broudou would see me. I only touched her when he could see. He had to buy the lie."

"And let me guess." James' disapproval was thick. "He tried to hurt this girl?"

I cleared my throat. It was my turn now. "He was going to rape her, but I came running by. I poured gasoline on his truck and set it on fire to distract him. Someone called the cops, and he was arrested. The girl testified against him."

"That's what put him away, and this guy wants payback now that you guys are back in Fallen Crest."

Logan gave him a half-grin. "Look at Pops here. All smart and catching on quick."

James shot him a look as he sat back down. "Not now, Logan."

Logan's eyes widened, but he shut his mouth and sat down, as did I.

Mason leaned against the wall beside us, crossing his arms over his chest. "Now you know the details. We need your help dealing with him."

"What's he doing?"

All three of us shared a look.

"I can't discipline him if I don't have a reason to," James said. "I need a reason."

"I don't want you to discipline him. I want you to promote him," Mason explained.

James fell quiet, staring for a beat. "You want him to have incentive *not* to do something. Give him something to lose, and he'll work even harder to keep it. Something like that?"

"Yeah. Something like that."

Logan snorted. "Something *exactly* like that."

"It's a good plan," James said. "Except it won't work."

"What?" Mason stepped away from the wall. "What do you mean?"

James pointed at the file. "Reading his history and last review comments, I'd say he's got a chip on his shoulder. You give him power, he'll want more. He won't be content to stay where he is, even if it does mean he'll lose a significant raise if he acts up. I don't know what he's been doing—" His hands shot up when Logan jerked forward in his seat. "And I don't want to know. What I do know is that this is not a kid you can bribe or threaten."

"What are you talking about?" Mason's tone was quiet, eerily quiet. I looked over to him, but he was watching his dad with rapt attention.

"Is it within reason that this kid is doing something illegal?"

Mason shrugged. "You mean besides assaulting people?"

"You can charge him with that?" James frowned.

Logan snorted again.

Mason sighed. "Nothing he can't charge us with, too."

"My sons," James bit out, standing up again. He gestured to both of them. "Such saintly examples." He turned to Mason, his neck becoming red. "You're fighting again?!"

And the pleasantries were over.

Mason jerked forward, but Logan was on his feet as well. He said, "Dad."

"Will you never learn? You're almost a senior in college, Mason! You're doing the same shit you were doing when you were a freshman in high school!" James' voice rose louder and louder. His hand curled in a fist, and he shook it in the air. "What's your excuse this time? You blamed me for the divorce back then. Well, you can't anymore. I'm not *whoring around*, as you like to say. I've been faithful to the same woman since—" He glanced over, and his eyes found mine.

In an instant I was back there, back to the first time Analise told me we were leaving my father. I felt the same emotion I had then. Nothing, because it was all too much.

His voice quieted. "I'm sorry, Sam."

I closed my eyes, hanging my head.

She had been on the floor, sitting in between boxes already. Two empty bottles of wine had lay next to her, and I knew she was only starting.

I barely heard myself as I said, "I remember feeling like I was suffocating when she told me we were leaving him." I'd never known it, but there were words I needed to say to this man, and right now he was listening.

Now was the time.

I took a calming breath. "You were the catalyst for all of it. I mostly blamed my mom. I knew she was the one who went after you. And I knew I'd find out Jeff was cheating on me, and I should've lost my two best friends, because it turns out they're really shady assholes. But I blamed you for ripping apart my family because you were stupid." I frowned, biting the inside of my lip for a moment. "I still think you're stupid."

Logan covered a laugh.

James' gaze had fallen to the desk.

I felt Mason next to me. He was right there, if I needed him.

But I was okay on my own. "She cheated during her entire marriage. You cheated during your entire marriage. How am I supposed to believe both of you won't cheat when you marry each other? How am I supposed to know that cheating's not a part of every marriage?"

Now I really felt Mason watching me, but I couldn't look. There was no way, because he'd know.

"Samantha," James started, his posture that of a broken man.

But I knew he wasn't broken. That was the problem. People like him never broke. They did the breaking.

"You broke your family. She broke my family. You guys are going to break it again."

"Is that what you think?" he asked.

I nodded. "That's what I know."

"Samantha." He started to walk out from behind the desk.

Mason was right there, blocking him, and when James looked over, Logan moved closer to me, too. Neither of them was going to let their father close to me. When he saw that, he nodded, a sad laugh coming from him.

"This, right here." He pointed to us. "This is how you know we won't be breaking another family. My sons love you more than they love me. I lost their love so long ago, and I'll never really get it back. I've made my peace with that. But with you, that love is solid. It's the only beautiful thing Analise and I have done together, and we can't take credit. You three found each other." He looked at Mason. "I know my son will never cheat on you, and my other son will never stop being your brother. We'll never break the three of you again."

He turned to sit back down. Some of the tension I felt from Mason ebbed, and Logan stepped back.

"But you will," I said, stopping everyone.

"What?" James tilted his head to the side.

"You're asking them to love you. And even though she hasn't verbally said anything to me, I know my mom is asking the same. You both want to be let back in, maybe not as deeply as before, but still behind our walls. That gives you the power to hurt us. Again." I looked at Logan and Mason. "They don't want to let you in because that's what you're going to do. Maybe not with my mom, but somehow, you're going to hurt them again. That's what you do. You hurt people."

"Samantha—"

I cut him off. "If you want to do something, help us with Caldron. He's a problem we need dealt with. Do that for us."

"And what do I get in return?"

"Nothing." I leaned forward, resting my hands on the desk to stare him in the eyes. "Because that's what parents do. They give without asking in return. Do the right thing for your sons, for once."

---

"Holy fuck!" Logan burst out as soon as we were through the main doors. "That was amazing, Sam! I don't care what I do; I want you to work with me. You're a fucking closer. You can end any shit you want."

I grinned, but I wasn't feeling it. I shrugged. "Once I figure out what I want to do, we can make a plan how to work together."

"You've inspired me," he said. "Fuck communications. I want to be a lawyer. What school is Quinn going to? I'm going to go there, just to piss him off on a daily basis." He snapped his fingers at us. "Maybe I'll even take a quick poke at Beck—ahhh, and I just went back to single Logan for a bit. Don't tell Taylor. She'll ream my ass for real." He pretended to take in the fresh air. "I was just so moved, Sam. I felt like we were back in high school, taking pieces of scum down one at a time."

He frowned over at Mason. "Why you so quiet? Your girlfriend kicked ass for us. Dad said he'd deal with Caldron, and we don't owe him anything for it."

I knew why Mason was quiet. He'd read between the lines back there, but he only grinned. "Maybe I'm turned on and trying not to let you see? Ever thought of that?"

"God, no." Logan groaned, wrinkling his nose. "And now I do. Thanks for that."

"Do you know how many jokes you make about being dick-deep in Taylor? You think I want to hear that stuff from my little brother?" Mason squeezed my hand a bit, moving ahead.

I knew what he was doing—distracting Logan for me.

"*Agh!* Shut up, Mase." Logan shook his head, moving toward the Escalade ahead of us. "You can't talk about my dick any more. No more dick jokes between us."

Mason let go of my hand, keeping pace with Logan. "What about all the hashtags? Hashtag limp dick. Hashtag my dick is in my girlfriend. Hashtag I'm the rocket man."

"Shut up!"

I had started to laugh with them when I heard a car door shut. They hadn't seemed to hear it, but I did.

Maybe I knew. Maybe I just felt it coming, or maybe it was finally right to face her, but when I looked over, I knew who would be standing there. I felt her there.

My mom. And unlike the previous two times, she looked prepared to see me.

She stepped up on the sidewalk, wearing a flowy red dress. The material whipped all around her, but her hair was pulled up under a black hat.

"Hello, Samantha."

"You can talk this time."

A small laugh slipped from her, and she looked down to the sidewalk for a second. "I wasn't expecting you at the grocery store, but I know Mason is interning here. I'm prepared to see you every time I come."

"Prepared?"

"Excited." Her eyebrows pinched together and she amended, "Hopeful. I'm hopeful every time I come here." She held a hand out, indicating me. "You look lovely."

"Not like you." I smiled. "You're always beautiful."

"So are you."

"Spoken like a true mother would normally say."

She heard my biting tone, and her smile lessened. "And we both know this is not normal, is it? You and me. Our relationship never was."

My anger was rising, rolling into a massive cloud. I couldn't hold it in. "Because you were never a mother, were you?"

Her eyes went flat, and she didn't respond. She drew in a deep breath, closing her eyes for a beat. "You have years of anger built up toward me."

She was damned right, I did.

"And you have every right to feel that anger," she added, her voice soft. "You have every right to have your say, to express that anger, and to have a mother who will finally listen to you."

Because I was feeling petty, I said, "Don't worry. I have a mother now."

The blood drained from her face.

I could see Mason and Logan coming back for me. "And unlike with you, I have no reason to be angry at her, so everything worked out in the end. Now, I have to go because if they see you here and think you're the reason I'm upset, you'll be dealing with all three of us." I stepped past her off the sidewalk, but I turned back around. I had one last thing to say. "I'm not scared of you any more."

She frowned. "You weren't before."

"I know. I just wanted to say that because this time, you should be scared of me."

"Hey." Mason was coming. Two steps and he'd clear the last SUV that blocked his view of Analise.

I waved him back, hurrying my pace. "I'm coming."

"What's wrong?"

Of course he'd know. I only shook my head, though. "Just thinking. I'm fine now." I moved past him and took his hand, pulling him behind me. "Let's go home."

# CHAPTER THIRTY-THREE

Two weeks went by.

No drama.

No fights.

No nothing.

It was an eerie calm, and it wasn't that nothing at all happened, just no bad stuff. There were parties. Heather and Channing came over, and we hung out at Manny's. There'd been no more sightings of Caldron, so Mason and Adam went back to working at the country club. The hotel was nearing its opening, and they'd been doing more and more events for it—radio interviews, newspaper interviews, ads, even a couple videos for Facebook. And somehow, during those three weeks, I got roped into helping with a bridal shower for Becky.

Heather brought in a package of silk flowers and dumped them on Malinda's table. "What are we doing here? We're not bridal shower friends. We're Vegas and bachelorette party friends."

Cass came over and picked up some of the flowers. "You're supporting friends, and Sam promised to support Becky."

Heather glared at her. "I hate you."

Cass narrowed her eyes.

"Go away," Heather added.

I smothered a laugh.

"You're still just as hateful as you were in high school." Cass sniffed.

"Like you would know," Heather countered. "You went to the rich, preppy school."

I was content to let this go on as long as necessary. Mark's girlfriend was a longtime enemy of mine. We'd come to a strained truce because of Becky, but nothing had been spoken between us. I was waiting for her attack. It'd come. It always did.

I had a lot of fires in my life. They were all simmering and contained, but at any moment, there could be an explosion.

Malinda came to watch the exchange from the kitchen, and my excitement died a slow death inside of me. I had to stop Heather from completely annihilating Cass, though it would've been so much fun to watch.

Clearing my throat, I grabbed a pile of papers that still needed to be folded and sat down. "I'm seconding Heather's request. Go away, Cass. We're busy folding these little suckers. We don't need you to boss us around."

Heather sat beside me, taking half the pile. "Yeah. Get stomping…" She waited until Cass had left with a huff before adding under her breath, "you prissy bitch."

I had to stifle another laugh. Today was not the day.

She looked at the paper as she started to fold and paused. "Wait. The Love Game?" She read one of the questions. "Who said *I love you* first?" She looked to me. "Are you serious? This is the type of game people play at bridal showers?"

I shrugged, starting on my pile. The questions were on the front of the page and the answers were on the back. No one was supposed to look, but Malinda had them printed this way on purpose. Everyone was going to cheat, but Becky would feel like everyone actually knew her that well.

"From what I Googled, this is common stuff," I told her.

She snorted, starting on her pile. "Too bad it's not Logan's bridal shower. This game would have questions like *Who offered to do anal first?*"

We looked at each other and said at the same time, "Logan."

I laughed. "That's a no-brainer."

Heather sighed. "I'm going to die of boredom at this thing. What did you blackmail me with to make me do this?"

I thought about it. "I threatened to tell Logan that Channing wants to marry you."

"Oh yeah." She shuddered. "I don't want to think about what he'd say if he knew that. He'd be on my ass all day long."

"If he didn't have Taylor, he'd be begging to be your maid of honor."

Heather barked out a laugh. "He would. He'd be stabbing you in the back, trying to get that position from you."

"He could have it. I hate weddings."

I cringed, realizing what I'd just said. The words slipped out before I knew I was even going to say them.

Heather paused mid-fold. "Are you serious?"

I looked around, making sure no one else had heard my flub. Then I shrugged, leaning forward. "Maybe."

"This is the wrong summer for you to be saying that. You know that, right?"

I nodded. "I'm not proclaiming it or anything."

"Becky got engaged. Channing's been bringing it up more and more with me, and your mom is actually getting married very soon."

"I'm aware. It's all around me."

She lowered her voice. "Has Mason mentioned the M-word to you?"

I shook my head, feeling some relief. "No. I think it's just overkill. That's all."

"Bullshit." Heather continued to watch me steadily. She wasn't giving me any room to breathe. "The whole wedding thing is usually contagious for girls. If you're around it, you suddenly want to do it, too." She studied me. "You look ready to bolt just having this conversation. You really hate weddings, or you hate your own wedding?"

I hated this conversation. "I'm not engaged, so this is a conversation I don't need to bother with."

"But he will ask you."

My heart jumped to my throat. "You know something I should know?"

She shook her head. "No, but it's Mason. He loves you—like, really loves you. He's going to want a ring on your finger."

I knew that, but the thought of marriage sent ice through my veins. "I'll deal with it," I told her.

The look in her eye said *bullshit*.

"It's not a big deal."

She snorted. Again. "You need to talk to Mason about that. For real, Sam. It's a big deal. It's on the same level as when a partner doesn't want to have kids and the other does. It's a deal breaker."

She wasn't helping. I felt a headache forming. "I know. I'll talk to him."

"Promise?"

I nodded.

"No, you have to say the word. I know you, and you'll try to get out of it somehow. Promise me, Sam."

I didn't understand the problem. Mason never brought up marriage or weddings. We hadn't talked about it, and he came from the same background as me. He'd understand. Right? But I remembered the fear I felt when I first realized how much I didn't want marriage.

I didn't want to promise, but Heather was waiting, watching me like a hawk. "I'll talk to him," I heard myself say.

She let out a sigh of relief. "Good." She squeezed my hand. "It'll be fine. I know it. That guy worships the ground you walk on. There's nothing he wouldn't deal with for you."

Yeah...I hoped so.

Heather went back to reading the questions and groaned. "Honestly? 'What's your idea of a perfect weekend?' Please. Hers is probably when there's a slight breeze in the air, walks on the beach, and cuddling in front of the fireplace. His is probably a blow job to wake up, a blow job at lunch, a backdoor rally in the afternoon, and a good scotch after dinner." She rolled her eyes. "I can't stand when couples like them get married."

I laughed, wondering just how far off her answers were from Becky and Adam's truth.

Then Becky walked in with Adam right behind her. They were holding hands and smiling, but the terror in her eyes and forced lines around his mouth were what caught my attention.

"Wait, wait, wait," Heather said. "Since when does the groom come to these things? This completely blows all of my white trash stereotypes about what rich folks do."

Malinda went over to greet them. As Adam hugged her, Becky glanced at me, and I stood.

"Something's not right," I told Heather.

"What?"

I was across the room before Malinda had finished gushing over the couple. She had an arm around Becky's waist and beamed at me.

"One of these days, this will be you and Mason, Sam. I can't wait."

"Yeah." My cheeks were hurting, my smile was so forced. I reached for Becky's hand. "Can I have a minute?"

An emotion flickered in Malinda's eyes, and she glanced down. I know she saw how tightly Becky held onto my hand, but she continued to exude warmth. She turned, pulling Adam over to where Cass and some other girls were helping put up the decorations. "Come on, Adam. I need your opinion about where we should put the cake."

Becky overheard. "There's a cake?"

I pulled her past everyone, motioning for Heather to follow, and tugged her downstairs.

We found Mark on the couch playing video games.

"Hey, wha—" he started to say, but I cut him off.

"Get out. This is girl time."

He paused his game. "Where am I supposed to go?"

"Logan's determined to create a new drink. Go over and be his guinea pig."

He groaned, but turned the game off. "I'm going to get wasted off my ass, aren't I?"

Heather patted him on the back as he moved past us, going upstairs. "Just have fun doing it. That's the trick."

He muttered something under his breath, but then the door shut behind him.

Becky bit her lip, hugging herself. She eyed Heather.

"Heather's fine."

"She's your friend, not mine," Becky said.

Heather snorted, sitting where Mark had just left. "If you want to start a fight, keep reminding me of that."

"Heather's loyal to me, and as long as I'm loyal to you, so is she."

Becky continued to stare at Heather, doubt evident in her gaze. Then she turned to me. "You pulled me down here. What's going on?"

"Something's wrong."

"I know. What's up?"

"No." I shook my head, sitting on the couch next to Heather. "With you and Adam. What's going on?"

Becky seemed to shrink as she sat on the couch across from us. "You noticed that, huh?" She rubbed her hands together, sticking them between her knees. "I thought I'd perfected the plastic look."

Heather laughed. "The fact that I know exactly what you mean makes me think Sam's not all that crazy for liking you again."

Becky looked up, warily, and shrugged. "Plastic and shiny. It's the fake look we rich people offer, isn't it?"

Heather lifted a shoulder. "It's the equivalent to the tough, I-don't-give-a-fuck look we not-rich people have."

A cloud came over Becky's features. "Adam might not be able to go to law school. We might have to stay here after we graduate. He's going to have to take over his dad's business."

This.

This was the moment—I could feel it—what Mason had been searching for since James had sicced him on Adam. I tried to quell my adrenaline.

I leaned forward, keeping my voice casual and steady, "What do you mean?"

Heather sent me a look.

Becky shook her head. "It's so messed up. I don't even know what to say." She looked at the ceiling. "It's nothing Adam's done. It's what's being done to him. His dad's fucked up in a major way."

Heather leaned forward slowly. She softened her voice. "What's he doing?"

"He's breaking the law."

"How?"

"He broke down and told Adam this morning. It's all complicated, but from what I understood, when he has to get permits to develop land somewhere, he bribes whoever gives him the permits. He found a copy of the emails on a computer somewhere. He doesn't know who made the copy, but he knows it's out there and everything could blow up in our faces. He'd go to jail."

"Bullshit." Heather leaned back. "Rich people pay fines. Poor people go to jail. That's a fact."

"Not with this." Becky suddenly looked so tired, like a slight wind could knock her over. "It's been going on for years, and there's enough to worry about that even I'm in the know." She shook her head, getting up and beginning to pace the room. "You guys can't say anything. I mean it. Adam would break off the engagement if he knew I was telling you guys this. No one can know."

"Yeah, of course." I nodded.

Becky sighed. "I mean, in the long run, it's not that bad. Adam could take over the company and run it until he finds someone else to step in for him."

"What would he do then?" Heather asked.

"He'd go to law school as he's planning. And then he'd go into politics after that. This would just be a speed bump along the way."

Heather shared a look with me. It sounded like a doable plan, but anything could be planned out on paper. Only sometimes life didn't turn out that way. I stood up and went over to Becky, pulling her in for a hug. Then I lied to her because that was what she wanted to hear at the moment.

"Everything will be fine."

She hugged me back, and as those words left me, she sagged in relief.

"Thank you, Sam."

The door to the basement opened, and Malinda called down, "Everyone's starting to arrive. Becky, are you down there?"

She took a deep breath as she pulled away from me.

"I'm here." Smoothing her dress and fluffing her hair, she flashed Heather and me a smile. "Thank you, guys." She squeezed my hand. "I mean it. I'm coming, Malinda!"

Heather stood next to me, watching her go up the stairs.

"Samantha? Heather?" Malinda called back down.

Heather asked softly, "Why do you look like you just killed her puppy?"

"Do you really want to know?" I kept my voice low so Malinda couldn't hear.

"Do you have to ask?"

"Girls?"

"I know who has the copy of those emails."

"Who?" Heather stopped me.

Malinda watched us, a slight frown marring her face. "Just come up when you're ready." She moved back, shutting the door.

"Sam," Heather prompted me. "Who has that copy?"

"Mason."

I went upstairs. He just might not realize what he had a copy of.

Heather was right behind me, and she took my arm and pulled me out to the back porch. "Are you sure you want to do this?"

I could see through the window. Becky's smile was more relaxed. She had a fresh glow to her, and she tipped her head up so Adam could drop a light kiss on her lips. She looked happy, and I was going to be the reason it was taken away.

I nodded. "It's her or Mason. I'll always pick Mason." I studied her. "Are you with me?"

She gave me a look. "You know I am. I just wanted to make sure you knew what you were doing. You recently decided to become friends with her again, and now you're going to do something I know you loathe."

"I know. I'm going to stab her in the back."

And with those words, I went back inside. Heather was right behind me. There was no confusion. I knew exactly what I'd just become, and so did she.

I was the bad guy now.

# CHAPTER THIRTY-FOUR

I was sitting on the back porch at Helen's house when the doors slid open behind me. I didn't look up from my position on one of the couches. I continued surveying the pool, pool house, and the second lower deck and veranda. None of it seemed impressive or surprising anymore to me. It was like the other mansions, and I couldn't remember the day when I *had* been impressed.

I was so far from that person now.

"Logan said you were out here."

Mason sat next to me. He lifted my legs and placed them in his lap, starting to knead my calves. "You okay?"

"I was just thinking about the beginning."

"That seems to be the theme this summer."

I looked over and felt my breath catch. The moonlight shone on him, casting him in a romantic, hazy glow. He was gorgeous.

"Sam?"

I gave him a quick half-grin. "What do you mean by that?"

"About the theme?"

"Yeah."

He shrugged. "Just that you're friends with Becky Sallaway again. Adam Quinn is in our lives. We're dealing with my dad and your mom. I know a lot has changed, but in some ways, nothing's changed."

"Well, I have."

He quieted. I knew he was waiting for me to say what I'd come out here to get the nerve to tell him. I laughed, and winced at how bitter it sounded.

"I have to tell you something, and I'm questioning whether I really want to. And then I'm questioning why I'm even questioning it in the first place."

"Sam."

I calmed, hearing his voice grow stronger, more authoritative. "Whatever it is, nothing is your fault. You don't have to worry about anything."

That wasn't true, but I said, "You know that illegal thing you're supposed to get on Steven Quinn?"

Mason's eyes sharpened, and I continued. After I told him what Becky had said earlier, he didn't comment for a moment.

"They know someone has a copy?" he finally asked.

"That's what she said."

"Okay."

"That's it? Just 'okay'? That's all you're going to say?"

"I don't want to put you in the middle any more. I'll handle it from here."

"Meaning you'll give the copy to your dad and tell him what transactions to look for?"

"Yeah." He nodded. "After I make a second copy for myself. I don't trust my dad either."

"So this might not even come out on us?"

He shook his head. "I don't know. It could, but more than likely my dad will use it as leverage to have Steven step out of some decisions. It may never come out."

"Isn't that illegal?"

A ghost of a smile teased across Mason's face. He continued rubbing up and down my leg. "Doing something illegal isn't exactly outside our wheelhouse."

I flushed, leaning back against the cushions. "I know. I just... I'm feeling bad. That's all."

"Sam."

I lifted my head to meet his gaze. His eyes smoldered, and instantly I felt a fluttering in my chest. My body warmed.

"Are you sure this is about what Steven Quinn is doing? Or is this about something else?"

My lips parted. My throat suddenly dried up. "What do you mean?"

"You know what I mean."

"About me being disloyal to Becky?"

"About whatever had you running for almost five hours the other day."

The fluttering picked up its pace. My heart was flying around like a damned rocket trying to take off inside of me.

I looked away, shrinking in my seat. "I can't talk about that." I could hear Heather as clearly as if she were out there with us. *Tell him, Samantha! Tell him!* I ignored her voice. "It was nothing anyway. It's stupid."

He stopped rubbing and cupped the underside of my leg. I looked over at him in reflex, and he leaned forward, making sure I couldn't look away.

"Anything you're scared to talk about is the opposite of nothing or stupid. And whatever it is, you don't have to worry. Unless you cheated. Then you need to worry."

I grinned, kicking him lightly with my foot. "You'd have to worry about that, too."

He caught my foot and held it. "So it's not that you were unfaithful."

"What?"

"You didn't flinch when I said that. I know that's not the issue." He leaned his head back, resting it against the side of the house behind us, still watching me intently. "What it is, Sam? Please tell me."

My heart stilled. This man—he'd been a boy, but I didn't think he'd ever been a child. He was already a man when I met him. Powerful. Alpha. A mastermind. Beautiful. His presence captivated so many, but right now he was under my control.

I leaned forward, though he still had my foot, and touched the side of his face. "I don't think I could love you any more than I do right now," I whispered.

His hand rested over mine. "You're not going to tell me?"

"Yes," I breathed out. "I will, but not now. When I'm ready."

"You have to tell me."

"I will. I promise."

My fear was real, but when Mason stood and lifted me with him, I knew I'd been granted time. I wound my arms and legs around him, kissing him as he carried me through the house to our bedroom.

It was a few hours later when he left the bed. I rolled over, able to see his silhouette as he dressed in the darkness. I didn't ask where he was going. I already knew.

He came over, dropping a kiss to my forehead. "I love you." His hand rested against the side of my face.

My hand covered his. "Just be safe."

"Always." He left, and a moment later, I heard Logan and Nate's voices outside. Headlights came on, and I heard the sounds of a vehicle leaving the driveway.

Whatever was going to happen had been set in motion.

# CHAPTER THIRTY-FIVE
## MASON

My dad hadn't wanted the meeting at his house, where Analise was, and that had been fine with us. We'd met at his office instead. I'd handed over the copy of the files I made for him, and he'd said he'd take care of the rest. I hadn't asked what would go down or how he'd use it. I knew he would, and I also knew James Kade had questionable connections. Probably better not to know.

With the meeting over, Logan, Nate, and I traipsed back outside, all quiet. I glanced at Logan as he bypassed me for the front passenger seat. We'd learned a year ago how far on the other side of the law our father could travel. He'd helped keep a crime boss off our backs. But this—something was nagging me.

I reached for the door handle on the Escalade and was about to open it when someone stepped out of the shadows.

"I can see I didn't do my job very well."

Caldron and a bunch of his guys surrounded us.

I stepped away from the door. "Excuse me?"

He held a bat in his hands and gestured with it to the office building. "That was you taking that copy of Quinn's files to your dad, right?"

"What makes you think that?"

These guys were here to stop us. I don't know how Caldron knew, what business it was of his, but if they were going to stand against us, I knew my dad wasn't safe either. I caught Logan's gaze and jerked my head toward the building. He nodded and began easing his way backward. He'd get James to safety—or try.

"No." Caldron pointed at some of his buddies. "Block him. We don't want the rich daddy dearest to get away scot-free, not after we wipe the floor with his sons."

"This is getting old." Nate growled, stepping toward some of the guys.

I did a quick count and stopped after I hit more than twelve.

"You came out in full force, Caldron." I turned back to him. He was the leader. He had all the answers. "Why don't you show some decency and say why?"

"Yeah." Logan stepped back toward us, but four guys hurried around to block him from getting to us. "How do you know about any of this? What do you know about Quinn? And why the fuck are you here?"

"That's right. Your rich prick of a father was supposed to 'take care of me,' wasn't he? Well, he did. He transferred me out to another job location. I was there last month when suddenly I got a call saying I was fired."

Logan and I shared a look. James wouldn't fire Caldron. There'd be no point.

He saw the look. "Oh yeah. That right there says I'm right. I got 'handled' just like I'm here to 'handle' you guys."

"Who fired you?"

Caldron looked at me, his arms folding over his chest. The bat hung down at his side. "The person who hired me to go after your asses." He pointed the bat at everyone around him. "That's what we're doing here—what I was hired to do in the first place."

"And that was?" I was getting tired of his chatter. A deep anger began to boil inside of me.

"Yeah." Logan shoved at the guy closest to him. "Get to the fucking point."

Caldron smirked, and I smirked back, but I glanced over at Nate. All the attention had been focused on us. Even the guys who were "watching" Nate hadn't been watching him. I caught a quick flash of light from his phone. He stashed it back in his pocket and nodded to me.

He'd called the cops.

It was the old system we had in place for times like this: Logan and I drew everyone's attention, and Nate called for backup. Sadly, our backup had to be actual law enforcement this time. These guys weren't just here to hurt us. They were here for blood.

We needed to hold them off long enough, or we were dead.

Logan rolled his shoulders and gave a small dip of his head. He was ready.

I squared off against Caldron. I wanted to fight, but I wanted answers, too. "Who really hired you? You're not after us because of Budd, are you?"

Caldron started laughing, tipping his head back like a hyena. "No, no. You guys did me a favor with him. Since he's out, I'm the guy in charge. With him gone, I'm on top." A serious look settled in his eyes, and I knew I was looking into a murderer's gaze. "Quinn hired me the same day he and your daddy had a meeting. He knew I was already working for your dad. We were supposed to do the landscaping for that hotel they're opening. Quinn thought I could keep an eye on you, but your dad messed that up. He postponed the landscaping. We don't start until this next week, now that everything's almost done with the hotel. But it doesn't matter, because this is the real job he hired me for. I was supposed to keep you from getting too close to his son."

"To Adam?" That was why he kept trying to attack us. "That's why you went after Sam so much?"

Caldron nodded, swinging the bat like he was warming up for batting practice. "Yep. She's your weakness. Keep going after her and you wouldn't be able to concentrate on whatever your daddy put you up to. You'd be too focused on keeping your girl safe."

He paused a moment. "My guess is your dad stuck you with little Quinn to watch him, right?"

I didn't offer a response, and he shrugged.

"Doesn't matter if you don't confirm it. I know it's true, just like I know I got a call an hour ago to be on the lookout if you made a move. I'm thinking you coming to your dad's office at midnight was the move. Am I right? I know I am. I also know there was a breach in security at some offsite location Quinn uses. I know your girlfriend had a cozy chat with Quinn Jr.'s fiancée, and that same fiancée broke down crying to Quinn Jr. earlier this afternoon. Now," he spread his arms, "I have no clue what you made a copy of, but that's what I was told to get from you. Since we got here too late and it looks like you've already delivered it, we're going to have to do this the hard way."

"You mean the bloody way."

"Whichever way you want. Either your daddy brings it out to save your asses, or we step over your bodies to get it. It's up to you."

I heard sirens in the distance, but they were almost coming too soon. I wanted this guy's blood on the ground. I wanted it all over, and I wanted to be the one who broke him in half. We'd had enough. I didn't need to hear any more to understand what had gone down.

"I would've thought you'd get tired of this, Caldron."

"What do you mean?" His eyes twitched, just briefly.

"This. You. Me. Fighting." I grinned, knowing it didn't reach my eyes. "You losing."

He swallowed, his Adam's apple bobbing up and down. "That's what you think is going to happen?"

Logan and Nate shifted. They were ready to fight.

I stepped away from the Escalade. "I know that's what's going to happen. I always beat you, Caldron. I always will; no matter how many guys you bring with you."

He moved back, as did his guys. It was like I had an invisible force protecting me. But if I'd heard the sirens, they must've, too.

"What?" I asked. "You know you can't finish this fight before those cops show up?"

"Who says they're coming here?" He tossed the bat up, catching it like he was going to swing at a baseball. He held it above his head.

I narrowed my eyes. "What are you talking about?"

"They have to prioritize their calls," he said. "It's a small police department. I'd think a burning nursing home would take priority over a text about brawling from someone's cell phone." He looked right at Nate. "I saw that, you know."

"You set the nursing home on fire?" Nate paled slightly.

"They'll get everyone out, I'm sure." Caldron didn't sound like he cared. "But that leaves us to our merry selves." He dropped the bat and caught it again, right around the handle. He hefted it back up. "How about we get this show on the road?"

And he swung.

I blacked out after that.

The bat swung down. I saw my hand catching it, saw Caldron on the ground. His face was bleeding. His eyes were swollen shut. There were hands at my shoulders, and I was swinging.

Time skipped.

Two guys were on me. I ducked down, ramming my shoulder into one of them. Someone's arm cracked, and he screamed in pain as it bent at an indecent angle.

More lapses in time.

Nate was on the ground. Three guys kicked him.

I pulled one away, slamming him into the pavement.

Time jumped again.

Logan threw a punch, and a guy's head snapped backward from the blow. Another guy swung a bat, about to hit Logan in the back of the head—another blackout. I came to again, and that same guy was unconscious.

I was holding his bat.

More blackness.

"Mason." I heard Logan's voice in the distance.

There was a buzzing sound. I looked around. What was that?

"Mason." Suddenly, the buzzing sound vanished, and Logan was right there. His voice was too loud, and he was clawing at my hands. "Mason, stop!" He sounded panicked. My brother never panicked. He kept pulling at my hands, and I looked—they were wrapped around a guy's throat.

Logan reared back and rammed his shoulder into me. He knocked me backward, but I'd let go of the throat already.

What had I...?

I didn't want to know.

I shook my head. There was a cloud there, a haze settling over everything. I didn't feel like myself, and I surveyed the parking lot and felt sick.

There were bodies everywhere.

Nate sat on the ground, his face covered in blood and only one eye open. He was holding his shirt to his head. The end was soaked in blood.

I looked for Logan. He was right in front of me, and he was bleeding all over, too. He fell into me, and he began to slip to the ground, but I caught him. Wrapping an arm around his back, I eased him down and sat next to him.

My hands were already bruising. They were covered in blood, but there was blood everywhere. Even the Escalade had blood on it.

"Logan." My voice was hoarse. "What did we do?"

He grunted from pain as he tried to stretch a leg out. "We fought. That's what we did."

The sound of someone walking over broken glass came from behind us. I didn't look. My body was beginning to scream in agony. Everything hurt.

James stepped in front of us, taking everything in. He sucked in a breath. "What happened?"

I wasn't sure. I kept quiet.

Logan glanced to me, then said, "Quinn knew you sicced Mason on his son. He sicced Caldron on us. We were supposed to be distracted." He had to stop to spit out blood. "He failed at his job." He looked up at our dad, his face misshapen and bruised. "You still have that copy, right? We didn't do all of this for nothing."

James held up the flash drive. "It's here." At that moment, a squad car lit up the parking lot in red and blue. "I was going to use it as leverage against him, get him to back down, but it looks like it's going to the district attorney instead."

Two cops got out and stopped a few feet from their car. They looked all around, and one slowly raised his hand to his radio. He called for an ambulance as James said, "Let me do all the talking. If you say anything, it's to ask for your lawyer. You got it?"

He looked down at us to make sure.

We nodded, and he strode forward, meeting the policemen halfway.

# CHAPTER THIRTY-SIX

## SAMANTHA

James called me and explained the situation, and when I parked in the police station's parking lot a little after three in the morning, Becky was the first person I saw. She hurried toward me, an angry set to her chin, and I was barely able to shut my car door before she was on me.

"You were supposed to keep quiet about what I told you," she hissed in my face, her hands balled into fists. She held them up like she wanted to hit me, but she only pressed one into my shoulder. She pulled her punch, if it'd been intended as one. "You weren't supposed to tell, Sam!"

"What'd you think I'd do? I had to choose between Adam and Mason." The choice was obvious.

She hung her head, her hands dropping to her sides. "The choice was between *me* and Mason. I trusted you."

"I'm sorry." And I was. "But this wasn't between you and me. It was between them." It was ultimately between James Kade and Steven Quinn. "We just got in the middle."

She sighed as a white SUV pulled in and parked next to her car. Adam got out. If Becky had been mad, Adam was furious. His jaw was clenched and a vein popped out along his neck. He started for us.

His eyes were cold as he turned to Becky. "I told you not to come here."

She stood a little taller. "I wanted to be here for you."

He turned to look at me again. "You wanted to yell at Sam."

"So? You would, too."

He shook his head. "I'm not the one she betrayed."

"If it's a choice between Mason and someone else, you know my decision." He always had.

"Yeah," he spoke quietly. "I'm well aware."

"Sam!"

Heather came out of the station, shielding her face with her arm against a sudden gust of wind.

"What are you doing here?" I'd called her, but... "How'd you get here so fast?"

"I already knew what went down before you called. Channing has a police scanner. We were already on the way."

She hadn't told me that on the phone. She flashed me an apologetic smile. "I figured it was just easier to explain when you got here."

I surged forward. "Are they okay?"

"James is the only one here."

"What?"

"They arrested my dad," Adam said. "They're bringing him in."

Two squad cars pulled into the lot and stopped right before the front door. But instead of seeing Steven Quinn in handcuffs, we watched as Nate and Logan were helped out of one squad car. Their hands were cuffed in front of them, and I gasped, reeling backward.

Their faces were covered in bandages, not to mention bruises on every bit of exposed skin, and their knuckles were scraped raw. They'd been fighting. A lot.

Heather stepped close and steadied me with a hand on my arm. "That's what I was coming out here to tell you. Everyone else went to the hospital first. All of Caldron's guys were admitted. Mason, Logan, and Nate—they were hurt, but they kicked ass."

Mason...

I searched for him, but couldn't find him. If Logan and Nate looked like this—the back door to the first squad car opened, and I stopped thinking after that.

A sob hitched in my throat. I couldn't even let that out.

Mason stepped out with his hands cuffed in front of him.

I couldn't breathe.

I couldn't do anything.

He had fewer bandages on his face, but one side was a giant bruise. His lip was busted, and I could tell he was in pain. He limped. I must've made a sound because he turned suddenly. His gaze found mine, though one of his eyes was covered by tape.

He stepped toward me, my name on his lips, but the cop yanked him back.

"Stop!" I ran to them.

Two cops moved to intercept me, but Heather and someone else stopped me before I could get to them. Heather shot a hand out to stop the police from coming closer.

"She's fine. We got her." She leaned close and whispered to me, "Chill or they might arrest you for making a scene."

I could only watch as they led Mason inside. Then I looked to see who else had stepped in to help me.

Becky. She released me, her eyes darting away. "No one else needs to get hurt…or arrested."

I reached out, saying a soft *thank you* before Heather started forward, and I went with her. I looked back over my shoulder. Becky watched us go, and I mouthed again to her, "Thank you."

She nodded, offering a faint smile.

Heather held my arm close to her. "We'll sing the friendship song with her later. Come on. We have to start harassing for bail."

But in the end, that was taken care of.

James Kade had called in an army of lawyers. They walked in wearing their three-piece suits like they were secret service—except with briefcases. Once they showed up, it wasn't long before Nate, Logan, and Mason were released.

I leaped into Mason's arms as he came out, rubbing at his wrists. He caught me, tucking his head into my shoulder and neck.

"This is worth the pain," he said.

I'd forgotten, and tried to pull away.

He only tightened his hug, holding me another moment longer. "God, Sam." He lifted his head. A raw and tender look appeared in his eyes, and he traced my face with his finger. "Caldron could've really hurt you."

Logan murmured, "He was more dangerous than we thought."

Mason didn't let me go, and Logan nudged him. "Buddy, I know we were in the clinker, but it's not like you had to hide some soap in your ass cheeks. Nate and I were there the whole time, and it was just a couple hours."

Mason stiffened and pulled back to glare. "Buddy?"

"It's the joint. I'm already a hardened criminal."

Mason released me, but his hand still held one of mine. "You've been arrested before, and excuse me for hugging my girlfriend when I realized how Caldron could've really hurt her."

Logan stepped in front of him, shouldering him out of the way. He pulled me in for a hug. "It's my turn."

"You have your own girlfriend."

"Who went back to see her dad. Remember?" Logan squeezed me. "Besides," he added as he let go, "Sam's going to officially be my stepsister after next week."

That was right. The big wedding was next Saturday. I didn't have the energy to deal with the tension that clung to me anytime the wedding was mentioned. Mason and Logan had been discreet in going to get their tuxedos fitted. Beyond that, I didn't know anything about the wedding. Malinda was helping, but I didn't live with her and my father anymore. I didn't have to see any of the decorations or preparations she might've been doing at her house.

Heather and Channing came over, his hand resting at the small of her back.

"What's going to happen after this?" Heather asked.

Nate and Logan shut their mouths and looked at Mason.

I felt tension flood him, though he showed none of it. "We're in the clear as long as those guys are okay."

"What guys?" Heather looked around the station. "Everyone's here."

We all looked over as Adam and Becky entered the station. Behind them two police officers brought in Steven Quinn. His hands were in front of him with a sweater laid over them. It didn't matter if we didn't see the handcuffs. We knew they were there.

"Ah…" Logan cleared his throat. "Mason means Caldron and all his goons."

"But Mason doesn't have to worry about that." Nate shot him a meaningful look.

Mason let out a silent sigh. I could feel the release from his chest. "You're not doing that."

Nate shook his head. "I don't care. I'll do it before you can."

"Nate—"

"Stop it, Mason. I mean it. You have football yet."

"What's happening?" I asked them.

Nate and Mason fell silent. Logan said, "We'll tell you later."

"Nothing's going to happen—" Mason started.

Nate cut him off again. "You're right because there's no way in hell I'm letting my best friend throw his life away because he was protecting himself and his loved ones. It will be self-defense. My parents are movie directors. They have good connections. If it goes to a trial, I won't get convicted. You know that."

"Nate—"

"For the last goddamn time," Nate snapped. "Shut up."

I was putting the pieces together.

Mason said *if* those guys were okay, so if they weren't… I looked up at Mason and horror struck me deep in the chest. If one of them died, or even if they had serious damage, he would be arrested, again. He would be charged. There could be a trial.

Feeling like I was in water, like an invisible force had slowed my movements, I looked at Nate.

He would take the fall. That was what he meant.

My lips parted. I felt a gasp, though no sound came from me, and I reached back down to find Mason's hand. I squeezed. I knew he was in pain. I knew I should loosen my grip, but I couldn't. I felt like I'd almost just lost him. And now, if that happened, I could lose him all over again.

He would never let Nate take the fall.

I looked at Logan to find him watching me. He knew what I was thinking, and I could tell he knew it, too. I looked again at Nate and saw the same look there. He knew it as well. No amount of convincing would change Mason's mind.

I wasn't waking up from a nightmare.

It was only beginning.

# CHAPTER THIRTY-SEVEN

When we got home, James followed us into the house, but he only repeated what he'd said at the station: Don't say anything. That was the bottom line, and judging from the exhaustion and pain on Mason, Logan, and Nate's faces, no one was going to argue with him.

Matteo had been sitting in the living room when we all went inside, but he waited until James left before standing up.

"Uh." He folded his arms over his chest, his biceps and chest muscles bulging a little. Glancing around, he seemed unsure. "Do you guys need anything?" He turned to me. "Bandages? Antibiotic cream? Are you stocked with all that stuff?"

Mason's hand came to rest on the small of my back. "I think we're good on everything. Thanks, though, Teo."

He nodded. "Yeah. Just let me know. If you need me to run and grab something, I can do that, too."

I fought against leaning back into Mason's hand. I wanted to. I wanted to sink into his warmth and reassure myself he was okay. I didn't. I didn't know the extent of his injuries, and I was grateful when Nate and Logan murmured they were going to bed.

Logan paused on his way to his bedroom. "I'm going to call Taylor."

I rested a hand on his arm. "That's a good idea." She left a week earlier to spend some time with her dad and her friends. "She'll want to know you're okay."

"Yeah." He sighed.

Matteo lingered as everyone dispersed. Even Mason went to our room, but I held back.

Matteo's shoulders fell. "I don't know what to do."

He looked lost, like a three year old whose mother was out of sight.

I knew that look. I'd seen it on others who'd thought they were in the circle and then realized they weren't.

I patted his shoulder. "Just be a good friend. That's it."

"I didn't—I know the three of them are tight, but I could've helped. They didn't even give me the option, you know?"

"You're a good guy. That's how Mason views you. He doesn't want to make you not good."

"That's what he thinks? Because it feels a whole lot like I'm not good enough."

I shook my head. "No. That's not it at all. Mason wouldn't let you stay here. He wouldn't have even called you if he thought that. He doesn't want to put you in a position where your future could be affected."

He nodded, his head hanging. "I get it, but I wouldn't mind. I know I joke that Logan's my soul brotha connection, but Mason's the brother to me, too. I love the guy."

"I know. He feels the same."

"Just let him know that if he needs anything—and I mean it, anything—I'm here for him. There's not a lot I wouldn't do for you guys."

"He knows."

He nodded again, and I left him there, looking defeated.

I found Mason in the bathroom, stripped to the waist as he stared in the mirror. I had to stop in the doorway once I got a good look at him. Reaching for the doorframe, I steadied myself.

His entire chest and stomach were covered in bruises. There were cuts and gashes all over. Blood had seeped through some of the bandages the hospital put on him, and I couldn't hold back a small whimper.

"I did worse than this."

I took his hand. "I know."

He was trying to reassure me, but as I led him into the shower, I knew what I could see wasn't the real damage. I put the showerhead on a softer setting so the water wouldn't pound down on him, and as he stood in the middle of the shower, I began removing his dressings. Once he was naked in front of me, I couldn't help myself. Softly, I ran my hands over every inch of him and kissed all of his cuts, everywhere he'd been hit or where his skin was torn. I wanted him to know I loved every inch of him, and when I was done, I looked up.

His gaze was dark, but there was pain in his eyes.

He was hurting. I touched the side of his face and whispered, "What you did was to protect us. You protected Logan. You protected Nate. You protected yourself, and you were protecting me, too." He leaned down enough that I could rest my forehead against his. "If anything had happened to you. Anything…" I closed my eyes, drawing in a shuddering breath.

I couldn't even—

I couldn't think about that.

My God.

I opened my eyes and stared right into his. "If anything had happened to you, you know how devastated I would be. You were protecting me, too."

"I could've killed someone."

He might have.

I shook my head. "You didn't, and you won't. Those guys will wake up. You were only protecting us. That's it."

"Sam." His chest rose as he drew in a ragged breath. His forehead rested a little bit heavier on me. "If you'd been there…"

A lump formed in the back of my throat.

I swallowed it. He couldn't think like that, and neither could I.

My hand trailed down his arm until it found his fingers, and I laced our hands together. "Everything will be fine. Everything will be fine."

I was lying to him. Everything might not be fine, but I had to believe it, and I had to make him believe it. There would be other enemies. There would be other times when Mason might have to fight, but he'd risen above the odds. There were so many against him and Nate, and Logan. Too many.

I moved closer, folding my body gently to his. As his arms wrapped around me, I found myself saying, "They might've killed you." My lips touched his chest. The water came down over both of us, and some of it hit my lips. I barely noticed. "The cop said sixteen guys came to attack you three. Sixteen to three. You defended yourself. That's all you did." I pulled back to hold his gaze again. I felt him searching. He needed to believe what I was saying. "Sixteen to three, Mason. No judge will convict you on those odds."

He nodded, closing his eyes.

"Everything will be fine."

Maybe I was lying to myself now.

# CHAPTER THIRTY-EIGHT

## SIX DAYS LATER

"I didn't expect to see you here, Sam."

I looked over at Nate. I knew what he meant. Here I was in the one place I'd been hoping to avoid all summer: Analise and James' wedding. More specifically, I was waiting in the back of the church for their rehearsal and dinner.

I snorted, moving down the pew so he could sit next to me. "Trust me. I came under protest."

He just grinned and patted my leg. The truth was, he probably understood why I was here. It wasn't about Analise or James, or even their sure to be wedded non-bliss, but about Mason. Since the last attack and his arrest, I hadn't left his side. I'd even quit the carnival. He never pushed to know why; maybe because he knew I wouldn't give him the real answer. But it was because I had to be at his side.

If anything happened, I would be there.

If one of those guys died.

If one of them slipped into a coma.

If one of them brought a lawsuit.

I was going to be at his side. I wouldn't be able to do much, I knew that, but I'd be there. I liked to think that would mean something.

So far, the guys had been recovering. They'd all woken, and most had been released from the hospital. The district attorney said they'd have a hard case since all those guys had gone to that parking lot with the purpose of assault. Mason, Logan, and Nate had been defending themselves.

I was also waiting for the day the incident was picked up and reported by media. Mason's name was big. The fact that it hadn't surfaced yet was miraculous. But when that day did come, I'd be there for that, too.

So even though I cringed every two seconds, I was here in the church, and I was watching as the woman who gave birth to me rehearsed how to marry the father who'd helped bring my soulmate to life. It was a whole clusterfuck, but I was here regardless.

"What are you doing here?" I asked Nate. He wasn't a groomsman.

He pointed at Logan, who was making a crude gesture at us with his hands and tongue. "Our favorite douchebag told me to come. Said there'd be good food and free booze at the dinner."

I paled. "We have to stay for the dinner?"

Nate grinned. "Logan said we did, but maybe you and Mason can slip out early." He looked around. "Is Taylor coming?"

"She'll be here tomorrow for the wedding."

She'd better be.

"Matteo took off, right?"

I nodded. "He starts training next week. Everything's going to be okay, so he headed home to see his family for a few days."

"He's a good friend to Mason."

"To you, too."

Nate smiled. "Same for you." He nodded toward the front of the church. "And Logan. I know Mason wants to protect him, but Matteo was there for us. He's kind of become family in a way."

He gave me a meaningful look, and I knew what he meant. Matteo had made it known that he wanted to be brought into the fold, but he wasn't out of the fold, even if he felt that way. I placed my hands together on my lap, looking up at Mason's back as he and Logan joked, standing to their father's right.

"Mason wants to protect him."

"Yeah." Nate shifted, lounging back against the pew and stretching his legs out. "I know what you mean, but it sucks being on the outside."

I glanced at him.

He didn't look at me, but he spoke as if feeling my gaze. "It was hard when I first came back in high school. Mason had been my best friend. I came back, and you and Logan had replaced me. It took me a long time to get back in." The lines around his mouth strained. "I messed up a few times, but I'm in again. I won't do anything to mess that up. I'm just saying, I feel for Matteo."

There was nothing I could say. I knew how close Mason and Logan were, but I wasn't around when it'd been Nate and Mason, not Logan and Mason. And he was right, I remembered the times when Nate hadn't seemed to like me, when he'd looked at me like I was the enemy. But I knew he didn't mean it. He came back around. He'd always come back. He loved Mason, just like the rest of us.

I nudged him with my shoulder. "Don't be leaving us when you find your girl, okay?"

I felt his surprise. "What do you mean?"

I shrugged. "Mason and me. Heather and Channing. Logan and Taylor. Even Becky and Adam. Everyone's found their person. Don't leave us when you find yours. Deal?"

There was a hint of a grin on his face. "Deal." Then he added, "Should we pinkie promise like Logan made me do one time?"

"Logan made you pinkie promise something?"

He nodded. "I can't tell you what. I made a promise." He was so solemn.

I cracked a grin. "I understand. I won't push you."

"So are we done then?"

Logan's voice drew our attention to the front of the church, and the pastor turned to him. "Yes, I believe so. We've already had you guys practice coming in once. Everything should be set." He gestured to Analise and James. "If you two could stay behind, we'll get the marriage certificate signed tonight."

Mason and Logan came down the side aisle toward us just as a man walked inside. He wore a three-piece suit and had slicked back hair, cologne that threatened to suffocate me, and a whole greasy vibe to him.

He boomed out, "James!"

James looked back and grinned. "Peter." A transformation took place. Gone was the guy trying to make sense of the pastor's instructions, the guy who'd been holding Analise's hand a moment earlier, and even the loving guy who'd kept rubbing her back before they held hands. Instead, a businessman took his place. I felt transported into a conference room.

Mason and Logan paused when they saw the guy, then slowly resumed their trek to us. Logan hopped into the pew in front of us, and Mason went to the back, resting his hands behind my shoulders. If I tipped my head back, I could look right up at him.

Nate half-turned to face Mason and me, but he was also able to see Logan. "Who's that guy? Do you know?" he asked.

Logan spared the guy a second look, disgust coming to his face. "It's the mayor," he sneered.

"The mayor?" Nate looked to Mason.

Mason watched the mayor shake James' hand, then be introduced to Analise. "That's the one thing our dad wanted," he said. "And he came out on top." He shot Logan a look, talking to the rest of us. "He wanted back in."

"He got back in," Logan confirmed. "Sure is helpful that Steven Quinn's been removed from his CEO position."

Nate asked. "Does that mean Adam took his place?"

Mason shrugged, folding his arms over his chest. "The hotel's opening was postponed. Adam and I are off the project, so I don't know. I'd assume, unless someone else moved in." He touched the back of my shoulder. "Come on. We don't have to stick around for the dinner."

I stood.

Nate did as well. "I thought that was the whole reason you called me here," he said to Logan, who smirked.

"Yeah, it's all set up," Logan assured him. "We're going to stop there on the way home."

We headed toward the doors.

Logan and Nate went out first. Mason held the door for me and was waiting outside when I heard my name called.

I looked back. Maybe I'd expected my mother, and when I saw she wasn't standing there, I felt a pang of disappointment. I frowned, shoving that away. I looked out to the parking lot and saw Becky. She was standing to the side, her hands twisted together in front of her. She eyed Logan and Nate, who had paused on the sidewalk as they waited for us.

Mason let go of the door behind me, and her gaze jumped to his face. Her mouth opened in a silent gasp. Most of his bruising had faded, but I understood. It was still shocking. She looked back to Logan and Nate. I could only imagine how all three of them looked to someone else.

"Becky?"

She turned to me. "Yeah. Um…" She bit her lip. "Can we talk?"

"Sure."

Logan stepped toward us, a dark look coming over him.

Becky took a step back.

"Uh…" I gestured to a bench in front of the church. "We can talk over there."

She seemed relieved until Logan called her name. "Hey, Sallaway."

She tensed, stiffening as she turned around. "Yeah?"

"Your fiancé. Is he the new CEO of his dad's company?"

Her eyebrows pinched together, and she glanced quickly to me before nodding. "Yeah. He is."

"So the two of you have to stick around here? He's not going to law school yet?"

"Uh. Yeah. I mean, he is, but not right away."

"When?"

I frowned. Why did Logan want to know?

"I don't know. I think he'll wait a year."

"He's still going to graduate this year, right? So he'll be going in three years?"

"I guess." She shook her head. "Why?"

He ignored her. "What school is he going to?"

"He got into Harvard Law."

"Good." Logan clipped his head in a nod.

"Why?" she asked again.

A cold look came over his face. "Because where he goes, I'm going. That fuck sent Caldron after my brother and Sam. I'm going to make his life miserable from here on out."

Her mouth fell open and stayed that way. She didn't seem capable of closing it.

Nate shot Mason a look, but Mason only shook his head. Adam Quinn hadn't sent Caldron after us. That was his father, and Logan knew that. Whatever he was saying, he had a reason.

Becky looked at me imploringly, but she wouldn't see any sympathy from me. "Did you still want to talk to me?" I asked.

"I…" She closed her mouth, swallowing. "Maybe not now." She turned back to her car, took a couple steps, then pivoted back to us. "We're never going to be friends again, are we?"

Remorse swept through me, but I couldn't let that show either. There might've been a fight between the fathers, and I didn't know how things were between Mason and Adam, but it didn't matter. Logan just threw a gauntlet down. Becky would be the messenger for it. Adam would know within the next five minutes that Logan Kade was his enemy now. That meant we all were.

All I could say was, "I think it's best if we're not."

I saw her swallow again. Pure frustration pulled on her features, and she looked down to the ground for a moment. When she looked back up, she just seemed defeated.

"I guess so." She headed to her car and swiped at something by her eye.

I couldn't help but wonder if it'd been a tear.

Once she left the parking lot, I rounded on Logan. "Did you do that on purpose?"

"What?" But there was a guarded mask on his face. He knew exactly what he'd just done.

"You said that to her on purpose because she'll be the one to tell him, and that'll make her have to take his side."

Logan shrugged. "So what?"

"So that means I can't be friends with her," I snapped.

"Like you would've been able to anyway," he shot back. His eyes were heated as they flicked to Mason's before coming back to me. He softened his tone. "I just did what you couldn't. If you tried to be friends with her, you would've betrayed her again eventually. You know it. I just did it so Mason didn't have to. Lines are drawn, Sam. The Quinns are our enemies, no matter who holds that name."

Becky Sallaway would eventually be Becky Quinn.

He was right.

But it still hurt.

# CHAPTER THIRTY-NINE

My mother was getting married today, and I stared at myself in the mirror with no clue what to wear. But it wasn't even the clothes. I had no idea what to feel, which is why I'd been standing here for the last hour.

There was a slight flutter in my chest, but that didn't make sense. Why would I be nervous? There was no reason for that.

A soft knock sounded on my door, and Taylor called from the other side. "Sam? You have a visitor."

I frowned. Who would that be? "Let 'em in."

The door opened, and my stepmother popped her head in first. "Sam? Oh good." She pushed her way inside, shutting the door behind her. She held a garment bag in her arms and hung it up on the closet door. "I wasn't sure if you had a dress for the wedding, so I brought a few over. Unless you do have one picked out?"

"Malinda." I frowned. "What are you doing here?"

"I knew Mason and Logan were probably already at the church to take pictures, and I wasn't sure if you needed a ride or not."

I felt faint as I answered. "I was going to ride with Nate and Taylor."

"That's right. I forgot Logan's girlfriend came back. I didn't realize Nate was going, but of course he'd go. Where you guys go, he goes, too."

There was a small bead of perspiration over her top lip, and she looked flushed.

"Are you okay?" I asked.

"Huh?" Her eyes darted around, and her lip trembled. She had to blink a few times before she could focus on me. "Oh. Yeah. I'm fine."

She patted my arm. "You have nothing to worry about with me, honey. Let's focus on you this morning. Now." She stepped back and scanned me up and down, frowning. "Have you lost weight, Samantha?"

I had, but I'd stopped running as much. I smoothed a hand down my tank top and pajama pants. They were soft, baggy, and heavenly. "I was running a lot earlier this summer." I made sure to hold her gaze as I answered. "I'm fine now." I wanted her to know I was telling the truth. She didn't have to worry about me.

Her hand ran down my arm, resting on my wrist. "I know you are." She pulled me in for a hug. "You are one of the strongest people I know," she murmured, pressing a kiss to my cheek.

I hid a grin. "You brought some dresses for me?"

"Oh, yes!" She snapped back to attention, and her eyes lit up. "Your mother's colors are teal and aqua. Such a pretty palette, and so rarely used if I do say so. Sooo…" She pulled out one of the dresses. "I brought you a teal dress, and I brought you an aqua dress. Your mother called me earlier in the week. She wanted to relay that if you wanted to wear white, you could. Mother and daughter kind of thing, you know. So I brought a white one, too. But you don't have to; not if you don't want to."

My mouth dried.

Analise wanted me to match her? It was a wedding. No one else would be wearing white. It'd only be her and me.

Seeing my indecision, Malinda reached inside her purse. She pulled out a small box. "She also said you could wear this, if you wanted. She has a matching one, and people will know you're not wearing white to disrespect her." She held out a sparkling teal-colored pendant with a dandelion on it. "I don't want to push you, but I also want to give you the option. It's completely up to you, Sam."

I took the pendant and held it up. "She has a matching one?"

"She does." Malinda reached for the necklace around her own neck. She pulled it out, and I saw it was identical to mine, but larger. "She wanted me to wear it, too. It was a gift since I helped her plan the wedding. And again, I'll take mine off if you don't wear yours. I'm with you, whatever you decide."

I...

I had no thought. No reaction.

Then I frowned. Suddenly, I wanted to wear it, but I didn't know why. "Let me see the dress again." I asked hoarsely.

"Oh!" She held it up by the hanger.

It was a simple dress, but it was beautiful. It had small straps that would circle around my arms and attach underneath them. There was a side pocket, and the dress fell to the floor. I shouldn't wear it, but I wanted to.

As if sensing my torn feelings, Malinda said softly, "Would you like to put it on?"

I nodded, and when I did, even I was taken aback by how I looked.

Malinda stepped behind me, resting her chin on one of my shoulders. She smiled, and I saw tears in her eyes. "Amazing. Absolutely amazing."

I couldn't speak, not for a moment. Emotion choked my throat, but I didn't want to identify what kind of emotions they were. I swallowed them down.

"If I wear this, then what?" I asked. "Is this a peace offering to her? Am I saying she can be in my life again?"

"No, sweetheart." She moved my hair to my other shoulder, still smiling almost sadly at me. "It just means you accepted her gift. That's all, and she knows it. The rest is when you decide to go to her. She knows that. She's waiting, for whenever you want."

My eyes fell on that necklace. Malinda had placed it on the bed, and I could see it in the mirror.

I missed my mom.

That was what these emotions were.

I missed her, but I was so goddamn angry at her.

I closed my eyes, feeling the tears there. I didn't want to cry for her.

Malinda kissed my bare shoulder, and whispered, "What are you feeling, honey? What are you thinking?"

Analise had two other women standing up as her bridesmaids. I'd noticed them last night, but I hadn't asked who they were. I couldn't keep the words in today. "Who are those women? The ones standing up for her today."

"They were patients with her at the treatment facility. They helped her through some rough times, and I guess she did the same for them."

"So she has friends? From that place, I mean."

Malinda nodded, holding my gaze in the mirror. "She does. Yes."

That was good.

My mom had friends.

I looked back down to my hands and murmured, "She never did before." And if she did, she'd lost them because she flirted with their husbands, or worse.

"They seem like real friends. Good friends."

"That's good." I looked down again. I didn't want to keep looking at that dandelion.

"Samantha? What's going on? Tell me what you're thinking."

I shook my head. Malinda meant well. Maybe letting myself feel these emotions was smart, but I didn't want to. Not now. There was a mountain of repressed shit, and all of it was beginning to swirl inside of me.

I cleared my throat, pushing the tears aside. "I'll be fine. Give me a moment and I'll be ready."

"I booked a hairstylist. If you come over, you and Taylor could both get your hair done."

"Really?"

She nodded and kissed my shoulder again. "I'll be in the living room. The wedding isn't till this afternoon. You have plenty of time to decide on the dress, so look at the others, too. They're just as gorgeous." She went to the door. "The stylist will be at my house in ten minutes. You and Taylor head over about fifteen after that. She doesn't take long to do my hair."

She slipped through the door, but I called out, "Malinda?"

"Yeah?" She leaned back in.

"Thank you."

I wasn't sure what I was thanking her for, but I knew there was a lot.

"Of course, honey. I love you; you know that."

I nodded. It'd been a long journey, but I didn't fight those words. I embraced them. I clung to them even, the way a real daughter would.

# CHAPTER FORTY

## MASON

"You ready for this?"

Logan sidled up next to me at the front of the church. The pastor had come out, so the music was going to change soon. My dad was to my left, and Logan to my right. All eyes had been on us, but now people began shifting in their seats. Analise was about to come down the aisle.

I grunted. "I just want to get this fucking over with."

He chuckled, folding his hands in front of him. "I hate tuxes. I hate weddings. Only good thing about weddings is the booze." He winked. "And having Taylor here. Have I told you lately how much I love my girlfriend?"

"You're becoming annoying."

"Good." He snorted. "It's payback for all of your and Sam's lovey-dovey shit."

"Lovey-dovey shit?" We weren't known for our public displays of affection.

He shrugged. "You know what I mean. All the sexing you guys do. I remember when we moved into Nate's parents' house. We heard moaning and groaning at all hours of the day." He leaned closer and hissed in a whisper, "Sickening, I tell you. Sickening."

"Didn't stop you from hitting on her every chance you could."

He paused. "She's my stepsister. That's gross, Mason. It's called joking."

I rolled my eyes. "She's your stepsister after today. That was three years ago."

"Was it three years? I thought it was four? Like this wedding—it's taking for-fucking-ever."

James shot us a look. "Shut up. Both of you."

Logan leaned around me. "Fine. I'll just go back to ogling my girlfriend."

"All eyes are supposed to be on the bride."

I gave our dad an incredulous look. Did he realize the door he just opened for Logan?

Not even a second later, he added, *"Don't* respond to that."

Logan groaned. "You give me that opening and then take it away? On this day? Analise Manning Day? Come on, Dad."

"Logan, just…" James sighed, turning back and smiling as the first bridesmaid came to the front. "Be nice for today. Please? I'll owe you."

"What'll you owe me?"

"Are you kidding me?!"

I shook my head. "You know better, Dad."

"Fine," he hissed out of the side of his mouth. "What do you want?"

"I want to use your private plane."

"Done."

"For a month," Logan added.

Our dad shot him a look. "Are you joking?"

"One full month, or I can be a complete ass to your new wife without blinking an eye. It'll be my pleasure."

James gave me pleading eyes as if to ask for me to step in. No way. I shook my head and moved back slightly so I wasn't right in the middle. This wasn't my fight.

"Fine," our dad bit out.

Logan added one more item. "And you'll cover all the expenses that go with it."

A low growl sounded before the fight left our dad. He refolded his hands in front of him. "Fine, and I swear, Logan, that's the last thing you get to demand. If you're not nice to Analise, I will rescind everything. There'll be no deal."

I could almost feel Logan's happiness. "I'll be so nice, she'll think she adopted me. Don't worry, Dad. Perfect charmer here. That's me as of right now."

The second bridesmaid arrived, and then the music changed. Everyone else stood with us, and it wasn't long before Analise started down the aisle.

"Oh, whoa," Logan said under his breath.

Despite her being a bitch of a mother, and someone who hurt her daughter more than she helped her, I understood what he meant. Analise was beautiful. But as she came toward us, I didn't really see her.

I saw Samantha in the way her black hair was swept up. I saw Samantha in the graceful slope of her neck. I saw Samantha in the way she walked, her petite shoulders set in a timid line, like she was taken aback by all the attention and felt self-conscious about it. And lastly, I saw Samantha in the love in her eyes. She looked at my father like he was her lifeline and she would drown without him.

I looked to the second pew where Sam sat, and was struck deep inside. If Analise was beautiful, her daughter was absolutely stunning.

Sam wore a similar-style white dress. It had the same straps, but not all the extra lace and other stuff Analise's dress had. As my gaze dipped to her neckline, I could see she wore a necklace similar to her mother's, too.

The look had been coordinated. Had that been her idea?

I made a mental note to ask about it later, but in the meantime, I couldn't tear my eyes off of her. Even when the pastor asked us to face forward, I shifted sideways.

She was the most goddamn amazing person, thing, creature— whatever word should be put there. Sam was it.

I was going to marry her.

We'd never talked about it, but I knew.

"Hey." Logan nudged me in the back with his arm. "Snap out of it, loverboy. You've got the rings, remember."

"Yeah." But I remained where I was. I paid attention to the ceremony and knew the time when I had to hand over the wedding rings, but I kept looking back at Sam.

It seemed too long before the ceremony was done. Analise and James were officially Mr. and Mrs. Kade, and Logan and I had our first official stepmom. Once it was over, I waited in the crowd until Sam was escorted out. As she stepped out of the sanctuary and was about to greet our parents, I grabbed her hand and tugged her behind me.

"Mason!" She grabbed my arm in surprise. "What are you doing? Where are we going?"

I didn't answer. I led the way through the small crowd at the back of the church and pulled her to the basement, to a back closet. Once inside, I was on her. Mouth to mouth. Hand to hand. As I was kissing her, claiming her, I reached behind me and locked the door.

I had to have her.

It was a primal need, and after a second's hesitation, she responded in kind.

"Mason." She groaned, raking her hands through my hair.

I needed more.

Skimming my hand down her arm, I hitched my fingers under her leg and lifted her. I wanted to be right there, and she answered my need. She moved with me, hoisting her legs to wrap around my waist and I was right at her opening.

"What are we doing? Here?"

I was beyond thinking. The door was locked, and it opened in. No one could get to us. I reached down, unzipped my pants, moved aside her underwear, and slipped inside. Both of us paused at the contact. My head fell to her shoulder, and I had to take a moment to breathe.

Goddamn.

I fucking loved this woman.

Then I began to move. In and out. I held on to her. She clamped tighter to me, and I began thrusting harder into her. I moved her from the door, just slightly, and braced my hand against it so I could hold her weight. I didn't want her to hit the door, but I couldn't stop, and I couldn't be gentler.

This was a desperate and almost frenzied need, like I had to claim her right here and now as mine.

"Mason." She groaned. Her hips were slick, but I kept sliding in and out.

More.

Harder.

Rougher.

Her hips moved along with mine, and then I felt my climax coming. I forced myself to stall. I wanted to make sure she came with me, and I reached down to touch her. I began rubbing, and she gasped, her head falling back against the door.

"Oh, holy shit!"

I kept caressing as I moved inside of her, and when she clutched at my shoulders, I dropped a kiss to her shoulder. "Sam."

She let out another deep groan, and her body began to come apart in my arms. She convulsed. Her orgasm seemed to rip through her almost violently, and then I started going harder for myself.

God. I came, and it wasn't until after I'd finished that I realized I hadn't used a condom.

"Fuck," I whispered, kissing her neck.

Her legs slowly unwound from my waist, but she couldn't stand. I held her steady in front of me.

"What?" Her eyes looked drunk. She reached down to adjust her underwear, then tucked me back into my pants and zipped me up. She smoothed a hand over my belt. "What's wrong?"

"I didn't use a condom."

"Oh." Her hand froze, positioned right over me. "Oh, no." It fell away.

"You're on birth control."

"Yeah, but still." She bit her lip.

I touched her mouth and smiled. "You know I love it when you do that."

"I know." She let her lip go, smiling, but her eyes were still worried. "Mason, what if—"

I shook my head. "Then we'll deal."

I tested to see if she could stand on her own, and when her body didn't immediately sway to the side, I stepped back an inch, just enough to breathe. Raking a hand through my hair, I looked down. She'd smoothed out everything. Nothing looked out of place.

"You okay?" I asked.

"I should stop in the bathroom for a quick cleanup."

I nodded. "I'll wait for you." We slipped from the closet, still holding hands, and Sam darted into a back women's restroom. I took position, watching to see if anyone came down the tiny hallway. I knew she'd be fine in there, but it was the least I could do.

I couldn't believe it. No fucking condom. I was fucking stupid.

"Hey." Logan came toward me, frowning. "Where'd you disappear to? We need to get to the reception. Nate and Taylor are waiting in the limo."

"What about Mark?" I gestured upstairs where we'd been standing. "I saw him sitting next to Malinda."

"Oh yeah. I'll grab him." He started to leave, but paused. "You okay?"

I nodded. "Just waiting for Sam."

The questions still lingered in his gaze, so I added, "She didn't want to wait in line or deal with other people. We found a bathroom down here."

"Okay." He was still frowning, but pointed back where he'd come from. "Anyway, I'll grab Mark, and we're in the limo. Hurry up—no quickies."

I shot him a grin. "You're going to tell us no quickies? Mr. Sex Machine himself?"

Logan smirked, puffing his chest out. "Well, maybe hold off till we get to the reception. You and Sam can get a room at the hotel."

"Uh-huh." My tone mocked him. "Or we can use the king suite you have booked."

"Fuck, no. Where do you think my quickies are going to be? I plan ahead, unlike some of us." He looked at me pointedly.

"Get out of here." I heard the door open behind me. "We're coming right now."

Sam stepped out next to me, her hand slipped into mine, and she leaned against me. She saw Logan walking away. "What'd he want?"

"They have a limo waiting for us."

"Oh."

I knew she was thinking we should go, but we stood together a moment longer. Her head rested against my arm, and I felt her entire body draw in some air.

"I know I should be worried, but what we did felt like the most natural thing in the world," she murmured. She tipped her head back, her dark and solemn eyes finding mine. "Why aren't I more worried?"

Because I loved her.

I kissed her lips. "Because we'll be fine, and whatever happens, we'll be fine then, too." My hand wrapped around her, holding onto her hip and anchoring her to me. "You know it'll all be okay."

She closed her eyes again, burrowing into me.

I could've stood there the rest of the day. I didn't care if they were waiting for us.

Finally, Sam pulled herself away from me, and she was the one who led me from the basement. Once in the limo, I kept us as far from the rest of the group as possible. There was space between us where seven people could've sat, and Logan stared at us, his head cocked to the side. He knew something had happened; he just couldn't figure it out.

It was none of his business this time, at least until it was ours first.

I pulled Sam onto my lap and held her during the ride.

# CHAPTER FORTY-ONE
## SAMANTHA

I suppose I should've been happy my mother was married.

She looked it. She glowed as she sat at the head table with James and their bridal party, excluding Mason and Logan. The boys sat with me at a table in the back, which also included Mark and Cass, and Taylor. Heather and Channing came for the dinner and were with us as well. James had his two ushers sit in Mason and Logan's empty chairs.

Drinks and appetizers appeared, and then the dinner was served. The maid of honor offered a touching toast for my mom, and I couldn't stop watching as she listened to those kind words being spoken about her.

Whoever she was, this woman didn't know her. They might've been in a treatment facility together. And they all seemed demure and perfect, but it was bullshit. I knew that much.

They'd shed a few tears, probably heard each other's sob stories, but did they hear from the ones they'd hurt? Did they know how my mom had lied to me all my life, let me fall in love with the man who raised me, and only after she left him did she tell me the truth? Or how she'd threatened him and my real father to keep them away? Or how she'd tried to ruin what I had with Mason? Or—I forced myself to calm down.

This woman. I wanted to destroy her. I wanted to hurt her the way she'd hurt me. I wanted misery to come to her, but I also missed her. I could remember the times we'd laughed, the few there were.

And I loved her.

I touched the dandelion pendant hanging from my neck, and feeling the whole storm inside of me, I could only sit and stare at my mother.

She turned, as if feeling my gaze, and she flinched. Her eyes widened and she turned away immediately to pretend she was laughing along with everyone else. The maid of honor had made a joke. Apparently.

I didn't need to look around my table. No one was laughing. Wait, I heard Cass giggle.

She quickly muffled it and hissed under her breath, "What?" One second passed. "Oh."

And my table went back to silence again. They all watched me, I couldn't stomach any of this anymore.

I shoved back from the table, and as the second bridesmaid started to give her speech, I left.

"Sam."

Mason came after me. I shook my head, not turning around. "Don't, Mason. I just—" I had no idea. I swept out to the parking lot.

"Hey." His hand caught mine. "Hey."

"I can't, Mason. I just can't." My chest heaved.

His hand tightened around mine, and instead of pulling me to a stop, he tugged me to an outside patio area tucked back between a bunch of trees—a little oasis. No one else was there. There were a few tables, and each one had a light sitting on it.

He sat down, but I couldn't. I wrapped my arms around myself, but then I yanked at my dress. "I can't stand wearing this now." Disgust flooded me. I was choking on it. "Fuck this matching shit." If I could've ripped it off then and there, I would've. I eyed the stream flowing nearby. The fucking thing would go in there. I didn't care what happened to it.

"Sam."

I wanted to punch him. Mason's voice was so calm and steady. I wanted him to rage with me, and then I remembered the police station. He had raged. It hadn't gone so well.

"What?"

He pulled me onto his lap.

I waited, but he didn't say anything. "What? No words of wisdom from the fucked-up son of James Kade?" I grimaced, hearing the bite in my words. "I'm sorry."

"Why?" He looked into my eyes. "I am James' son, and I *am* fucked-up regarding him. There was no insult in what you said, and even if there was, you know I'm not going to get mad." His eyes softened, and he pulled my head down so he could kiss my temple. "Not with you."

I turned so my back rested against his chest, and I watched the stream. I almost couldn't look away from that small trickle of water. "She killed my little brother or sister, then I called 911, and she pretended she'd tried to kill herself." I'd never forgive her for that. "I thought I was over that."

"Hey!" Heather came toward us. She dropped into another seat at the table and said, "Logan sent me out here." She turned to Mason. "He said something about owing your dad and to get your ass in there." She turned to me, a crooked grin on her face as she reached into her purse. "I came out to keep you company."

Mason looked at me.

I nodded. "Go." I gestured to Heather. "She's right, or Logan is. You owe your dad. You need to hold up your end of the deal."

He groaned, but I stood up, and so did he. He pressed a kiss to my forehead before heading back inside the hotel.

Once he was gone, Heather pulled out a cigarette. "Is this okay?"

"Yeah."

Grabbing an ashtray from another table, she lit up. She took a quick drag before leaning back and exhaling. "I normally wouldn't, but I'm a bit tense in there. This is a rich person's wedding? Weddings I've gone to aren't like that."

"That was a wedding, but I don't know." Though I knew what she was referring to. There were an inordinate number of tanned and fit bodies, boobs that didn't seem all-natural, and money. There was no other way to describe it. It was present in the clothes, the mannerisms, and even just the stuffiness in the air. James Kade was wealthy and important. It made sense he'd invite similar guests to his wedding.

"The women seem stuck-up."

Heather was putting that mildly. I grinned at her. "You don't have to be so nice."

"I'm not." She took another long drag. "But I think their dad is going to make them give a speech, so I'm not sure if you wanted to hear that or not?" She finished her cigarette quickly, grinding it out.

"You know me so well."

Heather laughed, and as we went back inside, Channing stood in the opened doorway to the ballroom. He'd been waiting for us.

"Mason just took the microphone," he said. "James made a point of saying they had to do a speech together. He won't allow Logan to do his own."

Heather moved to stand next to him. "Smart."

Mason stood on the platform behind the bridal party's table and laughed into the mic. Logan was right next to him.

"I have to admit, I'm shocked our dad's asked us to do a speech." A polite smattering of laughter came from the room, but Mason ignored them. His dad had turned to see him. "You sure about this?" Mason asked.

"Logan promised to be nice."

Mason brought the mic closer to his mouth, his voice even louder. "But I didn't."

The laughter doubled from the tables, but there was a tension in the air, too.

I held my breath.

Mason seemed to be considering something, then his eyes found me in the back, and a resolve settled in.

I let out that breath. I reached for the doorframe and held on.

"Okay. You asked for it, Dad."

I didn't look at anyone else. No one else existed at that moment.

"I know we're all here for these two, since they're now wedded, and hopefully wedded in bliss. But we'll all wait and see on that, won't we?"

There was another polite round of chuckles, but it was like the rest of them were cluing in. This might not go as most toasts do.

"I know I'm supposed to stand up here and say a bunch of nice things." Mason's voice grew serious; there was no forced lightness now. The room grew quiet. "But I can't do that. I *can* say a bunch of things about what I hope for their future. I hope they continue to be happy. I hope they'll remain faithful to each other. I hope Analise won't start drinking because even though that's not what her problem was, I know it might've helped. I hope she won't do anything to tear this family apart. I hope one day Logan and I will enjoy coming to the house again, the place we grew up. I hope our father will one day apologize to our mother for the endless stream of mistresses. I hope Logan will have a relationship with his father, because he didn't growing up. I hope Samantha won't fear her mother one day. I hope you both will be welcomed at my wedding one day." He looked at me then. "I hope you'll both be doting grandparents to my future children, and I hope I'll let you see them, and maybe even have unsupervised sleepovers. I hope for a lot of things."

His gaze swept out over the quiet crowd. Some of the women had their hands over their mouths. Some of the men were glowering. But others weren't reacting at all. Those were the ones who knew the real Analise and James, and a few of them looked at Mason and Logan with sympathy.

A hand grasped mine, and I looked over to see Heather giving me a reassuring smile. I realized I'd been crying. I used my other hand to wipe my tears away.

Mason's voice gentled as he held my gaze. "I know this wasn't the nicest speech, but I'm not one to be fake. My dad knows that, so he must've been expecting something like this. I can say a few good things. I can say that I used to hate my dad, and I don't any longer." He tore his eyes away to look at his father. "I don't have as much anger at you as I did, so maybe you wanted to hear that?" Then he looked at my mother. "And Analise…" I heard a woman suck in her breath at the nearest table. "I can thank you for giving Sam space, but I want you to let her go."

A ripple of murmuring rose from the room.

A couple looked at each other near me, and I heard the woman say, "How can he ask that?"

Someone else said, "Fuck this." A chair pushed backward.

Mason ignored everyone. "The matching dress, the necklace. You've backed off, but she can still feel the hold from you. Let her go. Once and for all, just let her go."

Logan cleared his throat, reaching for the microphone. Mason let it go without a fight, but he continued to hold my mother's gaze steadily.

"Uh." Logan laughed, moving a few feet away from his brother. He took the spotlight with him. "Thank you for that...very transparent speech, Mason."

More people began to talk, but Logan spoke over them, raising his voice. "Yeah. So. I'm usually the one who delivers the bomb. I don't think I can compete with my brother, and by the way..." He waited until Mason looked at him, "You should've dropped the mic. I don't know if you'll get a more perfect moment than after that speech."

Mason shrugged.

Logan laughed again. "I guess here's my turn. Everything Mason said was true. If you guys didn't know, there's not a good history between us and our dad. And the other thing he said was true, too. When Analise was walking down the aisle, Dad made me promise to be nice, so this is a little different for me. Mason's the quiet fighter, and I'm the talker, and I don't usually equate nice with Analise—"

"Logan."

He lifted a hand toward his dad. "Hold on, Dad. But I'm going to do that tonight." He gestured to me in the back. "And if you all didn't know this either, Mason and I are protective of Sam back there, who is Analise's daughter. So..." His eyebrows pinched together, and he turned to regard Analise. He held the mic up to his mouth so we could hear his soft breathing. "My speech is going to suck because I can only think of a couple nice things to say. One, thank you, Analise, for giving birth to my new stepsister. Not only is she my first stepsister, she's my first sister at all." He did a half-bow, which caused some laughter from the room.

"Thank you for that. Two, uh..." He raked a hand through his hair. "You got my dad to stop sleeping around. I give you two thumbs up for that." And he actually did, flashing her a grin at the same time.

More laughter sounded from the tables, along with an air of relief.

"I have one more I just thought of; it goes along with my dad's newfound fidelity." He suddenly grew serious. "For what it's worth, I do think my dad loves you. And through that, he's shown me a different side of himself, one that I respect."

He turned to his dad. "Kind of. I kind of respect you. I'm starting to respect you. Wait. No. Yeah. I do, somewhat. You're halfway there, Dad. I almost completely respect you. Not really. You're like an eighth of the way there. Maybe a tiny bit more than an eighth, but you know what I mean. It's more than before." He grinned and held his hand up, leaning down toward James. "High five to that."

James didn't move to slap his hand, and Logan looked at it. "You're leaving me hanging? I kept it nice about Analise."

One of the ushers took that opportunity to get the mic from Logan. "Okay. Thank you…both." His Adam's apple bobbed up and down, and he glanced over to a stage where the deejay was setting up. "I believe we're ready for our slideshow, and then the dancing will be starting soon. Drinks are on the house, so everyone drink up!" He turned around, but Mason and Logan were still standing there. The mic was down by his side, but it still caught him saying, "Get off the platform. You two are horrible sons."

Logan didn't move, so Mason began to move him to the edge. Logan twisted back around. "Dad, you did ask us to do speeches. What were you thinking?"

"I thought you'd have the decency to be polite."

"Logan, come on." Mason kept moving.

Logan stepped back, and as Mason hopped down and moved my way, Logan spoke again. "Hey. At least I'm calling you Dad again. Mase, too. That's a big step for us."

Mason was almost to me, but more movement on the platform caught my eye.

Analise had stood, and she moved in front of Logan, folding her arms over her chest. Everyone quieted, and I heard her say, "You protect

Samantha from me. This is my turn to protect my husband from you. Please leave, Logan." She glanced to me. "All of you."

I felt nothing. The Sam I used to be would've felt stabbed, taking those words as a personal blow, but the Analise before would've delivered them with that intent. They weren't this time. They really were just words from a wife who loved her husband and was protecting him.

Mason pulled me with him as he headed to the parking lot. Logan jumped down to follow. I knew Heather and Channing were coming as well, and for the first time ever, I felt like we'd overstepped.

Once we got outside, Channing clapped his hands together. "Remind me not to get on your bad sides and then ask you to do a speech at my wedding." He nudged Heather with his elbow. "Whenever that's going to be."

I sensed a storm inside of Mason, but I knew he wouldn't say anything until we were alone.

"James shouldn't have asked, and he knows it," I told them.

Mason's hand tightened on mine. He glanced down, like he could tell I wasn't sure about my own words.

"Yo." Mark was jogging to catch up. Cass was with him, and behind them Logan was holding hands with Taylor. Mark held up his phone. "I got the whole thing on vide—"

Mason rotated around, grabbed his phone, and smashed it on the cement.

"Dude!"

He brought his foot down, then glared. "You think I wanted to hurt my dad?"

Mark's eyes rounded. "I…well, yeah. That's exactly what you did."

"But I didn't want to. That's the difference. He put me in that position. He made us agree to be his groomsmen, and then he followed through to the last detail. A fucking speech by his adoring sons—that's what he wanted. He backed us into a corner because he thought we'd play nice. I didn't want to do any of that, but I'm not going to be fake. I'm not going to lie and put on a charade that he'll be able to play over and over again and to delude himself. 'I had two doting sons once. I wonder what happened to them?'" Mason shook his head. "He can't rewrite history, and he can't force a new future. That shit I said up there, that was me being kind. Trust me. I have a lot more I'd like to say, but I kept it in."

"My phone, man."

Mason kicked Mark's phone to Logan's foot. He bent and pocketed it.

"Sorry, man," Logan said. "There may be other videos of it, but it's not something we want to be a part of spreading." He moved forward, still holding Taylor's hand. "We might not like James, but he's still our dad."

The rest of us began moving, hand in hand. Mark and Cass held back a step, and then with a sigh, Mark took her hand, too. They began following us.

We had one last parking lane to cross before we got to Mason's Escalade when a squad car stopped in front of us.

Mason pointed to his vehicle. "We were just leaving."

Two officers got out and the one closest to us asked, "Mason Kade?"

"Yeah?"

He pulled out a pair of handcuffs and gestured for Mason to turn around. "You're under arrest for the assault of Jared Caldron."

"What?!" Logan lunged forward, like he wanted to rip the cuffs off of Mason. "That was self-defense."

The officer opened the back door, reciting the Miranda rights as he guided Mason into the backseat, covering his head with his hand. He stopped once to ask if Mason understood the rights as he'd stated them, and Mason nodded.

He turned back around to us. "Not for the incident that happened a week ago. For the incident that happened a month ago." His cold eyes landed on me. "You were there. Maybe you could fill him in? I believe it happened at your place of employment."

I narrowed my eyes. What did he mean...then I knew. When Caldron had been about to hit me at the carnival. "Mason was defending me." I looked at Mark. "Tell him."

Mark lifted his hands in a helpless manner. "I didn't see it. I wasn't there, remember? I came after it was done."

The cop shrugged, sounding tired, "Bring your argument down to the station."

The car left, and Logan kicked savagely at a rock on the ground. "Fuck! Fuck!" He rounded on Mark. "You couldn't speak up? You couldn't say you were there?" He lifted his hands like he was going to shove Mark.

Mark's nostrils flared. "Back off of me. I can't lie, Logan. You want me to lie?"

"It wouldn't have mattered anyway." Channing stepped forward, getting between the two of them, his hands out. "They came to arrest Mason. They would've arrested him no matter what Mark said. It's with the courts now."

Logan was still glaring at Mark. "You have experience with that, Monroe?" His voice had an edge to it.

"Yeah." Channing lowered his hands. "You think you're the only guys to get arrested around here?" He seemed to force a lighter tone. "Come on, know of any good lawyers we can call?"

Logan cursed. "Yeah, my dad's."

The dad he and Mason had just royally pissed off.

Logan looked at me. "I know of one other lawyer in the family."

I sighed, wanting to curse, too. "He's not this kind of lawyer."

"Don't matter. He's still a lawyer."

"Fucking hell," I muttered, but he was right. I didn't have my phone or purse with me, so Logan handed me his.

A second later, it was ringing, and my biological father answered.

"This is Garrett."

"Dad?" I felt like a little girl in that moment, but I didn't know why. "I need your help."

# CHAPTER FORTY-TWO

It took a few hours for my dad to drive from Cain, where he and his wife had been vacationing for the last month before heading back to Boston. When he arrived, he seemed frazzled, and after we told him everything, he seemed even more frazzled.

He shot me an irate look. "How many physical fights have there been?"

Before I could answer, he shook his head, holding up a hand. "Never mind. I don't want to know. I'll go in and talk to Mason, but..." He turned to Logan. "Why aren't your father's lawyers here? Is there something I should know about Mason's case?"

"Uh." Logan and I glanced at each other. He tugged at his collar. "James asked us to give speeches at his wedding, and well—"

Another head shake followed. "Don't say anything more. I got the picture." His eyes lingered on me. "I forgot your mom got married today. How are you?"

"I'll be better when we get Mason out of there," I told him.

"Got it. That's my cue." He scanned the rest of the group as he walked inside the station.

Heather and Channing were still here, and some of Channing's friends—Moose, Chad, and two others—had brought pizza. I was pretty sure it wasn't coffee in their thermoses. We'd taken over a corner of the police station lot. Some sat on the back of Channing's truck, some at a picnic table, and Channing's friends had brought lawn chairs, too. Mark and Cass were still here, too. I thought Cass would be bitching more, but she'd been quiet.

Everyone had gone home to change clothes once they heard my dad had a three-hour drive, but Logan and I stayed. Taylor brought both of us a change of clothes. Logan had changed in his Escalade, but I was still in my dress from the wedding.

I'd change when Mason could change. That was how my mind was working at the moment. I was only focused on when he would get out.

A couple hours later, I pulled myself out of my lawn chair as Garrett exited the station. His tie flapped in the wind, and he rubbed briskly at his forehead. Logan stood next to me, holding Taylor's hand on his other side.

"Bail?" I asked him.

"It's Saturday, Sam. And it's late." He rested his hand on my shoulder briefly. "The judge won't see him till Monday, and I won't be able to do much until then. I did find out what they have on him. There's a video showing this guy, and Mason comes in. He tackles him, and then the video zooms in to show him punching this guy. I have to say, this evidence is damning for Mason. That's assault and battery, and they'll probably bump it up to aggravated assault, too. That's not good, any of it. What happened that day?"

I looked for Logan, but he wasn't there. I shook my head. "I was working, and I saw—" Not a friend, not anymore. "—someone I knew. She wanted to talk, so we went to the side of the tent, then Caldron saw me. He was going to hit me. Mason got there just in time to defend me. It doesn't show that on the video?"

"No. Who else was there whenever this video took place? Who would want to do this to Mason?"

Logan snorted. He'd reappeared. "The question is who wouldn't." He indicated the group with a quick wave. "These people here wouldn't." He paused, staring at Cass. "She's still suspect, though."

Cass had been sitting forward, her elbows propped on her knees, but jerked up at that. "Are you kidding me?" Her mouth fell open. She flung a hand up, almost hitting Mark. "We left, and I could've stayed home. I didn't. Mark wanted to be here for you guys, and I'm here for him. I've been very nice to Sam this summer."

She had. She hadn't said shit to me. That was nice for Cass.

Logan quirked an eyebrow, and I shrugged. It was the only thing I could muster.

"Unreal." She stood up. "Mark, I'm out of here."

He caught her arm, pulling her back. "Stop. You two don't have the greatest history. Chill. Stay, please." He kissed her cheek. "For me?"

The fight left her before our eyes. Her rigid jaw and tight shoulders loosened at his soft request.

Logan rolled his eyes, turning back to Garrett. "No dice then? For getting Mase out?"

Garrett scratched idly at the side of his nose. "I don't have a lot of pull, at least not legally. What I can do is recommend that you talk to your dad. He can call in some favors, I'm sure, and get Mason released. I don't know if he can get the charges dropped, but I bet he can get them lessened." He looked to me. "Who else was there that day? There's been other history with Jared Caldron, correct? They mentioned another incident. Would he have the motivation to dig this video up and turn it in?"

Logan turned to me, too.

He could, but...I shook my head at Logan's silent question. I didn't think Caldron had actually done this.

As if reading my mind, Logan said, "Yeah, that's what I thought, too. It doesn't feel right, but Caldron has plenty of motivation. Mason beat the shit out of him last weekend."

"No charges were brought because of that, though?"

"Not against us. It was self-defense. Sixteen guys showed up."

Garrett's eyebrows raised.

"But this is a pussy move," Logan continued. "Caldron deserved the beat down Mason gave him, but he doesn't fight like this. Or he hasn't in the past."

"Yeah. I don't know much about him, but he could sue Mason in civil court." My dad's phone started ringing, and he pulled it out and turned it off. "Okay, here's the plan. Sam, I'm going to drive to Cain tonight, and I'll bring Sharon and Seb back with me tomorrow. You can see your little sister, if you'd like?"

Mason was in jail. He was my first worry, but the thought of seeing little Sabrina—I felt my first smile in the last six hours stretch over my face. I nodded. There'd been a few holidays and some random times when Garrett and his wife were in Cain while I was, too. That'd been the extent of my time with my little sister. I'd been there for her birth, and I was already anticipating holding her hyper little two-year-old body in my arms.

"I bet she's a handful now," I murmured.

Garrett grunted, chuckling. "You'll see for yourself tomorrow." He shifted toward Logan and held a hand up. "I don't know why I was about to tell you what to do. You weren't there." His hand came back to me. "You were there. Make up a list of who else was, too, and are you on good terms with the carnival? Are you still working there?" Then it hit him. "Why were you working at a carnival in the first place?"

Lost.

Hurting.

Bored.

And trying to avoid Analise.

"It seemed fun at the time," I said.

Logan's head dropped, and I caught a small cough. He was holding in a laugh. "Yeah." The corner of his mouth twitched up. "We'll head over there in the morning and see if they can help us."

"They might have a different video that shows Caldron about to attack Sam. You never know. Or sometimes these places have policies about the use of hidden cameras, too. They don't like being recorded themselves. You never know what you might find, and I'll be going to see them myself next week, too. Depending on when Mason can get in front of a judge, I'll try to get there even before that."

His eyes rested on me, a small frown showing. "You look tired."

My mom got married. I'd missed her at first, then raged inside. Then my boyfriend made a controversial speech and got arrested.

I lifted my shoulder and let it drop. "Typical Saturday night for us."

Logan grinned, holding his hand out. "Thank you for coming. It means a lot."

Garrett nodded. "Well, Sam is my daughter." The two shook hands, and he moved to hug me. "You okay, honey?"

Warmth from those words helped settle some of my nerves, but Mason was still in jail "I'll be better on Monday."

It was late, nearing midnight, and I knew most lawyers wouldn't have even come. I hugged Garrett back a second longer. "Thank you."

"Of course." His voice was hoarse all of the sudden. "I'd normally get a hotel room, but I promised to watch Seb while Sharon has brunch with some friends tomorrow, so I need to go. We'll be back here late afternoon." He stepped back as he was talking. "And, Logan, I don't know how bad the speeches were, but talk to your dad. I'd be shocked if he didn't still want to help Mason out with this. Aggravated assault and battery is a big deal; it's a life-changer."

"I will."

I stepped back as Garrett said that last bit to Logan, and I felt a chill coming on. I didn't know if it was from the evening breeze or something inside of me, but I felt it wind itself all around me. I hugged myself, trying to ward it off, but I couldn't get it out of my head. Mason was in jail. He wasn't coming out. He'd come out before. He'd only spent a couple hours in there, but this was different.

After Garrett left, I knew the others would come closer. They'd want to know what was going on, since they'd hung back to give us space. I only had a moment of privacy with Logan. Taylor was here, but she was a part of Logan now. I looked at him and said, "So this is what it's like to be on the outside."

He sighed, giving my arm a gentle squeeze. "I'll talk to James tomorrow. I'm sure he'll help."

He probably would, but not tonight, and maybe not even tomorrow.

I didn't know how things worked in the legal system, but I had to assume every minute counted. We needed someone to help, and there was only one person I could think of left to ask.

I held my hand out. "Give me your keys."

"Why?" Logan frowned, digging in his pocket.

He placed them in my hand, and I got into the driver's seat of the Escalade. He could get a ride home with someone else.

"Sam?"

I started the car, then opened the window. "Mark?"

He moved forward with Cass right behind him. "Yeah?"

"Go talk to Keifer. See if they have anything there that might help us. I know Petey will try to help."

He nodded. "Got it."

"Sam." Logan stepped close to the door, resting a hand over the opened window. "Where are you going?"

"We need help now. I'm going to call in a favor."

"With who?"

There was really only one person who owed me.

"My mom."

# CHAPTER FORTY-THREE

It was irrational to come here.

Logan would talk to James tomorrow, and he'd help Mason. But I wasn't listening to the rational side of me. I was all irrational at this moment, and that was why I was waiting in a hotel lobby at one in the morning.

The elevator doors pinged, and I looked up.

Analise stepped out, wearing a robe with her nightgown covering her feet underneath. She saw me, frowned, and pulled her robe tighter around herself. The lobby was relatively empty, only two desk clerks and me.

"Samantha?" She came over. "What's going on? Why are you here at this hour?" She glanced around, smoothing her hair. She hadn't taken out the pins, so it was still swept up in the curled twist she'd worn at the wedding.

I searched her face for any signs of sleepiness, but her eyes were alert, and none of her makeup looked smudged. "I didn't know if you'd be here or if you guys would've gone somewhere else for the night." I didn't know any of their plans, actually. I now felt like I should've. "I'm sorry if you were sleeping."

"No." She shook her head, still frowning. "We just settled into bed, but that's it. We were talking about the day. Sam." Her head inclined toward me. "What is going on?"

This was so stupid. The words, the urgency, all of it left me in a sudden *whoosh*, and I realized the real reason I was here.

"Mason was arrested tonight."

"What?!"

I glanced down to my hands, balled into fists at my sides. "We were leaving the hotel, and two cops showed up. It's because he attacked someone, but he was only defending me. The guy was going to hit me."

"Oh, Sam." She leaned toward me, her hand reaching for my arm.

I saw it coming, and I did nothing. I found myself leaning toward her, and then she realized what she was about to do. Her hand stopped, flexed a couple times, and returned to her side. She tucked it into her robe's pocket.

"I'm so sorry, Sam. I'm sure everything will be fixed, especially if Mason was only defending you. James always gets his sons off, you know that. He'd never let anything really hurt them."

A small laugh left me. I reached up, pressing my hand to my forehead. I felt a headache forming.

"What?" she asked me.

"Nothing. It's just—" I heard her words again. *James always gets his sons off, you know that. He'd never let anything really hurt them.* Oh, the irony. Mason and Logan were so angry at their dad because that was all he did was hurt them.

"He does help them, doesn't he?" I murmured.

"In his way, he does."

I looked up at her. She was saying *he*. I was saying *he*. We weren't talking about James.

There's a moment in life—when you become a certain age and see your future laid out before you—that you have to make a decision. Whatever fractures are inside of you, whatever emptiness or wounds there are, you must become whole again because it's time.

It was time to let go.

I felt that wave of realization now, and something fell from me. It was an old lens. I could now look at Analise a different way.

It was time to step into my future.

"You do love me, don't you?" I asked.

Her head lifted, and her eyes widened.

I saw it now. It was there in fragments. She loved me, but she couldn't love me the way a normal mother could. But it was still there.

Her mouth opened, no sound came out, and she closed it again. Then she whispered, "Yes. I do."

I sank down into one of the hotel's plush chairs and leaned forward, resting my elbows on my knees. She sat next to me.

I stared forward as I said, "I've been so tense, waiting for you to talk to me all summer." No, that wasn't right. "Actually since the Christmas before when you came home. And you haven't done a thing."

"That's not true, Samantha. I've done plenty, and you know it." She reached over, touching my hand this time. She was tentative, but when I didn't brush her off, her hand grew heavier. She took in a silent breath. "I've tried to let you go. What Mason said at the end of his speech tonight? He's right. I haven't let you go, and we both know it. You've felt it. Maybe that's why you came to me tonight. I don't know, but I'm grateful. I've had many nights with James, but I haven't had a night with my daughter in a long time. Thank you for coming."

"I came to ask you for a favor."

"I know." She patted my hand, squeezing it before letting go. "You want me to talk to James, have him help Mason as soon as he can."

I nodded. I still couldn't look at her, though. I didn't know why.

"I'll talk to him."

"Thank you." My tongue felt heavy on the back of my mouth.

"I'd like to say I always would've helped, but that's not true."

I looked now. The old Analise was there, but it was just in her face, her hair, the way she looked on the outside. Her eyes were new. That was the different person here. She even sat differently now.

"Before going to treatment, I would've used this favor against you. I would've agreed to ask James if you'd break up with Mason. That's what I would've done, but that's not what a true mother should ever do to her child." Her hand reached out, but pulled back again. "You have been justifiably angry at me. I was gone for two years, and then I stayed away for the last year and a half. The truth is, I never should've come back. You were better off when I wasn't here. James had someone watching you for me."

*What?*

She hung her head in shame. "It wasn't all the time, but every now and then. I just wanted to know what was going on in your life. You were happy. That's what I saw, and then you changed when I came back. You were always looking over your shoulder in his pictures. I can't help but think that was because of me. Like I was a shadow behind you."

Exactly. Everything she said was how I felt.

"Then you guys came back, and the last two rounds of pictures he sent to me were all of you running. There were a few others from during the day, but you looked so harried. That was me, too. The thought of seeing me. I couldn't bear seeing any more so I asked James to have him stop."

"You were at the driveway that one day."

"That was by accident. I went for a walk, and I didn't walk past Malinda's house with the intent of seeing you. She told me you'd been staying at Helen's house with Mason. I usually walk the other way, but that day I didn't. There you were, helping her load those gift baskets into her car." She leaned forward, a reflection of me with both our elbows on our knees. "I was so jealous. Malinda's been amazing. She's protecting you by knowing what's going on with me. I know a part of her feels for me—mother to mother, you know—but it's really about you. She wants to be in the know about what I'm doing. Almost like keeping your friends close, but your enemies closer. But it doesn't bother me. She's doing it for you." She paused a beat. "She's the mother I should've been. She's the mother you should've had."

I should've reached for her. I should've had words of reassurance at the tip of my tongue.

I didn't move.

"You don't owe me anything, Samantha," she added after a moment. "I used to think you did, but Mason's words hit me hard tonight. You don't. I'm letting you go. Officially. We're going to move. James and I talked about it tonight. Mason brought up the house, so you guys can have it. I know Helen's coming back at some point. She'll want to see Mason and Logan and if it's before they go back to Cain, I know you won't want to be there when she does. James and I will be gone by the end of next week. You can move in then."

*Mom…*

I almost said that word.

She patted my leg before standing back up. "If you ever want to get coffee, I'm here. I'm here for anything you need, okay? But you never have to do anything for me. You never have to see me. You never have to talk to me. If you see me in a store, you don't have to say hi. You can walk past me like we're strangers, and I will never get angry with you. I'm letting you go, Sam." She cupped the side of my face, and her thumb brushed over my cheek. "You'll always be my baby girl," she said lovingly, "but I'll be whoever you want me to be." She bent down, and I closed my eyes as she kissed me on the forehead.

I reached up, bringing my fingers to rest where she'd kissed me as she went back to the elevator. I tried to remember another time when she'd kissed me like that.

I couldn't.

The elevator opened. She stepped inside, and the doors closed.

I sat there for another hour.

---

"Sam."

I was finally leaving the hotel when I heard my name. Becky rested against Logan's Escalade. She twisted her hands together and straightened as I drew near.

"What are you doing here?" I looked around. The lot was full of cars, but it was relatively quiet, like the lobby. A party bus pulled up to the front entrance, and a bunch of people staggered off it, laughing loudly.

"It was Adam."

"What was?"

"Adam's the one who turned in that video of Mason. He saw that one of the workers there had his phone out, and later he tracked him down. He edited the video so it looks like Mason attacked that guy for no reason. Here." She held out a flash drive.

"What is it?" I took it.

"It's the rest of the video. It'll show that the guy's about to hit you and Mason is just protecting you. It should get him off."

"Why are you giving me this?"

"Because Adam's wrong with what he's doing." She looked away. Shoving her hands in her back pockets, she looked like half the person she'd been. "I'm really sorry, Sam."

I laughed. This had become the night of apologies somehow. "I... Why did Adam do that?"

"Because he's still mad about how Mason humiliated him in high school." She lifted her head, and her eyes swam with tears. "Because he knows you guys are behind getting his dad arrested, and because of Logan's threat to go to law school with him." She stopped and took a breath. "Adam's not thinking straight right now. And he's angry because..." She took another deep breath. "He's angry that I broke off the engagement. He's blaming you for that." She nodded to the flash drive still in my hand. "He wanted to hurt you guys. This is me trying to make it right."

She started to go, but I stepped forward. "Wait. You broke up with him?"

She nodded, her lip trembling. "He thinks it's because his dad's in legal trouble, but it's not. I've always loved Adam, even before I loved myself. And I've always chosen him, but I've been thinking a lot over the last week. I still love him. I think it's just in my DNA, but I don't know. I think I need to start doing things for myself, you know? I can't marry a guy and have our entire life already mapped out. I know it's sudden and random, but—" She lifted her shoulder and rested her cheek against it. "Maybe it's the fight with you guys. I'm just so tired of it. I don't know if Logan's really going to do the whole law school thing, but when he said that, it was like I got a wake-up call. Adam's always going to fight someone. Whether it's you guys or someone else. He hates Mason, and it's like he chooses guys at school to hate, too. I was shocked when he said he wanted to make things right with you guys, but it was all a sham. Adam did know what Caldron was supposed to do. James insisted the two boys worked together, and it was his job too. He was supposed to distract Mason, too. He wanted to do it by being friends with him, but we all know that didn't work out. I'm sorry." She went back to twisting her hands together. "This is a lot of talking, and I'm probably not making any sense."

"No. You are."

She stopped twisting her hands and held still as her eyes found mine. She almost looked like a statue, like someone I used to know when life was simpler.

"I can never be friends with you. I know that now. I've been missing you all these years and thinking what I could have done differently, or what I could still do differently, but that opportunity is gone. Even if Adam's my ex, I still have to be on his side. It wouldn't be right to end things with him and then try to be friends with you again. That's, like, unnecessary betrayal, you know?"

"So what are you going to do?"

She shrugged again. "Stay away from Adam until the end of summer. Try to figure out what I want to do. I went to that college because he went there. I think I need to decide if I want to stay there or transfer, and then go from there. Anyway…" She gestured to the flash drive, which I'd put into my pocket. "I hope that helps get Mason free. He might deserve to be in there for something else, but not this." She paused, then took a breath. She tried smiling, but it faltered. It didn't quite meet her eyes. "Goodbye, Sam."

I nodded. This was my second goodbye in the last two hours. And this one really was a goodbye. I knew I'd still see my mom at some point, but I honestly didn't know if I'd see Becky again.

"I missed you," I said. And I meant it, thinking back over the years. "I missed our friendship, and I was happy when I thought I'd gotten it back this summer. I'm sorry things turned out the way they did."

"Yeah." She sighed. "That's just how it is, huh?"

"Yeah. I guess."

She began backing away and held up a hand. "Bye, Sam."

I waved back, but I waited until she'd gotten in her car and left. Then I said, so quietly, "Bye, friend."

# CHAPTER FORTY-FOUR

Mason was released Monday morning, no charges pending.

The flash drive did what Becky said it would do: It absolved Mason of guilt. It showed Caldron about to hit me, and it wasn't alone. Logan ended up going with Mark when he went to see Keifer, and they got him to release the carnival's video recording. Garrett had been right. Apparently, they had security cameras set up, and the footage helped back up what the first video showed. The cops were now looking into pressing charges against Adam instead, but Garrett wasn't sure if that'd happen. He told us that afternoon, after Mason got out, that any charges against Adam were none of our business. We shouldn't go looking to start trouble because we had enough already.

I agreed with him.

I was just thankful Mason was out, and nothing had come of his stint in jail.

"So everyone's all good, Jeeves?" Logan asked.

He received a round of weird looks in return.

Seeing our reaction, he jerked a shoulder up. "What? I like the name. Sue me."

"Uh, yeah." Garrett narrowed his eyes just briefly. "Everything's good, Jeeves."

Logan grinned. "Sam, I think I like this dad more than the other one."

"Thanks." I frowned. "I won't tell David."

Logan shrugged again. "Tell him if you want. He knows Malinda holds my heart in their twosome fearsome."

"You're starting with that stuff again?" Mason asked.

"We need a new name since Nate is more in the fold. Are we back to the foursome fearsome?"

"Stop thinking about it."

"Why?" Logan asked his brother.

"Because I can tell it's upsetting you." Mason's hand settled more firmly on my hip, slipping under my shirt. Logan made a sound, but Mason ignored him. "Thank you, Garrett, for coming down and helping us."

The two shook hands.

Garrett's gaze fell on me. "You know I'd do anything to help you guys."

A warmth trickled through me, and I felt my throat choking up. "Thanks, Garrett."

Mason and Logan stepped back, so it was just my biological father and me. He turned to face me, his arms out at his sides, and I stepped into them. "Can you start calling me Dad?" he asked.

I nodded, my head moving against his chest. And when we let go, I felt some wetness on my face. "Yeah, I mean, I wouldn't want to confuse Sabrina," I teased, wiping the tears away.

"Ah, little Seb." His fondness was evident. "She's so busy. I always wonder if you were like that, too. She looks like you."

"Except for the blond hair that's almost white." I brushed some of my black hair off my shoulder.

"Yes, but her personality is like yours."

As much as a two year old's could be. But I grinned.

He gave Mason and Logan a wave and headed to his Audi.

As he left, Logan clapped his hands together, jumping up on the curb. "And now it's just the threesome fearsome again."

Mason's gaze was hooded. I didn't look, but I felt him studying me as he said to Logan, "I told you to stop worrying about that. It's the three of us. Nate's close, but he's not you or Sam."

Logan let out a breath of air, jumping back down. "Yeah, okay. I should go. Taylor talked about going back to see her friends. They called last night; something happened up there."

Mason focused more fully on his brother. I could feel the tightness in my chest lighten as he did. "Are you going with her?" he asked.

"I might," Logan admitted. "No offense, but I've got a feeling the two of you are going to do the 'couple' thing the rest of your time here. Unless you guys want to go back, too?" His eyes lit up. "Yeah! You should. Mase, your internship's done. Dad's not opening the hotel while you're here anymore, and Sam, you don't have a job. Come on. Let's all go back."

The reason he wanted to go was obvious. Taylor was there. And the reason we'd come to Fallen Crest was Mason's internship. He needed that credit.

"Your dad will fill out all your internship paperwork, right?" I asked.

"He already did. The only thing I need from him is a grade."

Logan barked out a laugh. "God, our dad sucks. You're going to have to go in and kiss his ass."

"I know. I'll apologize for the speeches, too."

"Fuck that. He knew what he was doing when he tried to force us to give him nice ones."

I remembered what Analise had said to me. I hadn't told either of them about that conversation. They knew about Becky, but I'd kept quiet about the reason Becky had found me at the hotel in the first place. I'd tell them when things quieted down.

"I think he'll do the right thing and give you an A," I told him.

Logan gave me an incredulous look, and Mason just pressed his lips together.

Their doubt was obvious.

"Okay. Right, Sam." Logan shook his head.

I shrugged. "I got a feeling."

"You okay?"

Mason's question came out of nowhere. I turned to look at him, momentarily speechless. "Yeah. Why wouldn't I be?"

"Because Mason was in jail for almost forty-eight hours," Logan offered.

Mason frowned at his brother. "We've done longer."

"Hey." Logan cocked his head to the side. "You said you were going to see your mom. Did you?"

Here it was. This was my opening to tell them she was officially letting me go. I opened my mouth, ready to share the joyous news... and nothing. No words came out.

"I did, but nothing happened," I said instead.

Mason's eyes narrowed.

"It doesn't matter. That flash drive Sallaway gave you and the video Keifer added was all we needed." He clapped Mason on the shoulder. "You're out, and I think we've learned a valuable lesson."

Both of us waited.

"We should always have our own camera guy around. You never know what lengths some piece of shit might go to the next time we're busting heads."

Mason shook his head. "Or we could try to stop getting into physical fights. If any of that video gets leaked to the NFL, I could be out before I was even in."

"Nah." Logan brushed that off. "You're good. Everything's all good." He snapped his fingers, pointing at us. "And on that note, I've been thinking about Taylor since I told you guys she wanted to head back. Now I'm hard." He glanced down. "You guys are my ride, so can we go? I'd like to spend some time with her before we hit the road tonight."

"We didn't need to know some of those details." Mason went to the driver's door as Logan reached for the back door handle. I went around to the passenger side.

As we all settled inside, Mason asked, "You guys are leaving tonight, then?"

Logan was looking at his phone. "Yeah, and she just texted. Something went down with Jason. He got jumped."

"Logan." Mason's tone held a warning. "Don't do anything stupid."

"Like jump the guys who jumped him?" Logan finished sending a text and slid his phone back in his pocket. "No. You're right. I'd never defend that little piece of shit, but the problem is that he's Taylor's family, and you know we are about family. Totally don't do shit to help each other out. That's us. That's the Kade motto: don't do shit."

Mason pulled out of the parking lot. "You can tone down the sarcasm. I'm not saying don't help. I'm saying don't physically fight. Get it done a different way."

"I know. I know, but it's so damn satisfying when the other guy is on the ground because of you, you know?"

"I know."

I looked over. Mason's voice had quieted.

"We got off track this summer," he continued in a more normal voice. "We tried going right before. We need to get back to it. You have a future, too, you know."

Logan smirked. "Damn right. I'm going to be a lawyer. It'll really piss Quinn off if I get there ahead of him, too."

I turned around in my seat. "You're really going to follow through with that?"

"Fuck yeah."

"That's a lifetime commitment to fucking with Adam Quinn."

Logan looked at his brother, their eyes meeting in the rearview mirror. "I know, but it's not about just fucking with him. Maybe it was getting hauled in that night, or you being arrested a second time, or even just Quinn saying he's going to be a lawyer. I don't know what it was, but that's what I want to do. I want to be able to stick it to anyone I fucking please, because I know my way around the law and they don't."

That made sense, and the subject was closed.

When we got home, Logan didn't sequester Taylor in their bedroom for the next hour like he planned. Instead, they made plans to take off.

Mason and I were in the kitchen when Nate appeared. He pointed over his shoulder with his thumb. "Uh, Logan and Taylor are packing. What's going on?" He pulled out a chair and sat across from me at the table.

Mason straightened from the fridge where he'd been grabbing a diet soda for me. Letting the door close on its own, he handed me the can and leaned against the counter. "They're heading back. Something's up with one of Taylor's friends."

"Oh." Nate's eyebrows furrowed together. His eyes skated between Mason and me. "What are you guys doing?"

Mason glanced at me. "We don't know. We haven't talked about it. You?"

"Technically, you *could* go," Nate said.

One of Mason's eyebrows rose. "Meaning you want to go back?"

"Well…"

So he did.

Nate spread his hands over the table, his palms up. "There's no real reason to be here anymore. We came for your internship, but that's over now. And the wedding's done, too. So…" He smiled, coaxing us. "Matteo's back there already for football training. There's no reason to stay."

"Except my stepbrother is here." I leaned forward, propping my elbows on the table. "Oh." I snapped my fingers at him. "So is my best friend, and my stepmother and David."

"You've had all summer to hang out with them, and you have. You've seen Heather a ton. Plus, Malinda and David were at the wedding last night, too. I mean, come on, guys. Let's go back. There are parties back there. We can chill for an entire month before classes start. Your internship ended early. You could start football on time. I don't understand why we're not going back."

"So go."

Nate looked at Mason. "What?"

"Go." He gestured to me. "Maybe we'll stay an extra day."

Nate slowly sat back in his chair and tipped it on its rear legs. "You're okay with that?"

"Why wouldn't I be?"

"I don't know. Caldron, for one. You won't want backup?"

"Caldron's the least of our problems now. He's going to be charged in the assault against us, and also for attempted battery against Sam."

"Quinn then."

"I can't know for sure…" Mason's eyes flickered to mine briefly. "But I have a feeling Quinn's got his own troubles going right now." Nate didn't know Becky had broken it off with Adam.

"All the more reason for you to come with us." Nate stood up. "Come on, Mason. Let's all go back to Cain. We had problems one year, but we don't get into trouble there anymore. Our biggest problem is Taylor's friends now, and those guys are tame compared to what we usually deal with."

"A crime boss was tame?"

"That was a one-time thing. You know it." Nate switched to me. "Sam, what are you thinking? You have to want to head back to Cain, too. Analise is just down the road, and she won't have a wedding to plan any more. She's going to have a lot of free time now."

"Actually," I cleared my throat, looking at Mason, "she's doing what you suggested."

"Really?"

"What?" Nate looked between the two of us. "What's going on?"

"Analise is letting me go."

"So you *did* talk to her."

"I never said I didn't," I noted, quietly.

He didn't call me out. "What else did she say?"

"She and your dad are going to move. We can have the house."

Nate's eyes widened. "What? For real?" A grin spread over his face. "Man, all those memories from that house." He turned to Mason. "Let's stay for a week and throw a massive party next weekend. One more big bash before we all head back. Logan would be down for that."

"Down for what?" Logan and Taylor joined us, leaving their bags in the living room.

"Sam just said your parents are moving. We get the house," Nate announced. "One last big rager. How about it?"

Taylor's eyes widened, and she seemed to pull into herself.

"Oh. Can you stay till then?" Nate asked.

"Well…" She looked at Logan. "I have to go back now. Do you—"

He shook his head. "No. I'm going where you go. If you can stay, I'll stay. If you want to go back, I'll go there, too. It's your call."

She bit her lip, obviously torn as she looked around the kitchen. "I'm sorry, guys. I really need to go back. Jason was hurt bad. I don't want him to—"

Mason stood up, cutting her off with a wave. "Then you go. It's decided."

"I'm really sorry."

Logan reached for her hand and pulled her against his side. "You have nothing to be sorry about."

"I know, but I'm pulling you away from your family."

Nate laughed, pointing to Mason and me. "Uh, do you not know us? We're all family. If something affects you, it affects all of us."

Taylor still looked torn, but Logan lifted his arm to her shoulder. "She knows, and she'll get over her guilt. So…" He nodded to the rest of us. "Party at the house this weekend? The one in Cain?"

Mason nodded, then gestured to Nate. "Do me a favor, Logan?"

"Anything."

"Take him with you."

Nate twisted back around. "What? Mason—"

"I don't want to hear it. You're going. Sam and I will be behind you." His gaze came to me. "I'd like to spend some alone time with my girlfriend."

"Then it's all planned. Nate and I will go back with Taylor. We'll take care of the fuckers who fucked with Taylor's friend, and then we'll all celebrate this weekend. Your training starts next Monday. I'm sure all the guys will want to let loose this weekend anyway."

And with that, the plan was set in motion.

Logan, Nate, and Taylor left that day.

Mason and I spent the rest of the evening in bed, holding each other and enjoying our first alone time all summer.

---

We stayed a few more days and the rest of the week passed quickly. I went to the carnival to thank Petey and Keifer for sharing the surveillance video. Both told me not to hesitate to reach out again, and Petey reminded me with a wink not to sell carnies short. I tucked that information away and gave each of them a hug. I didn't know when I'd be seeing them again.

After that I spent my days with Malinda, Mark, or Heather. I tried to get as much time in as I could with each of them. David, too. He'd been around all summer, but we hadn't spent a lot of one-on-one time.

I knew he was busy planning for football, and on our last night in Fallen Crest, I realized I'd taken him for granted. I expressed that to him on the porch, after we'd just finished a family dinner.

"No, Sam." He shook his head, relaxing beside me on the bench. "I'm always here. You know that. You never have to worry about putting in your time with me. If you want to see me, I'm here. If you've got other people to see, I'm still here."

"Thanks, Dad."

"No problem. Love you."

"Love you, too."

Malinda came out to the porch then, her face flooded with tears, and I rose. Her goodbye seemed to last longer than normal, and we were only going back to college. We weren't moving across the country. I knew Malinda would be up for parents' weekend, too. She came every year.

"I'm just going to miss you two so much." She hugged me, then Mason. "And you. It's your last year. I can't believe it. You guys are growing up too fast." Mark stepped through the door behind them, and she added, "You, too. Stop growing up. I don't like it."

"I'll get right on that, Mom. No problem."

"Oh, and Sam, too." She turned to me, the dam breaking and tears wetting her entire face again.

More hugs. More goodbyes. More laughter until finally, Mason took my hand and began walking across the yard.

Mark waved, then we heard, "Mom, you know you can't stop them from going, right?" They headed back inside.

The screen door closed, but we could hear Malinda say, "I can try.

I'm going to do the same with you, so don't get any ideas. You know long, drawn-out goodbyes are essential with me."

Mark groaned, but David waved, a kind and loving smile on his face as he saw me looking back, and then he closed the inside door.

Mason tightened his hold on my hand. "Come on. I want to take you somewhere."

"What?"

We crossed the street to Helen's house and went inside. "Dress in something warm," he told me. "It could get cold tonight."

*Tonight?*

It was nearing dark. But we were going to be outside somewhere. "What do you have planned?"

He grinned, and my heart skipped a beat. "Just get dressed, okay?"

I melted, like I always did with him.

"Okay."

# CHAPTER FORTY-FIVE

It had grown nearly dark as we made the trek up the hill, and there were a few spots where I worried Mason's Escalade wouldn't fit. The driving path kept getting narrower and narrower, but as he took the last curve, I saw where we were. Mason had taken me high up in the hills, back to the spot where he'd come to get me after I'd been running.

"Mason?" I just sat there, holding his hand. I could just barely see the path I'd come from that day, and I remembered that his vehicle had been parked right here.

"Stay here a minute," he told me.

He got out of the Escalade and disappeared behind it for a moment. I turned around, but I couldn't see what he was doing. Then a little light started to appear, and it grew until the entire forest and path were illuminated against the night,

My door opened, and Mason stood there.

My heart leaped against my chest.

With the fading light of the valley behind him and the new light shining against his side, I swear I fell in love with him just a little bit more than I already was. This wasn't the usual Mason standing in front of me. This wasn't the man who gazed at me so fiercely when we made love, or stood confidently, knowing whoever came at us, he could protect us. This wasn't the brother who raised Logan, or even the one who cussed out their father for not being a real dad. This Mason seemed gentle and maybe a little uncertain even.

He held out his hand for me, and as I placed mine in his, this sweet Mason dipped his head. He was feeling unsure about something. When

I stepped out, he held me a moment there. His lips grazed my forehead, so softly and gently.

I looked up, feeling my heart climb its way to my throat. "What's going on?"

His fingers laced with mine. "Come on."

He led me behind the Escalade and down a small path that headed off from the main driving lane. We didn't go far, just through a clump of trees to a clearing next to the edge of the cliff. The sun still hadn't completely disappeared, and we had a perfect view of the forest, the rest of the sunset, and over Fallen Crest. It was beautiful, and so was what he'd done.

Mason jars were everywhere, with tea lights inside and a large comforter spread among them.

"Mason, what's going on?"

His hand loosened, but two of his fingers remained holding mine, and he led me to the comforter. I stood there as he looked at me, his eyes suddenly forlorn.

"Mason?" I couldn't talk anymore.

My other hand started to tremble so I tucked it behind my back. I willed the one he was holding to be still. Be calm.

"I didn't start thinking about marriage until this summer."

*Oh...*

"The whole thing's kind of a sham," he continued. "I used to think that way, but it hit me when my dad was marrying Analise, at the wedding ceremony: I want to marry you, Sam. I wasn't planning on asking. I assumed we would talk about it at some point, but it hasn't come up, and when I was standing there and your mom was coming down the aisle, I got mad at first. It wasn't supposed to be her in that dress. It was supposed to be you."

*My...*

He knelt down, holding my hand. He looked up as the sun finally disappeared over the horizon. It was just Mason, me, and a bunch of tea lights that cast a romantic glow over this spot for us.

"Samantha—"

*...God!*

I knew what he was going to do. I just didn't know what my response would be. I started to reach for him. "I—"

His phone rang. But he only reached inside his pocket and shut it off. The silence was so damned loud afterward. This was on me. I knew what was coming.

My mom cheated. His dad cheated. I knew David didn't. I hoped Malinda never did. And other parent figures raced through my mind. Mason was waiting for me, but Garrett flashed in my head. He was a cheater. He'd cheated with my mom. I didn't know about Sharon, if she'd ever cheated on him, but...

I couldn't think.

A feeling of doom settled deep in my chest. It was the same sensation as when I knew I was going to backstab Becky.

I was the bad guy here.

I had become the villain somehow.

"Mason." I stopped, wetting my lips. What was I going to do?

His phone rang again.

He cursed and shut it off a second time.

Mine started ringing right after that.

Our eyes caught and held, and I frowned.

"Fucking hell." He stood back up, reaching for my phone. Seeing who it was, he pushed the button to answer. "This better be a damned emergency." He was silent, then fell absolutely still. "Are you sure?" he asked. Fear, stark fear, showed in his eyes a moment before he blanketed it. His jaw clenched. "Okay. Thanks for letting me know." He ended the call, handing the phone back to me.

I took it, not thinking as I put it into my pocket. I felt tension growing in my chest. "What's wrong? What happened?"

His voice was so faint. "That was Logan. He talked to Taylor's dad when he got home." His Adam's apple bobbed up and down, and he half-turned away.

I reached for him, grabbing hold of his hand before those last two fingers slipped away. I pulled him back. "Hey. What happened?"

"Quinn sent that video to Cain University's coaching staff."

Fighting wasn't tolerated. At all. It was their policy.

My stomach grew uneasy. I knew what that meant.

Mason finished, "I've been suspended pending a personal investigation."

"Mason, it'll be fine."

"No." He sat down on the comforter, resting his hands over his knees. He watched as I sat next to him. "The fighting's on my record. They'll get ahold of the case we have against Caldron. Then they'll start looking into the past. I was fucked before I even started."

"Mason." I reached for his hand. I needed to say more, but that seemed to be all I could get out. I didn't want to hear what he was going to say next...

"The NFL has a strict policy on scandals, and this whole shitstorm over the summer? They'll see it as one giant scandal. It's over for the NFL."

"Mason." I closed my eyes, just holding onto his hand.

Then the question came. I wasn't expecting it, though I should've been.

His voice sounded raw.

"Sam, will you marry me?"

### Continued... *FALLEN CREST FOREVER*
www.tijansbooks.com

# ACKNOWLEDGEMENTS

Oh, holy crap! I cannot believe I'm at this point already. It's very very surreal. Fallen Crest Seven is done as well, and I'm just numb. Cripes! Lol! Oh my gosh. Okay. I have a feeling I'm going to be a babbling idiot for the acknowledgments in Fallen Crest Seven, but I'm here right now and all the emotions are spilling out.

First—thank you to my agent, to Debra Anastasia, to all of my admins, to Cami, Kerri, Eileen, Heather, Autumn, Crystal, Stacey, Amanda B, and Amanda W. Thank you to Lisa Sylva for checking in and being my cheerleader. Gah! So many.

Thank you to all the girls in the reader group! You guys have no idea how much all the posts and comments help me to keep sticking to what I love to do!

Thank you to J and B, for everything!

# SNEAK PEEK

# COLE

# CHAPTER ONE

I was surrounded—by champagne, crystal lights, and beautiful people. And I wanted to die.

Not really, but I *was* huddled in a corner with my back turned to the party. This was Sia's job. She was the event coordinator at this art gallery, the Gala. I wasn't even sure what event she was throwing, but I was here because she asked me to be. This was her thing, a typical Friday night for my best friend. The rich and gorgeous people came together to drink, socialize, throw money at some charity and mainly gossip. This was not my thing, and among all these paintings and socialites, I wanted to disappear.

I moved to Chicago two years ago, but that seemed like a lifetime now. We came for Liam's job. He was the newest counselor at the Haven Center, but a year ago he was killed, struck by a drunk driver on his way home.

A shudder went through me as I remembered.

Liam had left a message that he was stopping to get flowers—he was a block away. The local florist had a booth in our grocery store. I'd had the genius idea to walk Frankie and meet him at the store. Our ~~dog~~ furry child could wait in the car while we got food together. It was silly, but grocery shopping was a favorite "date" for me. Liam thought it was ridiculous. He always laughed, but he'd humor me. And Frankie loved it. He got out of the house and could wag his tail to his heart's content in the car. We lived in a nice neighborhood, and it wasn't too hot, so I trusted our child would still be there when we returned.

When Frankie and I walked around the corner, Liam's car was waiting to cross the intersection and turn in to the parking lot. He smiled when he saw Frankie and me, and he looked so happy. He'd lifted his hand to wave. So had I. When the light changed, Liam started across—I saw his smile fall away. I saw his hand grab for the steering wheel. I saw the blood drain from his face. He'd started to mouth, "I lo—"

My heart twisted. It was being yanked out, slowly, inch by inch.

As I'd watched, my husband's car was T-boned by a truck.

I bowed my head and gripped my champagne glass now. I could still hear the sound of metal being smashed, crunching and grinding. Then the car had started in a roll.

Once.

Twice.

It had rolled three times before stopping. *He* had rolled three times before dying.

The terror—I'll never get that image out of my mind. His crystal blue eyes, high cheekbones, a face I'd always teased would keep the ladies hitting on him long after he passed fifty, had never looked so scared. Everything happened in slow motion. His eyes went to the truck, and then they found me. Frankie was barking. I couldn't move. My heart slowed.

I was told later that I'd kept Frankie from running in to traffic, but I have no memory of that. All I can remember is Liam and the look in his eyes when he knew he was going to die.

My future died that day.

"Addison!"

I had one second to ready myself, and I wiped away the tear that had leaked from my eye. Sia rushed to my side, hissing my name in an excited whisper as she grasped my arm. She moved close, turning so she could speak quietly to me but still watch her friends behind us. Her dress grazed my bare arm.

"I just got the best news ever for you! Seriously, I'm gushing like a twelve year old because it's that damned good." She paused, her eyes searching my face, and her head moved back an inch. "Wait. What are you doing all the way over here?" She glanced over her shoulder. "The street's beautiful and all, but the party's behind you."

I had to stifle a smile. She wouldn't understand. I was indeed facing downtown Chicago. Traffic was minimal due to the impending blizzard. Already the snow was falling, piling atop cars, sidewalks, people, and signs.

It was breathtaking. That was the art I appreciated. Sia loved people, or more specifically, she loved connections. She didn't just see faces when she met them. She saw wealth, their friends, and potential connections. I was the opposite. I seemed to notice everything except those things—or I used to. I had during my Liam era, when my heart was full and open and welcoming. But that was then.

Now I was in the after-Liam era.

Everything was dull. Grey. Black. White.

I sighed. I even depressed myself.

I tuned back in to what Sia was saying. She hadn't stopped to wait for my response. "...number, and I have to tell you, you'll love it. It's one of the most exclusive places I've heard about. No one knows about the opening, but I got the number for you. Can you believe it? How amazing a friend am I?" Her eyes sparkled. "I'm fucking amazing, Addison. Ah—"

"Okay, I got it." I gently pulled her hand off my arm, keeping it in mine.

She squeezed back, her body dancing with excitement.

"Say it again," I told her. "What'd you get for me?"

She tucked a piece of paper into my palm. Her voice was so hush-hush. "I got the number for one of the most exclusive buildings there is. It's three blocks from here. There's never been a vacancy, but there's one now. The third floor is open."

"What do you mean, the third floor is open?" I unfolded the paper to find a phone number scrawled on it, nothing else.

"It's the silver building."

"The silver..." I looked up at her as it clicked which building she was talking about. It was a building a short walk away, covered entirely in something silver. Sia had first thought it was a business, but once she found out it housed residents, it took on a whole other appeal to her. Her interest was piqued, and when that happens, Sia's like a detective, going after every tip she gets. Only she couldn't find any information about it. There was an air of secrecy about who owned it and who lived there, which only added to its appeal.

I'd been hearing about this building for the entire two years I'd known Sia. We'd met early on when Liam and I moved to Chicago, and she'd been the one friend who stuck with me as my life fell apart.

I was speechless for a moment. She'd finally solved her mystery? "Who owns it?"

A grimace flashed over her face, momentarily marring the image of perfection I knew she wanted for tonight. She'd swept her light blond hair up into a bun and rimmed her dark eyes. They looked smoky, but alluring and sexy. Exactly how Sia was. She moved closer to me, pulling her wrap tighter around her shoulders as she checked behind her. No one was looking, so she reached down to tug the front of her ball gown up. It had ridden low, showing a healthy amount of cleavage, but that was Sia. I'd just figured that was the look she was going for.

"That's the thing," she said. "I still don't know, and it's driving me nuts. You can find out, though." She clamped on to my arm again. "This was passed to me through a friend of a friend of a friend, but if you call that number, you can request to view the third floor."

"It sounds expensive."

"It's perfect for you." Her hand moved to her chest. "I can't afford it, but you totally can. You have the money Liam left you, and you've been wanting to get out of that house. I mean, all those memories. I totally get it. I know you've been looking to move."

I was, though it was a shameful secret of mine. Liam had loved our house. We were going to have our family there. The thought of leaving made me feel like I was leaving him. I'd been putting it off for a year, but it was becoming too much. I could feel him in every room. I could hear him laughing. When I was upstairs, I swore he would call my name as if he were just coming home from work. Everything was him—the furniture, the stupid expensive espresso machine he'd vowed we needed to live and then couldn't figure out how to use. Even his juicer—I still couldn't believe he'd bought a juicer for us.

My throat closed. The tears were coming, and I had to shut them down. "Yeah, but downtown?" I murmured, my throat raw. "That's a big change."

"It'd be amazing. You'd live three blocks from here. I'm here all the time, and my place isn't far away either. You can cab that easily." Her eyes were wide and pleading. "Please tell me you'll call. Do it! Dooo it."

I glanced back to the number. "What if this is some elaborate scheme to trap people and kill them? You said it yourself: you don't know who owns the building. It could be the Russian mob," I teased.

"Even better!" She rolled her eyes and dismissed that with a wave. "Come on, if it was the Russian mob, I would've heard about that. Besides, I heard one of the residents is the CEO of Grove Banking."

"The CEO?"

"It's his place in the city."

"Oh." Coming downtown was such a hassle. I loved seeing Sia, but I hated coming here as much as I did. But actually living here…

I'd dodge all the parking and traffic. There was something peaceful about living among the finest restaurants, museums, shopping and so much more. And although things were busy during the workday, I knew there were also times when it was quiet. After hours, it was a sanctuary within one of the most active metropolitan areas in the country. "It'll be so expensive."

"Your inheritance from Liam is ridiculous. You'll be comfortable for the rest of your life."

Yes, my inheritance *was* ridiculous—but not because it was twenty million dollars, because I'd never known about it. Liam had never told me. In fact, he'd kept all sorts of secrets. I hadn't known about the wealth until his family told me at his funeral, begrudgingly. I knew his mother had hated doing it. His grandmother had been a household name, as she'd invented a popular kitchen utensil.

I still couldn't believe it, even though the money had been transferred to my bank account. Most days, Sia was the one who reminded me about it. I had done okay as a freelance writer before he died, enough to have a small nest egg, but I'd had to dip into his inheritance over the last year. Just a bit, but I'd have to dip into it more for that place.

"I'll call." Sia took the piece of paper from me. "I'll set it up. We'll go together to see it. You won't be alone, and that way I get to see inside that glorious piece of heaven. You can decide afterwards."

I gave her a rueful look. If I saw it, and it was gorgeous, I'd probably want it. I liked to live simply, but I did appreciate beauty. And evidently I could afford it.

I sighed. "Okay. Call and set it up."

She grabbed my arm with both hands. "Oh my God! I'm so excited!" She yanked me to her, but the movement caused her hair to scoot forward too, looking out of place on her head. She stopped and quickly patted everything back into place—hair, boobs, dress, everything. Her smile never faltered. "We have to celebrate! The best fucking champagne I can find." And she was off, in the same whirlwind as she'd come. She signaled for one of the waiters.

She moved gracefully through the crowd among all the sparkling dresses and black tuxedos. Sia's world was beautiful. It was much livelier than mine, and it was okay to come and visit. I didn't think I could handle living in it, though. Would that be what happened if I moved downtown?

Or even if this place were something I loved, if it was as exclusive as she'd said, would they take me? Surely they'd want someone else, someone who was *someone*. I was no one. Hell, half the time I wasn't even me. But I'd go. I'd see the place and let Sia down easy after that.

I could see her approaching now with not one but two bottles of champagne in her hands. I eyed the one she held out to me.

"Take it." She linked her elbow through mine as I did, and guided me back through the event she'd organized. "We're going upstairs to my office, and we're going to get smashed."

"What about your clients?"

"I've wined and dined with all of them already. They'll be fine. The staff will take care of them. It's best friend time." She pulled me up the stairs and winked over her shoulder, her voice dipping down. "And besides, I've already made my evening plans, if you know what I mean. When you go home and I'm feeling lonely—aka horny—I'm supposed to give Bernardo a call."

I didn't ask who Bernardo was; she had so many boyfriends. I just smiled and followed.

I would do what she wanted. And when my sides were splitting from laughing too much later on, I'd call a cab. I'd go home, and I'd curl up under my blanket knowing that for one night, the booze would help me sleep.